## SHADOWRUN:
# SHADOW DANCE

### AARON ROSENBERG

SHADOWRUN: SHADOW DANCE
Cover art by Derek Poole
Design by Matt Heerdt and David Kerber

Published by Catalyst Game Labs,
an imprint of InMediaRes Productions, LLC
7108 S. Pheasant Ridge Drive • Spokane, WA 99224

# ONE

"Well," Cole Danvers muttered as he lowered himself down, his hands still grasping the ceiling three meters up and his arms at almost their full extension, "this is going sideways fast."

This hadn't exactly been the plan. The plan had been clean and simple. Rodrick dispelled the wards around the building. Tish rerouted the alarms. Mace stood watch outside, either distracting or, if necessary, dissuading any security patrols. And Cole and Lorelei stealthed their way in, walked soundlessly down the hall that could no longer see or sense them, and right up to the display case, where they would pick the lock and remove their prize.

That was what they'd mapped out.

Only, it had turned out the wards were a lot more complex than they'd been led to believe. A lot more complex than a low-level bureaucratic building in what had been the Ute sector of Denver really warranted. There were a lot more alarms, too. A *lot* more. Not everywhere, though. The regular office areas were fine, just the standard door alarms and motion sensors that got switched on when the last worker left and the lights went off. But the main corridor, perhaps because it was lined on both sides with display cases filled with items that presumably had some significance, value, or both, had alarms every few feet, and not just motion sensors. It also had temperature, light, metal, *and* magic sensors.

And, of course, the prize was displayed in a case midway down that corridor.

As a result, it'd taken Rodrick three times as long as they'd allotted to dispel, trick, or break the various wards. Tish had been working furiously at the same time, and had managed to spoof or short out or turn off all the alarms as well.

They hoped.

But that all meant they were way behind schedule. They'd expected to have two hours to leisurely stroll in and acquire the piece.

Instead, they had ten minutes.

And they still weren't one hundred percent sure they'd found everything.

So they'd come up with a new plan on the fly. Rodrick and Tish were supposed to be safely outside in the van, out of sight and ready to cover their tracks as soon as Cole and Lorelei returned. Instead, they had to be inside, closer to the systems each one was trying to counter.

Which meant Cole and Lorelei had been forced to herd the elf and the dwarf into the building, guiding the novice thieves through the more mundane elements of breaking into a secure site and keeping them from setting off anything from sheer clumsiness and inexperience.

Then they'd had to set the two up in a pair of adjoining cubicles while Cole and Lorelei headed toward the main corridor, trusting that neither the mage nor the decker would do something to put the whole building on lockdown and leave them all trapped and waiting for the police to arrive.

Trust, Cole had learned, was a dangerous, dangerous thing.

"What the hell'd they do?" he demanded when the alarms had begun to blare and the steel mesh had slammed down across the door they had just been reaching for. He jerked his hand back just in time to keep from losing his fingers to the descending barrier. "Rodrick? Tish? Status report?" But the comms produced nothing but static. "Balls, there's a jammer." *Why hadn't Tish caught that?*

"Doesn't matter," Lorelei had pointed out, sounding just as frustrated as he felt. "What's done is done. All we can do now is try to figure out how to get around it."

Cole had sighed, but nodded at his partner's comment. She was right. They'd find out later which of the other pair had set something off. And what. And how.

Assuming they all survived to regroup and discuss it.

For now, they had to figure out a way into what had been an office corridor and was now a deadly steel box, lined with who knew what other deterrents designed to keep them from getting anywhere near their goal. They wouldn't be able to take even one step through that place without setting something off, and that was assuming they could even get past the doors.

One step. Hmm. Cole had backed up a pace and studied the hallway ceiling. It was a standard drop-panel style, the panels forming an acoustic barrier to help keep the noise of so many people walking and talking and typing and working from becoming a distraction. Above those tiles would be a support frame to hold them in place, and then above that would be the actual ceiling proper.

That was something he could work with.

Tapping Lorelei on the shoulder, he'd pointed up. She'd frowned, her eyes following his gesture, but then she'd smiled.

"Yeah," she'd agreed quickly. "Let's give it a shot. Nobody ever thinks to look up."

They'd hurriedly backtracked a little further, into the nearest cubicle, and from there they'd hopped up on the desk. It had held Lorelei's slight figure just fine, but had creaked ominously when Cole added his own weight. It wasn't his size, he knew, but the cybernetic components built into him—even with lightweight metals and ceramics, they gave his slim build a disproportionate heft. Fortunately, the desk had held, and it didn't have to support both of them for very long.

Cole had extended his hands upward—the advantage of some of those same cybernetic systems—and had gently punched one of the tiles up and out of the way.

Lorelei had turned to him with a smirk. "Give a girl a hand up?" she'd asked with that slow, sensual smile she knew perfectly well he couldn't resist.

He hadn't been sure exactly what she'd meant—his arms were strong enough to support him even at full extension, but he didn't have much to grab onto up there—but nodded anyway. He'd nearly fallen over from surprise when she threw her arms around his neck, wrapped her legs around his waist, kissed him—and then stretched upward, both hands on his extended forearm, both legs shifting and pushing her higher, and shimmied up his arm like it was a fire pole. Feeling her lithe form gliding over and then past him, watching the smooth play of muscles beneath her silky skin, had been far too distracting. But Cole still hadn't turned away.

Instead, he'd made sure to keep his hand latched onto the support strut beside the shifted tile. It probably wasn't enough to hold his weight—it seemed to be bearing Lorelei's well enough for the moment, though that was probably because most of hers was actually dispersed along his arm and the rest of his body.

Within seconds she had reached the ceiling and was grasping the struts, though she still had her legs folded around Cole's arm as she stuck her head up and through the opening. "Looks clean," she'd called down, her voice muffled by the tiles. "I doubt the tiles will hold us, and not so sure about the grid either, but it's wide enough, and I'm not seeing any sensors."

Which made sense, actually. The only things likely to be moving through that space were rats, and the building personnel wouldn't want alarms blaring every time a rodent went darting around.

"Try this," he'd suggested, digging into the pack slung over his shoulder. He'd extracted what looked like pair of a disks with handles set into them, and had passed them up to her.

"Magnetic grapples? I doubt they'll help—ceiling looks like standard plaster, not metal."

"Sure, but there's got to be support beams," he'd replied. "Those'll be either metal themselves or wood with metal studs. I've souped up the magnets on those things, they should be strong enough to get a solid grip even through the plaster. And they're powerful enough that one can support my weight, once they're latched on."

He could tell she was still skeptical, but she hadn't had any better ideas so she'd given it a try.

And had let out a soft yelp of surprise when the first grapple had clamped on. "It worked!" He could just make out her giving the grapple a good tug. "And it's solid. Nice!" But she'd glanced back down at him, her pretty features twisted into a frown. "But there are only two of them, and two of us, and we're going to need two each to move forward."

Cole had thought about that, too, and he'd come up with what he hoped was a viable solution. "There's another way," he'd answered slowly. "I think. It's going to be a little tricky, though, and it'll be slow going." He'd explained what he had in mind.

"That's crazy," Lorelei had replied at once. But she'd grinned as she said it, and she'd laughed. "I'm up for a little crazy right now. And it's not like we have time to come up with anything better." It had been maybe a minute since the alarm had started, and despite their banter they both knew they didn't have a lot of time left.

She'd set the second grapple and then transferred all of her weight to the first one as Cole grabbed the second. He'd jumped off the desk, the surface groaning again from the weight, and then reeled himself up, retracting his hand into its forearm housing so his entire body was lifted toward the ceiling.

Once there, with his head and shoulders above the tiles, he'd smiled at Lorelei. "Ready?"

She nodded, and without a word reached over and again wrapped her arms around his neck. "I think you just wanted an excuse," she said teasingly as she switched all her weight to him.

Cole had smiled at that, and kissed her quickly, in part because he could and in part so she wouldn't see how concerned he actually was. He knew the single grapple could support him—he'd used them several times, and of course the standard method was to hold one as you detached the other and slid it out ahead of you, then switched to that one so you could move the first one again—but his and Lorelei's combined weight was probably pushing it to its limits. He'd have to be quick.

Reaching out with his free arm, he'd grabbed the second grapple and detached it. Then, still holding it firmly, he'd extended his arm as far as it would go, and planted the grapple there.

Next he'd reached into his pack again and retrieved the coil of tightly woven hemp rope. Only as thick around as a pencil, it was strong enough to hold easily three times his own weight.

Now came the tricky part. Normally, Cole would have attached a smaller magnetic clamp to the cord's end. But the clamp wouldn't work with the grapple—the two magnetic fields didn't interact properly—and he'd only now realized he should have tied the cord before moving the grapple. He could pull the grapple back and start again, but they didn't have time for that. He had to tie the cord securely to the grapple where it was.

Using only one hand.

It wasn't the easiest thing he'd ever done, but fortunately it wasn't the hardest either, and after a minute he'd managed to tie a good solid knot. A sharp tug had confirmed it would hold. He'd handed Lorelei the other end, and she'd quickly knotted it around the closer grapple.

Now they had a line stretching from one to the other, and their weight would be distributed across the two grapples. And the space between the ceiling and the tiles was big enough for them to wrap arms and legs around the line and shimmy their way across.

Lorelei had gone first, of course. Cole had followed, refusing to let himself be distracted any further by the sight of her gliding ahead of him. It had only taken a minute to reach the second grapple, and then Cole had grasped it firmly with one hand, twisting his body into a cross-legged, hunched position so he could still fit above the tiles. Lorelei slung herself into his lap, her arms around his neck again as he'd reached back, detached the first grapple, brought it to them, and then twisted so that he could sling it past him and connect to the ceiling farther down.

And then they'd resumed their sideways climb.

Halfway through that second leg, they'd passed the wall separating the office area from the main corridor. Fortunately, as Cole had hoped, the wall above the drop ceiling hadn't been completely finished—why bother, when you knew that area wouldn't be visible to anyone but maintenance?—and had been nothing more than a bare panel. Cole hung there, waiting like a hungry spider on its line, as Lorelei extracted a small laser from her belt and cut a hole through the panel in front of her.

And again, as they'd hoped, no new alarms went off. Those were all set in the corridor itself, down below the drop ceiling. The area up here had been completely ignored.

Lorelei carefully removed the piece she'd cut away, setting it gently atop several tiles so it wouldn't fall through, and they'd resumed their trek. Both of them had been keeping track of the distance as best they could, and they'd only gone a few meters into the third leg when Lorelei had stopped. "It should be right about here."

Cole nodded. That matched what he'd been tracking as well. Sliding forward, he'd nudged her past the spot a little so he was directly above it. Then, with his legs coiled around the line to support him, he'd reached down past his head and slid the tile out of the way.

Sure enough, he was looking down onto the main corridor. And even from here he could see the display cases lining the walls to either side. From their earlier reconnaissance he knew they held various holopics and certificates and medals and other small objects.

And, nestled among the rest, the amulet that was their target.

"Do you have another line?" Lorelei had asked, but Cole shook his head. "You could stick your hand out and I could slide down your arm again," she'd suggested next. But without something to grab hold of, Cole wouldn't be able to support her weight adequately. And if she fell, she'd wind up right in the middle of all the alarms and wards Rodrick and Tish had supposedly shut off, but were now probably back on.

"It has to be me," he told her instead. "I can lower myself down, look around, see what's been deactivated and what's still hot. If it's clear, I can get you down then—with my feet on the ground it'll be easy."

"And if it's not?" she'd asked. They both knew she was far better at disabling locks and alarms than he was.

He'd just shrugged. "Then I'll improvise."

Now, hanging from both hands, Cole glanced around—and his eyes went straight to a small, blinking red light almost directly across from him.

A light that was very clearly an alarm, and that also very clearly had just detected his presence.

"Okay," he muttered. "Time to improvise."

# TWO

A second light blinked into existence beside the first, and Cole winced. From years of studying security systems—so he could circumvent them—he knew exactly what that meant.

The first light was the sensor.

The second? That was a laser—rare, and expensive, and completely out of place here, but what wasn't? He was sure that's what it was, though.

Which meant he had maybe a second to act, at best.

Not enough time to pull himself back up, so instead he let go. With one hand, anyway. That shifted his weight, and he swung to the side—

—just as a beam of ruby light pierced the air right where he had been an instant before.

The beam only lasted a few seconds before winking out again, which gave Cole a brief respite as the laser recharged. But that would probably only be a few seconds at most. He had to get out of its path before then.

Lunging with his free hand, he managed to grasp the line again and start hauling himself upward. The laser fired again just as his legs were in its path, but he must have been twisting around just enough because he didn't feel a sudden, searing pain as a beam pierced flesh and bone. A second later he was clear, and then he was back up above the tiles, safely wrapped around the line.

"That didn't look good," Lorelei commented once he'd stopped swaying. She'd reversed her position so her head was next to his, her feet pointing ahead toward the farther grapple while his were aimed at the one behind them. "For a second there, I thought I might need to start shopping for a new partner."

"Nice to know you care." Cole leaned forward to wipe his brow against his forearm. But the motion caused his entire body to contort—and in the process, a small screw sprang loose from one of his many pockets.

"No!" Lorelei shouted, lunging for the stray disc, but her grasping fingers just missed it as the screw plummeted, gaining speed as it fell past them and out into the main corridor.

Cole could only watch, cursing silently, as it activated sensor after sensor in its descent.

The first laser missed it entirely.

The second caught its upper edge, carving a thin sliver off to drift down after the rest.

The third hit the screw just below the head, slicing that off so two pieces were now falling, a cap and a small cone.

The fourth was dead-center, slicing the body of the screw down the middle.

The fifth was waiting when the screwhead hit it, and neatly bisected that tiny dome, leaving two hemispheres to flutter to either side.

Apparently the remaining pieces were too small for the sensors to detect, because they didn't trigger any additional attacks on the last of their trip to the ground.

"That could've been us," Lorelei pointed out as they both stared down at the fallen coin. "Heck, it almost *was* you. When I find out what Rodrick and Tish messed up to switch everything back on, I'm going to—"

But Cole wasn't listening. Instead his eyes were still fixed on the bits of screw down below, and on what had happened to it as it fell. And on what that might mean for the lasers it attracted, their battery packs, and his and Lorelei's own safety.

"Quick," he whispered. "Do you have any data sticks on you?"

"What, you want to reprogram the lasers? I don't think that's how those things work, do you?"

"Data sticks," he repeated, ignoring her quip. "Or anything else around that size and weight." He was already digging in his own pockets, pulling out a handful of odds and ends like more screws, nuts, washers, and clips. You never knew when stuff like that might come in handy.

Lorelei grumbled, but a second later she handed over a small assortment of her own, data sticks and clips but also safety pins, barrettes, and a tiny tin of lip balm. "Stealing things makes my lips dry," she said with a shrug when he shot her a questioning glance.

Accepting the items, Cole studied the space below them. "We're right over it, I think," he said, and she nodded. "Okay, here goes nothing."

And he tossed the entire assortment directly below them.

Even though he'd braced for it, the sudden barrage was still enough to startle him. Sensors and lasers went berserk as what must have been twenty small items suddenly entered their field. The air was filled with the zap of the lasers, the sizzle of the beams finding targets, and the acrid tang of scalded metal and melted plastic. Smoke drifted up toward them, and Cole and Lorelei both fought the urge to cough as the small fog enveloped them. The onslaught lasted at least a solid minute, and Cole estimated that no fewer than a dozen lasers had fired—what kind of office building *was* this?—and each at least three or four times, maybe more.

Finally, all was silent.

"Okay, you've succeeded in slaughtering the contents of our pockets," Lorelei commented, breaking the quiet. "So what?"

Cole smiled in response. "Now for the real test." Taking out a single metal washer he'd held back, he flipped it up. It arced to eye-level, then curved and began to fall.

Together they watched as it dropped below the tiles and into the killing zone.

And nothing happened.

"Yes!" Cole resisted the urge to wave his hands over his head in triumph—seeing as how they were still clamped to the line, that would have been a bad thing. But he was thrilled.

So was Lorelei. "Clever," she admitted. "You used the chaff to burn out the lasers."

"They may still recharge," he pointed out, "but I think I've bought us a few minutes, maybe more. And a few minutes is all we need." He grinned at her. "Shall we?"

In reply, she leaned over and gave him a quick kiss. Then, hitching a line of her own to the one strung between the grapples, she slid down it like a spider intent upon its prey. "Try to keep up," she called as she dropped.

For half a second Cole worried he'd misjudged, he'd missed a few lasers, or that he'd underestimated their battery life or recharge time. But Lorelei descended quickly and smoothly, her way unimpeded, and after a second she lightly touched down upon the floor.

Which triggered a whole new wave of klaxons, and forced her to jump hurriedly back up as the floor beneath her gave way, revealing a deep, dark pit right where she'd landed.

"What the hell?" she demanded, glaring up at Cole as if he were somehow to blame for all this. "Who puts security like this in a bloody office building?"

Not having any sort of answer for that, he shrugged, already lowering himself down by his hands again. He glanced about as he got close to the floor, then switched the vision in his left eye to infrared. They'd been too high for it have much use before, but now he could clearly see the pit below Lorelei as a darker, cooler shape—

—and the rest of the floor around them as a solid mass.

"Huh."

"Huh what?" she demanded, still dangling from her rope. "What does 'huh' mean? Is it good or bad or 'oh my god we're so dead'?"

"More puzzling, but possibly good," he replied absently. After staring at the floor another second, he came to a decision.

And stepped down, planting first one foot and then the other firmly on the carpet.

"Wait!" Lorelei shrieked, but then stared at him standing there only a foot away from her. "Wait, what?"

"It's just in the one spot," he explained, reaching out to pull her toward him. She let him, releasing her grip on the rope as he set her gently on the floor, taking a half-step back so she had room past the pit. "The rest of it's solid."

"So they only set a pressure plate and a pit right there?" she asked, glancing around. "Right in the one spot we needed?" Her pretty features twisted into a grimace. "What the hell's so special about this thing, anyway?"

"Don't know, don't care," Cole answered. "Above our pay grade. We're just here to nab the darn thing and hand it off to the client."

"Right, right." With a sigh, Lorelei turned toward the glass display case on the wall ahead of them and just in front of the pit. "Well, you're going to have to anchor me, handsome—I can't very well pick a lock and hold onto a rope at the same time." And she leaped into his arms.

Cole just barely caught her in time, wrapping his arms around her waist even as her legs twined yet again around his middle. He held on, leaning back and keeping his feet planted well apart to take the added weight as Lorelei twisted and then leaned away from him, putting her head and shoulders right above the pit.

And directly facing their prize.

"Hello, my pretty," she whispered, lockpicks already in hand. The actual display case lock was fairly standard, and within seconds she had that undone and the glass panel swinging open. Then she reached in for the object they'd been sent to retrieve.

And tugged, first gently but then harder, frowning. "It's stuck."

"What?" Cole stared at their target. It wasn't much to look at—just a thumb-sized gold disc with what looked like a shard of ruby embedded in the center like a red cat's eye. And it appeared to be looped over a simple hook against the display's back wall, without a lock or charm in sight.

Yet Lorelei was now yanking on it with both hands and it clearly wasn't budging.

"Here, let me." Reaching past her, Cole wrapped the fingers of one hand around the amulet, keeping his other arm around Lorelei herself. He felt the disc in his hand, cool and oddly tingly, and then a faint jolt traveling up his arm into his chest as he brushed against the ruby.

And the amulet came free in his hand.

"Hey, that's not fair!" Lorelei protested as he extracted the amulet from the case and tucked it safely into one of his pockets, then secured the pocket itself. "I must have loosened it for you."

"Sure, that's it," he agreed easily, amused but careful not to show it. Lorelei, he had learned, could be prickly when crossed. "Okay, let's get out of here."

For just a second, she paused. "You know, part of me just wants to charge down this stupid corridor, shouting at the top of my lungs," she admitted with a wicked grin and a gleam in her eye.

"You'd be Swiss cheese before you got three meters," Cole reminded her.

"Spoilsport," she grumbled, but didn't argue further. Instead she clambered up onto his shoulders, using him for support as she grabbed her rope and began hauling herself back above the ceiling tiles.

Cole waited until she was safely gripping the line above before he retracted his arms and rose back off the ground as well.

And not a moment too soon, he noticed, as behind him several of the laser-sensor combos began to wink to life again.

But they had the amulet they'd come to get, and they were still in one piece. Provided they could get back out of the building unharmed and undetained, they'd done it. The job was almost over.

Still, considering how many surprises they'd had on this one already, Cole decided he wouldn't relax until the client had the prize and they had their money.

After all, better safe than sorry.

# THREE

Sure enough, they had no sooner headed back into the office area and dropped back down to the ground—retrieving the magnetic grapples and the line between them before they descended—when Rodrick and Tish rushed over to them. The former had light coruscating about his hands and eyes, a sure sign he was either about to cast something or in the process of maintaining an existing spell, and the latter had her deck in her hand and her stubby little fingers flying across the keys with shocking speed and dexterity.

"We've got a problem," Rodrick declared.

"Yeah, we kinda figured," Cole shot back. "What happened with the alarms? And the jammer? You guys were supposed to take care of those!"

"We did!" the mage replied, his narrow features flushed. "All the ones we knew about, anyway. There was a second set nested beneath, set to go active only if the normal level was breached or frozen. There was no way to predict that." He shook his head and echoed what Cole and Lorelei had already said while trying to get to the display: "Somebody went to an awful lot of trouble to protect this place. A lot more than you'd ever expect for a boring old office building."

Tish had yet to look up from her deck, but now she added her first contribution to the conversation, which was as blunt as ever: "Did you get it?"

"Yeah, we got it." Cole patted his pocket, but didn't pull out the amulet. They could all admire it later—if they got out of here. Which was the priority right now. "So what's the problem?"

"Yeah." Rodrick sighed and swept long, dark hair back from his face. He looked tired. Cole knew from working with other mages that magic could be exhausting, and the elf had clearly been forced to operate at a much higher level than expected since they'd broken in here. And from the sound of things, they weren't done yet. "The building's on lockdown."

"We kinda guessed from the steel bars and mesh panels over all the doors and windows," Lorelei said. She'd been lounging against one of the desks, but Cole could see she was actually coiled like a spring, ready to move at a moment's notice.

"It's more than that," Rodrick continued, giving her a brief glare. "Apparently they've got a protocol in place for something like this." He gestured toward the back of the wide office space, where a wash of white light swept across a distant hall. "It scans the entire place, bit by bit, for anyone and everyone left inside. Compares them to its personnel rosters, approves the ones authorized to be here—" He actually gulped, looking even paler than usual.

"—and fries the rest through a grid built into the floor," Tish finished for him. The dwarf looked more angry than afraid, but from what Cole had seen that was normal for her. "I managed to reroute it so it started at the far end first, but the rate it's going?" She shrugged. "We've got maybe five minutes, ten tops, before it hits us."

"Could we dodge around it?" Lorelei asked. "Head to a section it's already covered, and then just wait until it's done?"

But Tish was already shaking her head. "It's smarter than that. It doesn't leave an area once it's been scanned, it just expands into the next one. Like somebody painting a floor—the patch they did first isn't as wet by the time they reach the last one, but it's still gonna leave a mark if you step on it."

"What about going up again?" was Lorelei's next suggestion. "That worked before."

"Not this time," Roderick answered. "The electricity may start under the floor, but it arcs all the way to the ceiling. You'd get cooked as easily up there as down here."

Cole was thinking fast. "I'm guessing you're trying to shut it down and not having any luck?" he asked, and Tish nodded. "Right. Stop working on that."

That got her attention enough for her to actually look up at him. "What? But if I can't shut it off before it gets to us—"

"You won't be able to," Cole interrupted. "And you're wasting your time on it. I've got a better idea." He grinned. "Get us into the system instead."

"That's what I'm trying—" she started to say, but this time Lorelei was the one who cut her off with a sharp gasp.

"Damn," the elven thief whispered, straightening. She shot Cole a bright smile. "That's brilliant!"

"I'm missing something here," Rodrick muttered, glancing back and forth between them.

"Probably lots of somethings," Lorelei agreed, then covered that with a sharp but sweet smile to counter his glower. "What Cole means is break into the personnel records and create files that make us look like employees. You know, people who're authorized to be here. Then, when the sweep reaches us—"

"It'll pass right over us, because we'll be on the approved list." Tish was nodding appreciatively. "Yeah, that is smart. And those records have barely any protection at all, since that's not where they figure anyone's gonna try breaking in. I can have us set up in a jiff." She stopped talking again, her fingers moving at even greater speeds, her heavy features furrowed as she began work.

Two minutes later, the four of them stood in the hallway, side by side, as the white light of the scan swept toward them. "Either this is gonna be a piece of cake or it's gonna hurt like hell," Tish said softly. She had her fists bunched at her sides like she could fight her way through the security measure, but if she'd done her job correctly, she'd already won this fight. Still, Cole could hardly blame her for being nervous.

The light reached them and enveloped them in a blinding white glare. *"Individuals located,"* a computerized voice announced. *"Initiating scan."* The light intensified until all Cole could see was shrouded in a haze.

*"Matching to personnel records,"* came the next declaration, followed a few seconds later by *"Personnel records found. Individuals cleared for office activity."*

They all breathed sighs of relief. Then they all had to gasp for breath when the computer system spoke again, stating, *"Unauthorized item removal detected."*

*Oh, drek*, Cole thought, his hand going to his pocket. They hadn't even thought of that, but of course a place like this would inventory everything—and enter those items in its database right along with its employees. You could move a pencil or an eraser without a problem, sure, but in lockdown mode it would check to make sure expensive stuff like server racks were where they were supposed to be—and any relics and artifacts as well.

Like the one he was now carrying.

His hand snaked into his pocket and closed tightly around the amulet. Would the system fry them for having it? Or would it just demand that they return it? Or, more likely, incapacitate or otherwise restrain them until the authorities could come and retrieve it? Either way, they were going to have to—

*"Identity confirmed,"* the security system declared. *"Item removal authorized."* And the sweep passed over them, the sudden darkness leaving them all blinking as the wall of white light continued on down the hall.

"What was that?" Lorelei asked as soon as it had passed them by. She kept her voice to a whisper, as if somehow that would fool a security program capable of scanning DNA.

"No idea," Cole replied, releasing the amulet and pulling his hand out of his pocket. "But I'll take it. Let's get out of here before it changes its mind."

The others all nodded. "Which way?" Rodrick asked. "The way we'd planned, or—"

But Cole had already thought about that and dismissed the idea. "It thinks we're legit," he pointed out. "If we try sneaking back out through the air ducts, it's going to be forced to revise that assessment, and I'm not willing to assume it's too dumb to figure that out. Are you?" The others all shook their heads. "So we leave the way any good little office worker would—out the service entrance."

There wasn't anything that needed to be said to that, so they started walking. The office building had a main entrance, of course, but that led straight to the corridor he and Lorelei had just come from, and there was no way they were going back there, even with the computer thinking they were allowed to be here. There were two side entrances, however, and one opened right onto this office area. That was where they headed now, and when they reached the plain metal door they paused long enough for Tish to check the alarms and locks surrounding it.

"All clear," she announced, smirking. "Looks like the systems actually unlocked it for us when it saw us approaching. Helpful, that."

"Very." Cole grabbed the door's lockbar. "Once we're out of here—"

"Already done," the decker assured him smugly. "Our records are time-sensitive."

"Nice." And with that Cole pushed the lockbar and shoved the door open.

It was still the middle of the night—with everything that had happened, he'd half-expected it to be broad daylight outside, with people heading to work. He paused a second on the threshold to let his eyes adjust to the change in lighting, then dropped into a defensive crouch when someone large and hulking loomed into his peripheral vision.

"You bozos about done?" Mace—Stonemace Lifecrusher to his close friends and associates—demanded, stepping into the light above the door just enough for them to see it was him, his signature stone mace hefted in both hands. "'Cause I've already had to put one patrol down, and sent another off on a wild goose chase, and there's a third on its way. But I figured you'd hit a snag when the comms dropped."

"Yeah, we did, but we got past it," Cole replied, stepping all the way out of the building and heading toward the ork and the comforting shadows around him. "Let's get the hell out of here."

He heard several mutters of agreement behind him, but didn't look back as he followed Mace along the exit route the big ork had cleared for them. At this point, the job was done, so the team wasn't really a team anymore. Just a handful of individuals all hired for the same purpose, and all interested in getting away and getting paid. That meant it was in each of their own best interests to make it away from here safe and sound, so he'd let the others worry about that themselves. Even Lorelei. Anyway, she was a big girl. She could take care of herself, and wouldn't appreciate him suggesting otherwise.

Besides, he had the amulet. As long as he got out of here okay, he'd get paid. And if some of the rest of them— particularly the two newbs, who had nearly gotten him killed— were too slow or stupid to escape? Well, that just meant a bigger cut for him.

Cole thought he could live with that.

# FOUR

"Right, the meet's set for tomorrow, nine a.m. sharp," Mace reported as he stomped back in through the door, tugging it shut behind him. "Meet here at eight-thirty and we'll all go over together."

"Go where, exactly?" Rodrick demanded, but the big ork shook his spike-adorned head. "Oh, come on," the mage practically whined. "You're not even gonna tell us that much? What's it gonna hurt? You've got the damn thing already!"

That had been the odd thing about this job. Mace was the one the client had contacted in the first place. He was the one who had come to each of them and invited them into it. And he'd been the only one in contact with the client throughout the process. It had been Mace who'd told them what building they were hitting, and Mace who had then—once they'd cased the place the first time—revealed what their exact target was. Cole had wondered more than once whether the whole "client" thing was just a smokescreen, and Mace himself was the one behind this job, but although the ork had proven himself surprisingly savvy for someone as rough and tough as he was, he hadn't struck Cole as the mastermind type.

Not that it really mattered in the end. As long as the money was real, Mace could have the amulet all to himself for all Cole cared. Still, it seemed like an awfully elaborate ruse to maintain, especially now when they had the amulet. And if there wasn't a client, why wait until tomorrow to pay them off and send them on their merry ways? So Cole had to assume that there was a client, and they would in fact be doing the handoff tomorrow as Mace had said. He didn't see any harm in their knowing where the meet would take place, either.

But still Mace refused. "Meet here at eight-thirty," was all he said. "That's it." He waved a heavy hand toward the door. "In the meantime, get the hell out."

This time it was Lorelei who protested. "Why?" she asked, rising to her feet to confront the ork. Which didn't really help all that much, seeing as how she was almost a head shorter than him. "This is a good, safe place—you said so yourself. Why can't we just all wait here together until the meet?"

Mace glowered down at her, a veritable legion of spikes, chains, studs, rings, and tattoos covering him in what amounted to modular armor, his right hand clutching the handle of the stone mace where it rose from its sheath on his upper leg. "'Cause I said so," he growled through his tusks, "and it's my place."

Lorelei stood her ground for a second, but when it was clear Mace wasn't going to budge, she shook her head. "Fine, I'm out of here." She glanced back at the rest of them where they were sprawled on the assorted couches and chairs clustered about the central table, her eyes lingering on Cole perhaps a half-second longer than Rodrick and Tish. "The rest of you coming? Unless there's something that says we can't all hang out together either?" she demanded of Mace, but he didn't reply.

Cole pried himself up from the couch. "Yeah, all right, sure. Come on, you two." Then he reached into his pocket and extracted the amulet. "Here, you'd better hold onto this," he said, offering it to Mace.

But, much to his surprise, the ork shook his head. "Naw, keep it till tomorrow," he said. Then he grinned, which was, if anything, more fearsome than his scowl. "Builds trust an' all that. 'Sides, you don't even wanna think about trying to cut me outta this deal...it'd be the last thing you ever did."

"Never even crossed my mind." Cole continued dangling the amulet between them for a moment, then returned it to his pocket with a shrug. "Okay, fine."

Rodrick and Tish were standing by now, and Lorelei was at the door, so the three of them joined her and, after one last glance at Mace left standing alone in the room, pushed the door open and stepped outside.

It was early morning—Mace had left at dawn to contact the client, apparently not trusting the rest of them enough to have the conversation in their presence—and Cole had cat-napped on the couch for a bit after they'd gone to ground here, so he felt reasonably well rested. But hungry.

"Who's up for breakfast?" he asked. Fortunately, Mace's place was in the PCC sector as well, so they hadn't had to worry about crossing borders after pulling the job.

"You buying?" Lorelei hit him with her devastating smile, wrapping one hand around his arm to add further impact.

But Cole had built up at least a small tolerance to her charms. "After we get paid, sure," he agreed easily, patting her hand but not removing it. "Until then, it's everyone for themselves."

"Food sounds good," Tish agreed, cracking her knuckles. "Coffee sounds even better."

That drew appreciative sounds all around, and Rodrick nodded. "I know a place not far from here," he offered. "Cheap, decent, not too loud. And they won't care if we hang there for a while."

"Lead on," Lorelei commanded, and Rodrick turned and headed off down the sidewalk, the rest of them falling into step behind him.

"So what'll you do with your share?" Lorelei asked Cole as they walked, her hand still on his arm. "Besides buy me breakfast, of course."

"Haven't thought about it much, honestly," Cole replied. He saw Rodrick straighten slightly and Tish tilt her head, so he kept his voice pitched loud enough that they could all hear him. "Get out of Denver for a while, to start. Both because there might be some heat from this and just because—" he shrugged, "—it might be nice to travel. Buy some new mods, maybe?"

"Guns," Tish suggested, not bothering to turn around—she had moved up to walk beside Rodrick so they were two by two, just like they had been during the job itself. "You could use some guns."

"I suppose." She wasn't the first person to tell Cole that—Mace had as well, and he'd heard it from other people over the years, too. He'd even been turned down for a few jobs because of it. Most cyborgs had built-in weaponry, after all. And some kind of armor or other defensive tech. Other than his arms and some of his optics, most of Cole's modifications were more basic. More of the life-saving variety—his, not anyone else's. He had an artificial spine, several synthetic organs, and part of both legs, as well as his arms and eyes and a few other odds and ends, weren't original equipment. Even bits of his jaw and cheekbones were add-ons.

In other words, before Doc had gotten to him, he'd been in bad shape. Most likely the result of some accident. At least that's what Doc had guessed, and Cole had agreed it made sense. It wasn't like he remembered anything different.

Or anything at all, before he had woken up in recovery.

Whatever had happened, it'd very nearly killed him.

"What about you?" he asked Lorelei, shifting the focus away from him. "What're you going to do with your share?"

"Ooh, that's easy," she answered, a happy little smile touching her lips. "I'm going to buy me a penthouse somewhere. Maybe here, maybe some other city, I haven't decided yet. But it's going to be high up and have huge windows all around so I can look down on all the poor little people, and I'm going to fill it with expensive furniture and even more expensive artwork and then I'm going to throw massive parties that only the best people get invited to and everyone else is dying to attend." She was practically bouncing with excitement just from picturing it.

Cole laughed, half at her enthusiasm and half at the future she'd painted. "I don't know that we're getting paid *that* much," he joked. Though initially he had felt they were getting paid a stupid amount for what was supposed to have been a simple break-and-enter and snatch-and-grab. Now, given how much added security there had been, he was starting to think they'd actually earned the inflated paycheck after all. Still, even 150k, divided five ways, wasn't going to buy *that*.

Lorelei punched him in the arm with her free hand, which didn't hurt at all thanks to the metal coils and other fibers running through his limbs. "Don't ruin my fun," she insisted, flouncing as if she were just some spoiled little rich girl rather than a danger-seeking professional thief. "If I can't afford to do all that here, I'll move somewhere smaller, where I can." Then she hit him with a pout that would have done any debutante proud. "And you'll come and visit me wherever I am, won't you?"

"Sure, if I'm on the invite list," Cole agreed. Half of his brain reminded him that she was just manipulating him, but the other half—and the rest of him—still didn't care. Not when she was standing this close to him, the heat of her slender body warming his side, her smile and her gaze heating him up even further, her scent of lavender and lilac washing over him and making his head spin...

"I'm gonna get me a brand-new deck," Tish declared, smacking her hands together. "Fairlight, top of the line, all the bells and whistles. And the inputs to go with it." Unlike most deckers, Tish didn't have any implants to link her directly into her deck or the systems she used it to invade. She'd claimed it was because she was old school, but Cole had suspected all along that it was more a matter of funds than principles. It sounded like he'd been right, but he generously decided not to point that out right now.

"What about you, Rodrick?" he asked instead, tagging their guide into the conversation. "What will you do with your share?"

"Some of it I'll save for enchantments and the like," Rodrick answered, still leading them toward the spot he'd chosen. "Some new formulae, reagents, things like that. The rest I'll send to my mother."

"Your mother? Seriously?" Lorelei made a noise somewhere between a laugh and a snort, and even Tish rolled her eyes. "You couldn't come up with anything better than that?"

"She's sick," the mage replied, his tone a lot sharper than before. "She needs an operation, but the family couldn't afford it. That's why I took this job. It's not exactly my regular gig." He left the "unlike the rest of you" unsaid, but it still hung over them like a pall, killing the good cheer they'd all had a second before.

"Well," Cole said after the silence had dragged on a few seconds, "I for one am glad you were there. I'd hate to think how much drek we'd have been in if you hadn't canceled those wards for us."

"The ones I managed to take out," Rodrick pointed out, but his voice had softened a bit. "But thanks."

They didn't say anything else until after they'd reached the café Rodrick knew and had chosen a table in back of the nearly empty restaurant, but at least it wasn't as awkward as it had been. And once they'd all ordered food and coffee, their good moods seemed to miraculously resurface.

"Can I see it?" Rodrick asked, holding out his hand. He didn't have to say what "it" he meant.

Cole didn't even hesitate. "Sure, why not?" he pulled the amulet from his pocket and set it on the table between them all, careful to arrange the menus and water glasses and napkin holder to hide it from view to anyone passing by.

"It's not all that pretty," Lorelei commented, poking at the medallion with one slender finger. "I think that's a ruby there, but it's not even faceted properly, more like a rough cut, and without inspecting it I can't even tell if it's got flaws or not."

Tish nodded. "I kind of like it, but if you'd told me it was junk jewelry, I'd believe you."

But Rodrick was staring at the amulet, clearly entranced. "Oh, no..." he whispered, his eyes huge. "You can't feel it? The energy coming off this thing—it's immense. Absolutely insane."

Cole studied the amulet with the rest of them. Lorelei was right, it didn't look all that special. Or that pretty. Or that valuable. But it had sure had enough security around it to mean something to someone. And now that he really concentrated, he thought he could feel something from it, though it was faint.

"Is it like a tingling in the back of your head, but also almost a glare off it like it was a bright light stabbing at your eyes?" he asked.

Tish and Lorelei both looked at him like he'd gone nuts, but Rodrick nodded. "Yeah, that's it," the mage agreed, switching his gaze to Cole for a minute instead, one arched eyebrow rising even higher. "You must have some magic sensitivity in you, then. I had no idea."

"Me either," Cole admitted. "So what does it do, then?"

"I don't know," the mage answered after another minute. "It's big, though. Really big." He frowned. "What's weird is, I couldn't feel it all until you set it on the table. It's like it was shielded before that." He squinted at the amulet, holding it close to one eye, the other squeezed shut. "There's some sort of writing here, I think," he said after a few seconds of scrutiny. "I can't make it out, though. I actually wouldn't have noticed it all, but the script itself feels like it has some power to it. Strange. Normally you only see that in incantations, but I'm not sure why—"

Tish interrupted, grabbing the amulet out of Rodrick's hand and tossing it back to Cole. "Incoming," she hissed.

Looking up, Cole spotted the waitress approaching with their orders and nodded thanks to Tish even as he stowed the amulet back in his pocket. No sense risking everything now by letting someone else see the piece and possibly report it—and them.

After the waitress set everything down and left, Cole raised his drink. "To a job well done," he said, and the others clinked theirs together. "And to a handsome payday soon to come."

"Hear hear," Lorelei agreed. She took a quick sip of hers, then smiled at him, her eyes devilish over the top of it. "I think I'll get a hotel room for the night, rather than go back to my place. Seems safer that way. Care to join me?"

Cole was proud that he didn't actually spit or choke in surprise, and hoped his 'ware prevented him from turning too red when he answered, "Uh, okay, yeah, that'd be great." But he had a feeling his augmentations could only do so much, and even they weren't up to working miracles. Especially with Tish laughing openly at his discomfort, Lorelei smirking, and even Rodrick chuckling behind his hand.

Still, an invite was an invite, and Cole could think of far worse ways to spend the intervening hours.

They stayed at the coffee shop another hour or so, chatting about this and that, drinking coffee and nibbling food, before Lorelei downed the last of her latest drink and rose gracefully to her feet. "Time for us to be off to bed," she declared, making Cole flush again as he floundered to his feet after her.

He could hear Rodrick and Tish laughing at him again as he followed Lorelei out, but right now he really didn't care.

# FIVE

Mace answered the door on the first knock. "You're late," he greeted them, but still pushed the door open enough for first Lorelei and then Cole to duck under his powerful arm and into the hideout.

"You said eight-thirty," Cole replied, double-checking the digital readout that constantly showed in the upper corner of his right eye. "It's eight twenty-eight."

"You tell him," Tish called out, and he glanced around to finally locate her leaning against a counter in what was presumably the kitchen. "I got here twenty minutes ago and he told me the exact same thing."

"Where's Rodrick?" Lorelei asked, then nodded as the mage held up a hand from where he was ensconced in a low-slung chair off to one side. "Hey, the gang's all here. Back together again and all that. Did everyone have a good night? Because I know I did."

She leered at Cole, which he suspected was only because she knew it would make him blush again. Not that he hadn't had a good night. It had been a very good night, in fact—one of the best he could remember. Not terribly restful, but very, very good. But he didn't think the rest of the team really needed to hear all about it.

Clearly Lorelei disagreed.

Tish laughed at his obvious discomfort, then fist-bumped Lorelei as she passed by. Rodrick didn't say anything, but did look mildly amused. Mace didn't even crack a smile.

"Let's get going," was all he said. "It's gonna take us a good twenty minutes to get there on foot, and we don't wanna be late."

Twenty minutes? That made Cole's ears perk up, and he could see that it had piqued the others' interest as well. Since they were already close to one edge of the city, twenty minutes could easily put them outside it altogether, even on foot, and he wondered if that might be where they were headed. Most places inside the city were too well-watched to hand off stolen goods, especially something as hot as this amulet. And there was the issue of the sectors, each under a different government's control, each with its own rules, its own law enforcement, and each with a strong prejudice against outsiders. Using any of the other zones for a handoff would be asking for trouble from the locals, if they found out. Outside the city was completely open, though, and there were a ton of places they could go that would provide good cover and easy access. And if they were on foot they'd be harder to spot and harder to track.

Sure enough, Mace led them toward the city's western border. The spot he picked had walls instead of the usual double fence line, but even though they were sturdier, the walls here weren't policed or even juiced—they were more there to serve as a demarcation than as a real barrier. It was a lot more difficult to move between zones than to get in or out of the city in general (and even that could be managed if you knew what you were doing). If people wanted to leave Denver so badly, the prevailing attitude was that they were welcome to take their chances outside, and if they made it this far, they could always enter the Outer Boundary at one of the border crossings. Those tended to be open to everyone during the day, so there wasn't a whole lot of point to trying to sneak over instead.

But that was exactly what they did now, scaling the walls and dropping down on the other side. The walls here were only three meters high, so Cole simply extended his arms, grasped the top edge with both hands, and hauled himself up. He actually paused when he was only a couple meters off the ground and turned to offer Lorelei a hand, but the elven thief slid past him at that very moment, walking up the wall like it were a level floor, and grinning down at him to clearly say "what's taking you so long, slowpoke?"

Meanwhile Rodrick was levitating himself to the top, Mace had tossed a grappling hook up and was now scaling that, and Tish—well, Tish was climbing, using no equipment at all, only her fingers and toes, boots strung together and slung around her neck as she free-climbed faster than most people could ascend a flight of stairs. Which made sense, Cole realized. After all, decker or not, she was still a dwarf. They were good with stone, weren't they?

Since he clearly didn't have to worry about any of the others, he concentrated on climbing the wall himself, and within a few seconds had retracted his arms and was straddling the top. Then he just hopped down, his hands still latched onto the wall as he lowered himself slowly down to the ground again.

He was the second one down. Lorelei was already waiting at the bottom, and Mace, Rodrick, and Tish all dropped down a few seconds after him.

"This way," Mace declared, stomping away without another word, coiling his rope around his forearm as he walked. The others fell into step behind him, doing their best to keep up with the ork's long, aggressive strides.

Denver was at the base of the Rocky Mountain range, and Mace seemed to be leading them up into the mountains proper, hiking higher and higher, skirting trees and bushes and boulders toward some destination only he knew. There wasn't much point in complaining about it, though, Cole knew. So they followed without a word and with only a minor amount of grumbling.

Finally, after ten solid minutes of hiking, Mace slowed to a stop. Their surroundings looked to Cole like any of the other areas they'd just passed through: rough, rocky terrain punctuated by short scrub brush and tall evergreens, the ground thick with fallen pine needles that muffled footsteps nicely, the air crisp and clear.

"This is the place," Mace said. The ork looked around them, then nodded. "Yep." He pulled a scrap of paper from his pocket and thrust it at Cole. "Here's the password."

Cole just stared at the paper, making no effort to take it. "Uh, okay, so? And what do we need a password for?" He hadn't even seen anyone around except for them—who were they going to read the password to, exactly?

But Mace was still shoving the paper in his face. "Just read it," he insisted. When Cole still didn't move, the big ork sighed. "Look, that's what the client said to do, okay? We come here to this spot—" he held up a small GPS, which showed their current coordinates highlighted in red, "—and you call out the password so they know it's us and we've still got it and weren't followed. Then they give the countersign, and we wait until they meet us here, we give them the amulet, and they give us the cred. That's it." He waved the paper. "So let's do this and get rich, huh?"

Cole frowned. This didn't make a whole lot of sense, and he'd never heard of anyone doing a drop this way before. But Lorelei nudged him. "Just do it," she said softly, batting those big eyes at him. "Like he said, let's get it done and get paid and get gone."

Cole couldn't really find any fault with that idea—though his part in the plan still made him horribly uneasy—so he finally accepted the paper. He read it, glanced up at Mace, then read it again. "I don't even know what this says," he pointed out. "It's gibberish."

"Who cares?" Mace replied. "This is what the client said we had to read to confirm." He'd drawn his mace from its sheath at some point, and hefted it now. "So read it."

With a sigh, Cole pulled the amulet from his pocket and held it up in front of him. "I possess the amulet!" he shouted, feeling like an idiot to be talking to empty wilderness. "Here it lies in my hand. *Kichisi Igluhica!*"

As he shouted the words, the sun beat down on him through a break in the heavy foliage, and the ruby caught the glare and reflected it straight into his eye, blinding him with what felt like a spear straight through to his brain. He flinched and shifted away, wincing at the sudden, stabbing pain in his head and the shudder it sent into his chest.

Because he'd turned a little, Cole saw Rodrick standing just a little behind him. The elven mage's eyes had gone wide. "What?" he muttered, staring at Cole. "No! That's—"

And then Rodrick's head exploded.

# SIX

"Get down!" Mace shouted even before the elf's death had really registered. He shoved Cole with one huge hand, slamming him to the ground with a force that took the breath right out of him. Cole saw Rodrick's headless corpse still twitching only a couple meters away.

"Don't shoot!" Mace bellowed next, standing tall and holding his mace level above his head with both hands. "We're here to deliver the amulet! You said—"

This time Cole saw the impact strike the ork, knocking his head back. Amazingly, the big man didn't fall, even though Cole had also seen the bullet exit the back of his skull in a spray of blood and bone and hair. Instead Mace took a step forward, then another. But a second bullet struck, his head jerked forward and then back again, and the massive stone mace dropped from his hands as Stonemace Lifecrusher finally succumbed to the devastating effect of not one but two bullets to the brain.

As the ork's limp body pitched forward, Cole managed to get his feet back under him. Twisting, he saw Lorelei and Tish both crouched behind rocks and bushes nearby. "We need to get out of here!" he yelled, even though the woods were actually silent despite the recent onslaught. *Too quiet,* he realized after a second. There should have been the report of gunshots echoing among the trees, but there had been nothing, no warning or aftershock, nothing but the sight of his two teammates falling lifeless to the ground.

That meant this wasn't a random attack, or even the client suddenly deciding to save some money by taking them out. Whoever was shooting at them was set up somewhere nearby, probably with a good vantage point down on them, and had a silenced rifle. A high-powered one, if it could put a bullet clean through an ork's skull.

This was an ambush.

"We need to move," he repeated, rising to a crouch himself. The other two nodded. Cole scuttled toward them, the amulet still clutched in one hand, and wished now more than ever that he'd listened to Mace and the many others who'd suggested he get armaments built in. He had a gun, of course, but he rarely used it, and even now there wasn't a lot of point in drawing it when he couldn't even see their attacker. Their best bet was to stay low, use the trees for cover, and try to get out of range before the sniper could get a clean shot on any of them.

"This way," Tish called, straightening behind the boulder she'd chosen as a shield. "It looks like there's an old trail a few meters back, if we follow it, we might be able to stay low enough to avoid getting shot." She spared a quick glance at Rodrick's headless body and shuddered.

Cole didn't bother to reply. Instead he just quickened his pace, crawling over to her. Lorelei did the same, and soon the three of them were all huddled behind the same large rock. The dwarf gestured behind her, and now they could make out what she'd meant—a spot perhaps a dozen meters away looked more worn down than its surroundings, the twigs and leaves and needles crushed by the repeated tread of many feet. The path twisted out of view behind a clump of short trees, which Cole took to be a good sign. Right now anything that got them out of this mess was a good thing.

"Come on," Tish said, and sprinted away from their cover, her short legs moving with surprising speed. Lorelei was right behind her, and Cole brought up the rear. He kept expecting a bullet in the back, or one through his skull, but the woods remained quiet, and all three of them made it to the path safely. They didn't straighten up, though, keeping as low as they could without stumbling as they hurried away.

"What the hell was that?" Lorelei demanded once they'd been moving for a few minutes without any sign of further attack. "That had to be the buyer, right? Nobody else could've known we were here."

"Definitely," Tish agreed from in front. "That was a sniper rifle, no question." She frowned as she shoved a wayward branch out of her way, not even noticing when it whipped back into place and nearly struck Lorelei across the nose. "And they clearly targeted Rodrick first, then Mace. Take out the mage, and then the heavy. Smart."

Cole nodded, not even a little offended at her assessment. She was completely right—Rodrick and Mace had been the biggest threats in a fight, no question. But they'd also left him and Lorelei for last, which could prove to be a fatal error on the client's part—they were the fastest, quietest, sneakiest members of the team, after all. And he still had the amulet. He hadn't tucked it back away in all the confusion; it was still in his hand, which throbbed in time with his wildly beating heart. His head still hurt as well, and all of his senses were awhirl. It was as if he'd been tossed about in a blender and he was still shaken, barely able to put one foot in front of the other.

They continued on in silence a few more minutes, before the path leveled out, the trees around it thinning. "Think we're far enough away to be safe?" Tish asked, turning around and walking backward so she could speak to them more easily.

Which was how Cole—and Lorelei as well, judging by her gasp—clearly saw the bullet hole appear dead-center in the dwarf's forehead.

Tish pitched backward, her eyes already dulling as that quick spark faded from them, but Cole was no longer watching. Instead he was diving to the side, Lorelei sprawling in the opposite direction. "Shit!" she shouted as she fell, leaves billowing up about her. "Shit shit shit!"

"Yeah," Cole agreed, though he doubted his reply reached her, since he was speaking at a whisper. Not that keeping quiet had helped Tish any, but he couldn't help it. He glanced over at Lorelei, now several meters away from him, and he could tell from her panicked eyes that she was thinking the same thing he was—the sniper had either been tracking their progress the whole time or had already been set up to cover this trail which they had so conveniently spotted. Either way, they weren't safe here.

And with the trail unsafe to follow, their choices were to strike out into the woods in some random direction, hoping they could get under enough foliage to prevent the sniper from getting a clean shot, or go back up the way they came. Or just lie here, waiting for someone to come along and finish them off.

"We can't wait around," Lorelei called, and Cole nodded. "We're going to have to chance it. Ready?" She looked ready to lose it herself, her face pale and her lips twitching. But she was holding it together somehow, and Cole couldn't let himself do any less. He rose into a crouch again, silently indicating that he was ready to follow her lead.

She'd barely taken a step when she staggered and fell back, dropping onto her butt amid the leaves.

"No!" Cole ran to Lorelei's side, momentarily forgetting his own danger. Apparently the sniper hadn't trusted a head shot here in the trees, because the bullet had struck her in the chest. A dark stain was already beginning to spread across her tunic, and a matching shade trickled from her lips as she struggled for breath. Cole propped her up in his arms, knowing there wasn't anything he could do for her now but not willing to let her spend her last few seconds alone.

"Sorry," she whispered, trying to lift a hand to his face and failing. "Guess I can't invite you along on this one." Then she slumped, her last breath whistling out of her perforated chest, and she was gone.

"Damn it," Cole whispered, stroking her hair back from her face and planting a last kiss on her forehead. "Damn it!" Laying her gently on the ground, he rose to his feet, stunned by the brutal loss of something that had only just begun to show such promise, and the casual end to such a bright, vibrant soul. Was this how it ended for him, too? Well, if so he wasn't going to go down without a fight—nor was he willing to get shot cowering in a corner.

"You want me?" he shouted up at the sky, turning in a slow circle. "You want this?" He raised the amulet up high, so that the sunlight again glinted off it. "Come and get it!"

He didn't hear the shot that hit him, but he felt the impact—though it came from behind rather than in front. The force of it knocked him off his feet as it struck his lower back like a sledgehammer. The pain was already beginning to erupt before he hit the ground, the breath once again forced from his chest.

Then everything went mercifully dark.

# SEVEN

Cole stood on a mountaintop.

He couldn't remember how he'd gotten here, or exactly where here was, though it looked familiar. He wasn't sure what he was doing here, either. So for the moment, he just stood and looked around, taking in the beautiful vista spread out before him, of sky and clouds atop an array of lesser peaks interspersed with valleys and plateaus, snow and ice decorating their tips and the trees and rocks dotted about them like festive caps.

The wind was fierce up here, strong enough to not only tug at his clothes and hair but to push and pull his very limbs, and he was forced to brace himself to keep from toppling. The wind redoubled its efforts, pushing harder, then suddenly swooping around behind him to attack from the rear.

Almost as if the wind itself were alive, and angry, and determined to knock Cole from his perch.

*Or*, he thought suddenly, *like it's a child, and this is its favorite game.*

A powerful gust took him by surprise and lifted him right off his feet, and for a second Cole hung in the air, suspended by the gale that had built up around him. As he floated there, trapped in its crushing embrace, he was startled to see something else hovering above the peak just in front of him. It was small, and red, and glowed like intense flame, but somehow he knew it wasn't actual fire.

It was an eye.

And it was staring right at him.

"Wha—?"

Cole started awake, the image of that glowing red eye still burning into his mind, and for a second he couldn't remember where he was or why. Was he on the mountaintop? There were trees all around, and rocks, and dirt, and open sky.

Then he glanced over and saw a body lying only a few feet from him, slender limbs limp, long, pale hair in disarray, lovely face just visible beneath the hair, eyes closed, but lips still parted in surprise.

Lorelei.

And he remembered.

*I've got to get out of here*, Cole determined with a jolt of panic. He struggled to sit up, but something was wrong. His arms and legs felt like they'd been wrapped in cotton—he could still feel them, but only faintly, and they weren't responding to his urgent commands.

Then he recalled the pain he'd felt right before he'd passed out. A pain to his lower back.

*I was shot*, he realized. *In the back. Apparently in the spine.*

*I'm paralyzed.*

That was going to make escape tricky.

He gritted his teeth and concentrated as hard as he could, making his head throb even more than it already did—and his left arm twitched.

Yes!

So, not completely paralyzed. But close to it. Of course, some of his nerves and tendons and everything else were synthetic—maybe that was why he could still feel and move even a little bit? It was possible that the bullet had damaged but not destroyed his spine, but that it had forced some sort of system shutdown. And now things were starting to wake back up. If that was the case, he might regain mobility before too long.

But when he heard the voices, Cole knew that it wouldn't be soon enough.

"Over there," someone said, and he heard the rustling of feet through the leaves and needles. Several people, not bothering to be quiet. *Why should they, after all?* he acknowledged. Everyone was dead except for him, and he couldn't move.

A mass of shadows fell across him, blocking part of the sky above, and Cole squinted to make them out against the glare. At least four men, all peering down at him.

"This him?" one asked—a big, bulky bruiser of a man.

"Clearly," one of the others responded, and something in the tone made Cole focus on him. He wasn't as hefty as his three companions, and his long hair was silvery where its braid fell over one shoulder and down his shirt front. But his tone had an air about it, one Cole had heard before.

The air of command.

This was clearly the boss.

"He's awake," another pointed out, nudging Cole with what felt like a sledge to his side but was probably only a boot tip. "You want we should finish him?"

Cole winced and tensed, expecting the end, but instead the boss said, "No, just truss him up and let's go. Time's a-wasting."

Wait, they weren't going to kill him? Cole was still trying to process this idea when hands reached for him, several lengths of rope held between them. Even though he'd just heard the order to the contrary, the sight of the rope convinced Cole that they were about to tie him up so they could kill him later. And once he was bound, he wouldn't be able to escape even if he did regain the use of his limbs.

This was the end of the line for him.

He panicked, thrashing around as best he could, trying desperately to avoid those fatal bindings.

High above, the sky rapidly darkened. Black clouds rolled in like a rushing tide, filling his view with the angry turmoil of a brewing storm. A bad one.

"Hurry up," one of the men said, grabbing Cole's right wrist and wrapping a length of the rope around it. "It's getting nasty out here, and I don't feel like getting soaked."

Anything else he might have said was interrupted by the massive thunderclap that filled the clearing—and Cole's head— with its monstrous sound.

And the lightning bolt that seared down from the heavens, spearing the guy right through the top of the head. His whole body jerked and spasmed as the lightning arced through him, all his hair standing on end and then crisping and burning, his eyes sizzling and popping, his entire body browning and charring in an instant.

Then the lightning was gone, leaving the world dimmer by comparison, and the man's blackened corpse toppled to the ground mere centimeters from Cole's unresponsive form.

"Holy—" one of the other thugs stumbled to his feet and backed away, the rope slipping from his fingers. "Did you see that? Atlow just got fried!"

"Yeah, I saw it," the other replied, not rising from where he was kneeling and trying to grab Cole's other wrist. "Tough luck for him. Now get back over here and help me with this stiff."

The one who'd moved off paused, clearly torn between self-preservation and obedience.

His dilemma solved itself when a second lightning bolt lanced down and struck him full in the chest. He was dead before he could even protest that he hadn't decided to comply.

"Shit!" Now the third thug, the one who'd remained, was the one to fumble upright and stagger back. "What the hell?"

Cole watched all of this, puzzled but pleased. If the storm wanted to fry anyone who came near him, well, that was fine by him!

The boss came back into view. He leaned over Cole, studying him with cool blue-gray eyes—one of which had a red pinprick in it. A laser sight, Cole realized. This had to be the sniper. He didn't look scared like the remaining thug had before he'd jolted out of view. "Interesting," was all he said. Followed by, "I suppose I should have expected that. I'd better call this in."

"Expected what?" the guy demanded, echoing Cole's own thoughts. "What the hell's going on here? This isn't what we signed up for!"

Which made Cole wonder what they *had* signed up for. To ambush him and the others and take the amulet by force? The steely-eyed sniper hardly seemed to need any help— he'd downed every one of them on his own. Perhaps he'd just wanted them as a contingency, though, in case Mace or Rodrick had proven tougher than expected, or somehow ducked the shots.

Or maybe, the thought struck him, the sniper had realized he might need extra hands and muscle to pry the amulet from Cole's paralyzed grasp.

Something they had yet to do, since the chain was still wrapped around his fingers and the amulet itself was pinned between his hand and his chest.

While he'd been pondering this, the sniper had stepped away, out of sight but still within hearing. "We've got a complication," he'd said to someone, and then he'd lowered his voice and continued, no doubt explaining about the freak weather conditions—which now seemed to have dissipated, Cole noticed, leaving the sky above them clear and sunny once more.

"—Yeah, I can do that," the sniper said after a minute, apparently having just gotten new instructions from whomever he'd called. So he wasn't the boss after all, just the enforcer. But still important enough to speak directly to the actual client, it sounded like.

Which also meant he was someone Cole very much wanted to have a long chat with.

Sadly, he wasn't exactly in a position to do that right now. And even if he had been, his specialty was breaking and entering, not interrogation.

Another minute of hushed one-sided conversation ensued, and then the sniper called out, "Right—time for Plan B."

"Plan B? What's Plan B?" the thug asked, which explained who the sniper had been talking to after his other conversation.

"Allow me to explain," he said now, and this time at least the back-and-forth was all taking place in one location, as the sniper explained the plan to his hireling. Cole strained to make out details, but could only pick up sounds, nothing that would resolve itself into actual words. He had visual enhancements, though some of them seemed to be a bit outdated now. Nothing audial, however.

Now the conversation had apparently devolved into an argument. Specifically, the thug asking, "Why me? Why don't you do it?"

"Because you're the expert," the sniper replied. "And this will absolutely require both your finest skill and your fullest attention. Just do it fast and it should work out fine."

"Should isn't a whole lot of comfort," the thug insisted, but from his resigned tone Cole guessed that he'd finally been swayed.

Cole tried again to move, and was heartened when both of his hands shuddered slightly in response, and his right foot pivoted to the side. He was starting to get control of his limbs again! He could feel that thick, swaddled sensation fading a little as well. A little more time and he might be able to move properly. It would still be two on one, admittedly, and he'd never been much of a fighter—at least, not that he could recall—but he was certainly highly motivated right now. They might not be expecting him to put up any resistance at all, considering how he hadn't previously. It was something, at least, and Cole was more than willing to take it and use it for all it was worth.

Sadly, he never got the chance.

The sky was just starting to darken again when, mixed with the thud of running feet, a shadow raced across Cole. The thug loomed over him so quickly that he could only blink stupidly at the man's heavy features before a thick fist came crashing down, robbing Cole of his recently recovered consciousness.

The last sound he heard was the clap of renewed thunder, and the sizzle of lightning.

# EIGHT

Once again Cole found himself trapped in mid-air, battling the wind that both battered at him and kept him aloft. That great red eye still stared at him, its fiery gaze stabbing into his brain like a needle right between the eyes, and he knew he was wailing in pain even though he could hear nothing over the howling of the wind. He twisted from side to side, struggling to pull loose, but the tempest had his arms pinned to his sides and he could not gain enough leverage to free them. His legs had enough leeway to kick, but there was nothing for them to shove against or slam into, only the swirling air all around.

That left only one avenue of attack. Cole forced himself to stop squinting from pain and to level his own glare right back at the eye he faced. He put all of his concentration into his stare, channeling his will through his eyes and directing that mental push at his airy adversary. He could almost feel his thoughts and emotions and personality, his every shred of self, being honed into a mental spear that he then thrust at his foe.

For a second, it worked. The eye jerked back as if startled, and it widened, then narrowed, like it had been surprised. Even hurt.

But then it narrowed further, before flaring brighter. Now it was truly enraged.

The wind tightened around Cole, his arms crushing against him, his lungs laboring for breath. Stars started to dance in his vision, but through the pain-haze he saw three shimmers form to the right of the eye, one above the other. They were mere ripples in the air, yet he could still tell they were not only parallel to each other, but tapering in slightly toward the center.

Like the three talons of a cruelly clawed hand.

The eye glowed, and somehow it looked as if it were laughing at him as those barely visible talons suddenly reared up and then lashed forward—

—and Cole screamed as white-hot agony pierced his chest and ripped through him, tearing his consciousness away like so much tissue paper and scattering it to the hungry, angry wind.

"*AHHH!*" Cole bolted upright, clutching at his chest as if his grasp could staunch the pain tearing through him. His hands came away sticky with blood and he fell back to the ground, gasping for breath, fighting to clear his head from the haze and shock still wrapped around him. It was only after he'd managed to draw in several long, deep breaths that his brain recognized what he'd accomplished without conscious thought.

He'd sat up! And grabbed at his chest! He could move again!

At least, he could a little bit. When he tried to push himself up to a sitting position again his head swam, his vision blurred, and he was forced to lie back down, close his eyes, and count to ten. Slowly.

So, still not fully functional. But at least he could move a little. His arms and legs were pins and needles where they weren't hurting outright, but they were no longer cottony. His back still hurt, but it was more of a dull throb compared to the terrible burning in his chest.

He was in bad shape. But he was conscious, which was good. And not paralyzed, which was also good. And his internal systems seemed to be running, which was excellent, because it meant he could do this—

Reaching around to his left forearm, Cole fumbled at a small bump just above the crook of his elbow. Pressing his thumb and forefinger firmly to either side of the protrusion, he twisted, then pulled. A small piece of artificial skin peeled away, revealing a slight depression—and a large red diode nestled inside.

Cole jammed down on that with his thumb, and it lit up. Then he collapsed again, all of his energy spent in that maneuver.

He just hoped the rest of it still worked. And that it had enough range to reach.

Otherwise, he thought as the darkness claimed him again, he might not be waking up from this one.

The talons were embedded in his chest, and Cole could barely think from the pain. But in order to hurt him, those same talons had been forced to take on some solidity, so now he could reach down with both hands and grab hold of them. Using every ounce of his remaining strength, he pried them out of his flesh. The tips came away bloody.

Then, holding the top talon in his right hand and the bottom one in his left, he took as deep a breath as his wounds and the wind still encircling him would allow—

—and yanked his arms apart as wide as they would go.

This time it was the wind that shrieked in pain as its talons tore free, the eye going wide and pale as the tempest fought to maintain itself against such an unexpected, and most likely unprecedented, injury.

Even though he was still faint from pain himself, Cole couldn't help but smile.

"Ah, there you are! Was starting to wonder if I'd lost you for good."

A gruff voice greeted Cole as he swam back to consciousness, blinking to clear his sight and his mind. The lingering image of a glowing red eye finally faded, to be replaced by a wide, craggy face sprouting whiskers from almost every possible location—brows, nose, upper lip, cheeks, jaw, and chin. It was a hairy, unkempt mess—and the most welcome sight Cole could imagine.

"Hey, Doc," he rasped, his voice emerging hoarse and dry and barely above a whisper. "Guess you heard me call."

"Hard to miss," Erasmus "Doc" Cragtop replied, his voice as grouchy as ever, but his eyes twinkling. He tapped a blunt finger against Cole's arm. "Wouldn't be much good as an emergency beacon if it went unnoticed, now would it?" The dwarf scowled, making his mustache droop even lower. "Be glad I did, too, or you'd'a been crow food for sure. What the hell kinda mess you get yourself into this time, boy?"

Cole frowned, tried to lift his head, then gave up and lay it back down on what he guessed was an examining table of some sort. "A job gone bad," he finally answered when he could draw sufficient breath again. "Really bad."

"Yeah? I could tell that much from the dead bodies everywhere," Doc snapped, stomping off to get something but returning a minute later. "The ones with the bullet holes, I get what happened to them, that's easy. But those other three, what did that? Some kinda spell? Energy beam? Laser?"

Cole shook his head and instantly regretted it when black spots appeared across his vision. "Lightning," he managed to gasp out, squeezing his eyes shut until his head stopped spinning. "At least, that's what it looked like." He wasn't sure how much of what he remembered had been real and how much had been hallucinations brought on by shock and pain and blood loss.

Except for the sniper. Him, Cole was sure about. The steely-eyed man was real—and Cole intended to find him.

Once he was back on his feet, that was.

Which led to his next question: "How bad is it?"

He could tell from Doc's expression that the answer was going to be "pretty bad."

"Not the worst I ever seen," Doc answered first. His eyes twinkled again. "That was this young fella I found out on the streets, tossed aside like yesterday's trash, mangled and torn and barely alive. Not even sure he could properly be called alive, to be honest—more like 'too damn stubborn to lay down and die like he ought.' But I figured that kinda determination oughta be rewarded with at least a solid try." He snorted. "Couldn't save half of him, but the rest, well, I patched that together okay, I guess."

"Way better than okay," Cole argued weakly, though he couldn't help the smile that tugged at his lips. "And you know I appreciate it, Doc. You saved my life, made me whole again. I can never thank you enough."

That made the dwarf scowl even more fiercely than before. "So this is how you repay me?" he demanded, jabbing a finger at Cole's chest but stopping just short of actually touching him. "Look at you! What'd you do, get yourself in the middle of a fight, literally? You got wounds front and back, boy—how'd you manage that one?"

So Cole told him what he remembered: the job, the ambush, the shot to his back, waking up mostly frozen, the voices, the lightning, the sniper, then the fist. "And then I woke up and they were gone and I was bleeding," he finished, brushing a hand lightly over the bandages now wrapping his chest. "I managed to hit the distress beacon before I passed out again."

"Well, you were damn lucky, that's all I can say." Doc held up a portable screen so Cole could see it. "Shot to your back grazed your spine, but didn't sever it. Blew out some servos, shorted out some linkages, shut down a relay or two—that's why you couldn't feel much or move nothing till it all rebooted and rerouted. I fixed all that good as new, though you'll be a mite sore along there for a few days." He flipped to a different image, one of Cole's torso. "This, though—this is a whole other thing."

Cole stared at the picture. He'd seen scans of his body before, of course. They were some of the first things he could remember after Doc had found him and dragged him in and patched him up, removing everything that was too damaged to repair and replacing those parts with artificial ones. So now his eyes zeroed in on the anomaly at once.

"What's that?" he asked, gesturing toward the spot on the screen.

"That," Doc replied, using thumb and forefinger to zoom in on the spot, "is some kinda shard, gotta be from whatever stabbed you in the chest. Missed your heart by less than a millimeter. Must've glanced off the breastbone and snapped." Over the years Cole had gotten good at reading the dwarf's facial expressions despite all that hair, and he could see Doc was worried as he continued. "I can't get to it, can't remove it, it's in too deep and it's too close, could tear your heart open if I try."

"Is it likely to move on its own?" Cole asked. It felt like the shard was throbbing against his heart with every beat, but he knew that was just his mind playing tricks on him.

Doc shook his shaggy head. "Naw, it's nestled in good. I'll wanna check it again in a few weeks, make sure, but if it hasn't shifted by then, it's not gonna." His brow furrowed so deeply his eyebrows almost touched the tip of his nose. "If it does move, though, and angles in...well, you may not even get enough time to push that beacon again."

Cole nodded. "Message received. Thanks." He pushed down with his arms, trying to lever himself up, but failed and fell back on the table again. Not giving up, he took several deep breaths and tried again, this time managing to force himself into a semi-reclining position. "How soon before I can get back on my feet?" he asked once he could speak again.

"At least a day afore you can walk," Doc answered, as no-nonsense as always. "Prob'ly two or three 'fore you're up to doin' more'n stumbling to the drekker and back. Why, you got someplace you gotta be?"

"Yeah." Cole frowned, eyes squeezing shut against the pain, but his mind already awhirl. "I've got some friends to avenge."

"Friends?" That drew another snort from the stumpy scientist. "What, those bodies I found with you? I ain't never seen 'em afore—how close could you be if you hadn't introduced me?"

"Fine, maybe not friends," Cole admitted, though an image of Lorelei in that hotel room flashed through his mind and made him wince. "But we could've been." He thought of sitting in that café with her and Rodrick and Tish. "We were starting to be." He glared at Doc. "And they were my teammates. We were on the job together. They're dead, and I'm not. That leaves it up to me to put things right."

"Attitude like that's gonna get you dead sooner rather than later," Doc pointed out. "Safest thing'd be to walk away, forget about it, and hope whoever did that to you does the same."

But Cole shook his head. Slowly. "I can't do that," he argued. "You know I can't." He managed a weak grin. "Any more than you could leave some poor sap to die on your doorstep when you could maybe save him."

"I just didn't want him bleedin' all over the walk," Doc grumbled back, but they both knew he didn't mean that. And he didn't try talking Cole out of anything again.

Which was good, because Doc had certainly been right about one thing. Cole was way too stubborn to just lie down and die—and he was way too stubborn to just let this go, too.

# NINE

Just as Doc had predicted, it was a full day before Cole felt mended enough to even stagger between the bathroom and the cot Doc had transferred him to now that he was awake. Anything more than that was clearly beyond him, since even that much left him pale, shaking, and covered in sweat.

The second day was better. He was only winded and a little shaky after a bathroom break.

By the third day, Cole was able to use the facilities and, instead of returning to his cot, sink into a battered old rocking chair nearby. His hands didn't shake at all, both vision and breathing were steady, and he could think clearly again, though his head still hurt and his chest still throbbed beneath the bandage.

On the fourth day, Cole dragged himself out of Doc's garage-workshop-sickbay and into the street. It felt good to be out in the open air again. He stood just outside and took a long, deep breath, enjoying the mix of cooking, exhaust, sweat, and metal that made up humanity. Then he squared his shoulders and started on his way.

But there was a problem. Denver was a big city. Even ignoring the issue of the different sectors, Doc's place was all the way over on one side in the UCAS sector—and Cole's destination was clear on the other, in PCC.

And even though he was healing, he knew there was no way he'd be able to walk from here to there. He might make it a third of the way before collapsing, and he wouldn't put it past Doc to just leave him out on the street this time, probably with a note pinned to his chest that read "serves him right." But he also had no money to hire a car.

He'd just have to get creative about transportation, then.

Fortunately, a block away he spotted a nice little bar, with a wood-paneled front, brick elsewhere, and a row of narrow stained-glass windows up above to allow in just a bit of light—but too high for the patrons inside to see out easily.

And that meant whoever owned the battered but still serviceable motorbike chained to the rack out front wasn't able to see Cole size it up, walk stiffly over to it, and then carefully hoist one leg over to straddle the seat.

It took him a few seconds to pick the lock on the chain. *Lorelei could have done it in a heartbeat,* Cole couldn't help but think, feeling a pang. Engines and ignitions he was good at, though, and he had the bike purring to life before that sharp stab of loss had faded.

Then he was riding off. He made a mental note to return the bike when he was done. With any luck, the owner would still be inside, and would never even know he'd borrowed it.

One of the augmentations Doc had given Cole when he'd saved him was a built-in GPS. Cole marked the places he'd been as a matter of course, so he had a full map of everywhere he'd gone inside the city, as well as the places he'd visited the few times he'd set foot beyond its borders. After losing all memory of whatever he'd done before he got his cybermods, Cole wasn't about to forget anything that had happened to him ever again.

Those mods made it a snap to navigate the safe passages between sectors, the alleys and narrow streets that were deliberately "overlooked" by guards and left open to all traffic as a means of maintaining smuggling and other less-than-legal activities, and then find Mace's hideout. Getting inside wasn't much harder—again, Lorelei could have beaten the physical lock faster, but Cole was an expert at electronic systems, and he had the alarms disengaged and the door open before anyone could wander by and wonder why he was standing outside for so long.

Once inside, Cole slid the door shut, breathed a sigh of relief, and took a few seconds to rest his weight against the door. That had taken more out of him than he'd expected.

Still, a minute later he'd recovered enough to push off and look around.

When they'd been here before, he'd only seen the main room and the bathroom. The main room took up the bulk of the place, with couches and chairs grouped around a low table in the center, a space for a motorbike—which was still here. Cole decided to take it with him when he left, since it was bigger and nicer than the one he'd stolen and it wasn't like its previous owner was going to need it anymore. The place also had a weapons and armor rack in the front, and a kitchen at the back. The bathroom was to one side, and on the other a flight of stairs was built into the wall, leading up to a small, open sleeping platform.

Cole started there.

He wasn't entirely sure what he hoped to find—a scribbled address, a business card, a dedicated phone. Instead all he saw was a mattress with a sweat-stained pillow and mussed sheets, and some cast-off clothes. He dug through the clothes anyway, just in case, but came up with nothing more than a few coins, a few rumpled bills, a packet of breath mints, and a folding knife.

Next Cole searched the living room area. Not surprisingly, that was also a bust. The kitchen didn't have anything except a few beers, some moldy food in takeout containers, and some ill-used dishes and utensils. The bathroom contained even less of use, and upon entering it Cole was reminded why he'd only used it once and very hurriedly during his last visit. Ork piss was apparently even more pungent than human, and Mace wasn't very big on cleaning up. Or aiming.

Finally, Cole checked the armory and garage area. Mace had left a nice shotgun and a good pair of pistols behind, and Cole packed those to take with him when he left. There was some armor, too: a heavily plated vest Cole couldn't even imagine wearing, much less fighting in. A shelf held some ammo and one grenade, and then there was the bike. And that was it.

Cole was just about to give up when something occurred to him. He glanced over at the bike, then stepped closer to examine it.

Sure enough, it was a nice bike. With lots of nice features, including a sync feature for your comms, whether internal or self-contained. That way, if someone called, you could see the number and caller's image projected onto the bike's windscreen, and you could voice-command it to call a number logged into your system.

Which meant it also kept track of your calls.

Cole bypassed Mace's password easily enough—the ork had used his own name in reverse, no doubt thinking he was being clever—and pulled up the call history. Mace had contacted him a week ago now, so he started looking a day before that. Several of the numbers came up as bars, one was a mechanic's shop, another was a gunsmith, and a whole bunch were takeout places. Then there was his number, and Lorelei's shortly after that, and two others Cole guessed were probably Rodrick's and Tish's.

And then there was one that was unlisted.

Cole hit *Call* on that one and crossed his fingers.

*"Yes?"* The voice that answered was female, Cole would guess middle-aged, and sharp enough to carve through steel. It didn't sound at all familiar, but Cole figured he'd started this roll of the dice, the least he could do was let it ride.

"This is Cole, Cole Danvers," he replied. "Mace is dead. So are the others."

*"What about the item?"* the mystery woman demanded. *"Do you have it?"*

So this was the right number, at least. Cole had hoped it would be. Mace had been clever enough to go outside when he'd called his contact after the job was done, but Cole had figured the ork wouldn't have bothered to hide anything beforehand. Why would he, when the team wasn't even assembled yet?

Unfortunately, Cole didn't think he could bluff something this critical. "No," he answered. "The guys that cut us down, they took it."

*"I'm sorry to hear that,"* the woman said, though she didn't sound particularly sympathetic. *"Without it, the deal is dead."*

"I figured," Cole told her. "That's not why I'm calling. I want to know—"

But she cut him off. *"The deal is dead,"* she repeated. And then she hung up.

Cole sighed and banged a fist against the bike's console, but he knew it wouldn't do any good. Nor was there any point in trying again. If the woman was half as canny as he expected, she'd have blocked Mace's number already.

Her own number, however, Cole now had on file. And although it was unlisted, that only meant there wasn't a name or address associated with it in the public databases.

Fortunately, even though he wasn't a hacker, Cole knew how to access some of the databases that weren't so public. The kind you had to give a name for, under the assurance that the information would never get out.

If he could dig that up, he could find out who she was and confront her in person. All he wanted was an idea who had hit them and why, and where to find them. Then he'd go after them and—Cole only had a vague idea of what to do then, but it involved avenging his teammates and taking back the amulet and probably a whole lot of hitting and shooting. He figured he could make that part up once he got there.

He was tinkering with the bike's computer, trying to get into its memory so he could pull up the number's routing code, when a door slammed outside.

Acting purely on instinct, he dove behind the weapons locker, dragging the bike down to the floor as he did.

That split-second decision saved his life.

Gunfire erupted through the hideout's door and even through the front wall. Daylight appeared through the holes as bullets pierced metal and brick with ease and streaked into the room, racing across to embed themselves in counters and cabinets and appliances at the other end.

Through the loud reports Cole heard someone shouting orders outside, though he couldn't make out the content. There were at least three of them out there, though, from the sound of things.

And this place only had the one exit.

Cole knew it was only a matter of minutes before they stormed in to make sure they'd finished the job, so he had even less time to find a way out of here. Preferably alive.

He quickly took stock of the situation. He wasn't in any shape to fight anyone, even if he'd been a fighter to start.

But he did have a motorbike, already unlocked and ready to go.

And an armored vest.

And a wall that had been weakened by a hail of bullets.

And a shotgun, two pistols, and a grenade of his own.

It was the kind of stupid plan Doc would give him hell over, he knew. And if he survived to make it back there, Cole decided he'd be more than happy to take that abuse.

But right now it looked like the only chance he had.

He crawled to the armor stand and hauled down the vest, draping it over himself as best he could. He swam in the oversized garment, of course, but at least it wasn't going to fall off. Then, feeling a little more confident now that his torso was covered but still worried about the continued barrage, he quickly slung the shotgun over one shoulder by its attached strap, grabbed the two guns and the grenade, and lifted the bike back to an upright position. Then he hopped onto it, crouched low—

—and threw the grenade.

Straight at the front wall.

*Bam!*

It went off with a burst like a small thunderclap, momentarily making Cole wonder if another storm had miraculously appeared to save him. But no, it was just the explosives taking out what was left of that wall, leaving a large, jagged hole right in its center.

A hole that Cole gunned the bike's engine and headed straight for at top speed.

He looped his extended wrists around the handlebars to steer so he could hold the pistols in both hands, and fired as he burst out of the hideout and onto the street, surprising the men gathered there. He saw at least two of them drop before he'd shot past. He dropped the pistols and retracted his hands so he could grip the handlebars properly and guide the bike out of the alley onto the main street, weaving between slower traffic as he quickly put as much distance behind him as he could.

Once he'd gotten at least a kilometer away, Cole slowed to a more normal speed. Then, spotting another alley, he pulled into it long enough to disable the bike's GPS and ditch the armored vest—which, he only now saw, had taken several hits, each of which had scuffed and dented it but not pierced through.

The shotgun fit into a holster along the bike's side, so when Cole re-emerged, he looked like anyone else out for a ride instead of some armed and armored madman fleeing a violent gun battle.

It took another klick before his hands stopped shaking, but he knew that was the adrenaline, not his injuries. Adrenaline—and fear.

There were only two ways those men—and Cole had caught a fleeting glimpse of the sniper on his way past—could have caught up with him, and so quickly. Tracking him to Doc's wouldn't have helped, since he hadn't told Doc where he was going.

They'd either planted a tracker on Cole himself, which was highly unlikely since Doc had done a thorough scan and would have found a bug as a matter of course, plus he would've detected any outgoing transmissions.

Or they'd been tipped off as to where Cole was.

And the only person who could've done that was the one he'd just called. From the bike he'd still been leaning against and was now riding away.

Which meant the woman—the client—was the one who'd sent the hit squad.

Clearly she not only wanted the amulet, but also wanted to make sure nobody knew she had it. Not even the thieves she'd hired to steal it for her. And she was serious enough about that privacy to send the sniper to finish Cole off after she found out he was still alive.

That didn't tell Cole who she was, though if he could track her LTG he'd at least have somewhere to start on that.

And it didn't answer the even bigger question: why? What was so important about that amulet that she'd kill Cole and the others to make absolutely sure they couldn't ever track back to her?

Cole didn't know, but he intended to find out.

# TEN

"Damn it!" Cole slammed a hand on the desk, making the ancient computer's keyboard jump and the monitor wobble.

"Whoa, there!" Doc called, hurrying over from whatever he'd been doing on the far side of the lab. "Don't break the equipment, yeah? 'Specially since it ain't yours, and it also ain't to blame for whatever's got you all riled up."

"I know, you're right, sorry," Cole said, reaching out to straighten the keyboard and push the monitor back to a more stable position. "I'm just running into some stumbling blocks here. Whoever this woman is, she's done a damn good job of making sure her number can't be traced."

He'd told Doc what had happened when he rolled up on Mace's bike, after first riding around the city for a while in random directions to make sure he wasn't being followed. Then, using an old computer Doc had salvaged and which he swore couldn't be traced or hacked by anyone, Cole had started trying to track back that unlisted number.

Every avenue he tried turned out to be a dead end.

"I'm going to need help," he was finally forced to admit, pushing away from the table and scrubbing at his face with one hand. "I know some tricks, but for this I'm going to need a full-on decker."

Beside him, Doc nodded. "I might know a guy can help," he said slowly, scratching at his chin and making his whiskers quiver. "I can call him, see if he'll meet you."

"Great. Thanks, Doc." Cole forced himself to stay seated, even though what he really wanted was to pace back and forth. He hated waiting, hated not knowing, and really hated the thought of having to rely upon someone else. He'd always survived just fine on his own, without anybody's help.

Except now he wasn't only interested in surviving. He was interested in revenge.

And for that he was definitely going to need some help.

First things first, though. Right now he wanted to figure out where that number was, and who it belonged to. Then he'd figure out what came next—and whether he could handle it solo or if he needed to recruit some extra arms. And guns.

Doc must have worked fast, because he was already walking back over when Cole glanced up. "He says sure," the dwarf reported. "Macon's Bar, back right booth, one hour. I told him to look for the guy with more metal than brains."

"Gee, thanks." But Cole actually meant it. Hopefully this guy could get him the info he needed, and put him on a real path for some payback.

An hour later, Cole strolled into the bar, sidestepped, and stopped just inside the door, scanning his surroundings. Thanks to his mods, he didn't need much time for his eyes to adjust and could study the bar and its occupants almost instantly. What he saw didn't exactly reassure him.

"Rundown" would have been a kind understatement. "Run over" would probably be more accurate. The entire interior looked like it had been smacked around a few times and then left to dry by the side of the road. The long bar against one wall was chipped and faded and looked like someone had stripped away its copper and brass fittings long ago. The stools were all cracked and torn, and several were missing tops altogether. The wall behind the bar had probably been covered with glass and mirrors at one point, but now it was just unpainted plywood, with rough shelves in front to hold the booze. The floor was covered in some sort of dark tile that stuck to his shoes, the ceiling fan had a broken blade that made it wobble and hitch in its path, only half the lights worked, and he guessed the garbled hiss he heard every so often was all that remained of the place's original sound system.

On the plus side, it wasn't crowded. And even though a few of the other occupants turned their slow gazes toward Cole as he walked in, they just as lazily glanced away again, back toward their drinks or whatever vids they were watching on their heads-ups. The bartender did give Cole her attention, however, at least long enough to find out if he was planning to drink.

Cole had never been a big drinker, and this didn't exactly strike him as a good place to relax, but he figured it was better to look like he belonged, so he stepped over the bar. "Let me have a beer, whatever you've got that comes in a bottle, the lighter the better," he told the bartender.

She smiled, hauled a dark green bottle from under the counter, and slid it down the bar's length into Cole's waiting hand. He scooped the drink up with one hand and tossed down a few nuyen with the other, then studied the room again. There was the back right booth—and even in the dim lighting, Cole could make out movement.

Apparently Doc's decker friend had beaten him here.

Taking his beer with him, Cole lengthened his stride and covered the distance to the booth in a few long steps. The blue-haired elf sitting there glanced up at his approach as if startled, but then nodded and gestured for Cole to slide onto the opposite bench. Cole did, and they studied one another for a second before the elf spoke.

"You're Cole?"

Cole nodded.

"Fine. Wouldn't normally work with someone I don't know, but Doc vouches for you. Name's Alaric. Alaric Kaine." He stared at Cole a few seconds longer. "You were working with an ork named Mace?"

"That's right." Cole wasn't sure what game his new companion was playing, but whatever it was, he wasn't in the mood to play along. He pulled a datachip from his pocket and slid it across the table. "That's the number. I've already tried all the usual traces and bounce-backs and other basic methods. Plus a few nonstandard ones. But I've gotten nowhere."

Alaric frowned down at the datachip but made no move to pick it up. "What happened to Mace?"

Now Cole was the one frowning as he relived the ambush yet again. "He got shot," he answered sharply. "So did everybody else. I got shot too, but not enough to finish the job. Happy?"

The elf nodded, then changed his mind and shook his head instead. "Happy?" he asked, putting his hands on the table and curling them into fists. "No, I ain't happy. And I won't be, until you promise me something."

"What's that?" Cole had absolutely no idea what was going on here.

Alaric looked up and met his gaze, and there was something eerily familiar about the decker's cool green eyes. "Promise me that, once I help you figure out who these bastards are and where they went, you'll let me come along." He shook his head, sending his blue hair flying about him. "I don't care about whatever you stole for them. You can keep that. Money, too. I just want the guys who did this. I want the ones who killed my brother."

Cole reared back in his seat, startled, but a part of his mind chided him for that. Now that he knew to look, the resemblance was obvious—Alaric was narrower in the face, and wore his hair longer and dyed electric blue, but a quick squint and it was like Rodrick was sitting there instead.

"I'm sorry," he told the decker. "I didn't know." With a pang he realized he hadn't even known Rodrick's last name until just now.

Alaric waved off the apology. "They took him out first, didn't they?" He sighed when Cole nodded. "I always told him this would happen. 'They always go for the spellslinger first,' I said. You're just painting a big old target on your chest every time. But he wouldn't listen." The elf glared at him. "So promise me you'll let me go with you."

"Uh, I promise." Even as he said it Cole realized Alaric was right, and had been right all along. He was going after the guys behind this, the steely-eyed sniper and the woman on the comm and whoever else was involved. He could tell himself he was doing it as a form of proactive protection, taking them out before they could try for him a third time. Or that it was justice, or honor, or some other noble cause. But if he was honest with himself, it was just payback, simple as that. They'd hired him and Rodrick and Tish and Lorelei and Mace to do a job. They'd done that job. Then, instead of paying them as promised, these people had gunned them all down and walked off with the amulet. That wasn't right, it wasn't fair, and he wasn't going to stand for it.

So yes, he was going after them. And when he found them, he'd make them pay. Maybe with blood, maybe with more money, but they owed him, not only for the job but for the double-cross. They would pay up somehow, he'd make sure of that.

And he had absolutely no problem with Alaric coming along for the ride.

"You need anything else?" the elf was asking, and the question drew Cole back to the present.

"No," he started to say, then stopped himself. "Yes, actually. The thing we stole, it's an amulet. A gold disc with a red crystal spike in the middle. It was in the Public Works building downtown. Your brother said it was powerful, but that was all he could tell without really studying the thing. I need to know everything you can find out about it. Who donated it, when, and what they knew about where it came from." He stared down at the bottle in his hands, which he had completely forgotten was there. "I want to know what made this thing worth killing us over."

"You got it," the elf promised. "I'll get you everything they've got. I can run a global search on it, too, once I have the official docs, see if anything else pops up anywhere." He nodded at Cole, finished his own drink, and then slid back out of the booth. "I've got Doc's number, I'll be in touch soon as I know anything."

"Thanks." Cole didn't turn around as Alaric left. Instead he sat there, staring off into space, thinking about dead friends and surviving family and what was already turning into a complicated process of getting revenge.

He hoped the elf would be satisfied by whatever they managed to achieve in the end.

And that he wouldn't be sitting here afterward instead, mourning two brothers instead of one.

# ELEVEN

Two days later, Alaric called Cole to say he'd found something interesting. Rather than go back to the bar and risk people guessing they were working on something together, Cole suggested the decker stop by Doc's. He figured since Doc had been the one to introduce them, that wouldn't be a problem.

"Fine by me," Doc had said when Cole told him. "This way I get to hear what sorta crazy trouble you're in firsthand." The dwarf had also been good about not pushing Cole too much about his plans; instead, he'd mostly contented himself with running diagnostics and physicals to make sure Cole was healing properly and that the repairs to all his other systems were holding. "Not happy about that piece of whatever it is," the old man groused each time, "but as long as it ain't moving anymore, I guess you'll just have to live with it."

"That's fine, I barely even feel it anymore," Cole claimed, but he doubted the lie was fooling the canny old dwarf. Truth was, he had a constant ache in his chest from that shard. He wondered if it was pressing on a nerve because his whole body felt jangly, like he'd touched a live wire. It wasn't exactly painful, but he was always aware of it, and always on edge.

Still, right now being on edge wasn't such a bad thing.

"Did you track that number?" was the first thing he asked when Alaric showed up, barely waiting through exchanging quick hellos before he got to the point.

The elf shook his head. "Still working on that part." He dropped into one of the many mismatched chairs decorating Doc's living space. Like a lot of tinkerers, Doc didn't exactly keep his work and his personal life separate—his bedroom was simply a larger curtained-off space over by the back wall, with slightly sturdier furniture than the cot and folding table Cole rated. The living room area, such as it was, occupied both the largest partition and the most central one, with the outer door opening directly onto it. Cole had always thought the place was too sterile and too claustrophobic, but he suspected Doc didn't pay much attention to his surroundings. As long as he had his tools and something—or someone—to experiment on, the dwarf was happy.

"If you don't have anything, why'd you say you did?" Cole demanded, taking one of the other chairs and perching on its arm. Doc settled into his own favorite seat, a worn wooden rocking chair sized so even his stubby little legs could reach the ground.

"I didn't say I wasn't getting anywhere," Alaric insisted, "just that it wasn't done yet. Number's rerouted all over the place, got a ton of firewalls and privacy shields blocking it. Whoever this lady caller of yours was, she definitely don't want her name getting out." He grinned. "But I found some other stuff that's real interesting. Weird, but interesting."

"Yeah?" Doc waved a hand from his chair. "Let's hear it."

The elf looked at Cole, one eyebrow raised, but when Cole nodded, he shrugged and pulled out his deck. "Check this out, then." He typed in a quick series of commands, and a holographic image rose from the top of the keyboard—an all-too-familiar gold disc with a wedge-shaped ruby at its center. "Look familiar?"

"Not to me," Doc replied, studying both the image and Cole, "but I'm guessing from what you told me that this is the little doodad that landed you in this mess?"

Cole nodded. "One and the same." Just seeing it made his heart beat faster, and his head throb in sympathy. "So you found something on it?"

"You could say that." The decker hit a key and a second image popped up alongside the first, this one a screen filled with lines of data. "This is the official record for the thing," he explained, gesturing at it. "Lists it as a 'genuine Native American talisman from the early days of the Native American Nation.' Says it was donated by a Raphael Stillwater back in 2044, sat in Acquisitions for three years, and then was put on display. It's been in that glass case ever since. Well, until you guys stole it, anyway."

"Okay." Cole frowned and rubbed at his jaw, staring at the two images. "So?"

"So..." A giant grin split the elf's face. "Everything I just told you? It's all a lie."

"Wait, what?" Cole glared at the decker. "You just made all that up?" He'd thought Alaric was serious about helping, and about avenging his brother, but maybe the elf was just a sick little prankster who liked to screw with people's heads and waste their time.

But, apparently sensing Cole's rising anger, the elf quickly held up his hands, the grin vanishing from his face. "Not me," he insisted, speaking quickly. "Whoever entered all this. Here, look." He did something on the deck, and the record changed—now it was showing not just the entries but the codes and keystrokes that had created them. Cole rose to his feet and moved closer so he could read the lines of text more easily.

It took him a minute, especially since he could feel Alaric dying for him to ask and absolutely refused to give the elf the satisfaction, but finally he spotted it. "The creation dates," he said, stabbing a finger at one of them, his fingertip breaching the hologram and causing the image to distort slightly around his flesh. "You said this was donated in 2044, but the input date is off by years."

"So they didn't get around to typing up a report right away," Doc offered. He hadn't bothered to get up or move closer. "Big deal. People're lazy."

"That would make sense," Cole agreed, glancing back at his old friend. "Except that these records were made years *earlier*, not later. In 2040, according to their tags."

Doc scowled. "They wrote it up four years before they even got it? That don't make no sense."

"Exactly." Alaric was clearly fighting to keep that grin from resurfacing, but his eyes still gleamed with the thrill of the hunt. "And the bit about Acquisitions was added in 2050, which would've been three years after the thing was put on display if its donation date had been right in the first place." The elf was practically twitching from excitement. "So that got me curious, and I did a little more digging." He paused a second, obviously hoping Cole or Doc would ask what he'd found, but was too eager to show off to wait longer. "This Raphael Stillwater? I couldn't find a single mention of him anywhere but here. The guy didn't exist—or else he was a complete ghost. And even thirty years ago, that was near impossible, especially in a place like the FRTZ, where everybody's keeping an eye on everybody else. Also? The Public Works building in the Ute sector didn't even have an Acquisitions department until 2050."

Cole was still staring at the screen, but he barely saw it anymore. He was looking through it, his eyes unfocused as he tried to puzzle this out. "So whoever donated this used a fake name, and somehow got the city itself to put down a fake date?" he said, working it through. "Or somebody else went back and changed the record later, probably in 2050, and altered the donor's name at the same time." He frowned. "Which means somebody didn't want this thing being found."

Doc snorted. "Didn't want it found? It was in a bloody glass case in the middle of a hallway in a public building! Not exactly buried down the bottom of a well, was it?"

"No, but it was hidden in plain sight," Cole countered. "That hall was lined with display cases on both sides, all kinds of photos and knickknacks. But this was the only case that had extra security—and a whole lot of it, more than anything in a building like that should ever need. So they knew what they had, and they were making sure nobody could get to it, but they did their best to make it look like it was just another old curio." He glanced over at Alaric. "Is there a way to tell who made the changes? Or revert to whatever the record looked like before they did?"

But the decker shook his head. "System's too old, that data's long gone," he explained. "I might be able to figure out which terminal got used, but that's about it. And that's assuming they're still using the same computers they had back then, which would be crazy even for a cheap-ass government building. This is all I've got."

That drew another snort from the dwarf. "That's the problem with you young'uns," he insisted. "Can't get your heads out of your own rear ends. You think everyone does things the same way you do, and always has."

Cole turned to study his friend. "You've got a better answer? Let's hear it."

"You think, just 'cause we're in the digital age, everything's all digital all the time, and always was," Doc replied, shaking his head so his eyebrows, beard, and mustache flew all about. "But not everything's kept in a cloud. Especially not when you're dealing with bureaucracy."

Cole got his meaning at once. "You think there's a paper trail," he said softly. "That they filled out a physical form first, and then entered it later. Or at least compartmentalized, kept a copy of things on a separate system as a backup." He considered that. "Could be," he agreed after a few seconds. He studied the screen again. "But if there was one, you really think they'd still have it lying around? More than twenty years later? And where'd they keep it, if they did?"

"Actually," Alaric offered, "Doc's got a point. And bureaucracies, they're famous for never getting rid of anything. If they had a paper form once, chances are it's still buried in a box somewhere."

That made Cole remember something. "I think I know where, too," he said slowly. "When we cased the building, there was a lower level. One of the rooms was labeled 'Archive' on the map. That's got to be where they keep their old files, right?"

The other two nodded, and this time it was Cole's turn to grin. "Guess I'm gonna have to break in," he declared. "Again." His smile turned wolfish as he considered his two companions. "And you two are going with me."

# TWELVE

"Tell me again why we have to do this?" Doc grumbled as Cole shoved him back up against the building. "I don't have anything to do with any of this nonsense!"

"You said you wanted to know what I was doing," Cole reminded the surly dwarf, checking to make sure no one had seen them. "This is the best way to find out."

"You could just tell me about it after!" Doc complained, but he kept his voice down and didn't move out of position again.

Alaric had a different question. "Why are we waiting? I spoofed those personnel records like you asked. Far as the building's concerned, we're just three more civil servants toiling away, trying to make a living. So why aren't we walking in there like we own the place?" He gestured down at himself, and the suit he was wearing. "Especially when we're dolled up all pretty-like."

"Because when your brother and I and the rest of us went in there before, we found a whole lot more alarms than we expected," Cole replied, not taking his eyes from the building's side entrance. "If we run into anything like that again, I'd prefer it happen when there aren't as many people around to witness it—and ID us later. And even though your files will hopefully fool the computers, they won't help if we run into one of those busybody types who knows absolutely everybody else's business, and they don't recognize us. The fewer people around, the less we have to worry about making anyone suspicious enough to call it in."

"And you don't think it'll look weird that three guys are heading into work when everyone else is heading out?"

Doc asked. Which at least meant he wasn't bellyaching for a moment.

"We did a thorough recon on the building the first time," Cole reminded his friend. "They've got people on different shifts for most of the day and night. We went in at three in the morning because that was when the last shift ended and before the first one started again, but that's the only window when nobody's inside. So no, it won't look at all funny for the three of us to be there. The night shift's small, though, so we should be able to get by without running into anyone."

He watched as a cluster of four left the building, then one person alone, then two together, then another one alone, then another couple and another, and finally one more solo employee. "Right," he declared as soon as that metahuman trickle had cut off. "Time to go."

The three of them straightened and rounded the corner, heading directly for the back door. Cole already had his tools in hand, and made straight for the keypad. The good news was, he still had the digits he'd recorded off the door before. Even if they no longer worked because the code had been changed, it was doubtful the government had altered the way the door worked, or its basic programs. Which meant he had a template to measure the new code against. He knew the style of code, its core structure, which would make it that much easier to hack.

Cole wasn't surprised when the previous code didn't work—even in the normal course of things they'd have switched to a new password by now, and of course they would have overhauled all their security protocols following that first break-in. He was just about to start the codebreaking process again—sorting through the programming of the door's security system, isolating its password generator, and then backtracking to find or figure out what password it had created last—when he heard a noise on the other side. A steady, rhythmic sound. And it was getting louder.

"Back up!" he warned his two companions in a quick whisper, and stepped back a half-dozen paces back himself. Doc and Alaric were right beside him, and Cole quickly turned toward them, tugging each by the shoulder until they were all more or less facing each other.

"I couldn't believe he would ask me about that after the last meeting," he started loudly, stepping closer to the door but keeping his face and body tilted toward the other two just as the door clicked and swung open.

A short, heavyset young man stepped out, a windbreaker slung on over his suit, a briefcase clutched in his hands. He glanced up, startled, when Cole approached, but seemed to relax as Cole's complaining reached him, and after he'd taken in the type and style of their clothes.

"Thanks, man," Cole said over his shoulder as he grabbed the door seconds before it could shut again. "So anyway, I told him after that to remember if he ever—" The door finally clicked closed, but this time with Cole, Doc, and Alaric safely inside. The second it was closed Cole dropped the inane drivel. "That did the trick."

Doc stared up at him, the look on his face somewhere between disapproving, horrified, and impressed. "Always knew you were good with words," he said slowly. "Didn't think you could use 'em to sweet-talk your way into a government building, though." He shook his head. "Is that how y'normally do it? Just talk to people, get 'em to let you in, then rob them blind?" It was clear from his tone that he didn't approve of the thieving, but Cole had known that for years.

Still, he took the time to answer honestly. "When everything's working, yes, this is how I like it—no hitches, no complications, and no need for magic or guns or anything. Just slip in, get what we need, and slip right back out, no muss, no fuss."

Speaking of that, through the whole discussion he'd been looking around, trying to see past some the art adorning the walls so he could watch the corridor ahead for any other late-night workers. No sign of anyone else, or any guards yet, which was good—they were one security feature Alaric couldn't hack.

At last, he reached an all-metal firedoor right where the building schematics said it would be. Taking a deep breath, Cole tried the knob, and almost laughed with relief when it turned easily.

The door, which had no access to sensitive areas of the building or the outside, had been unlocked.

Leading the other two quickly but without running, Cole headed down the metal and concrete stairs the open door had revealed. He wanted to break into a sprint, but forced himself to maintain his current pace instead. The key here was to preserve the illusion of normality as long as possible.

They encountered one other person in the stairwell, a dwarf woman wearing slacks and a blouse and studying the screen of a small reader as she ascended. She barely even glanced up when their paths crossed, and then only long enough to make sure she wasn't about to run into any of them.

After she'd gone, Doc let out a little sigh. "I can't believe this crazy plan of yours is actually working!" he whispered loudly.

Cole rolled his eyes, but decided not to say anything. What would be the point? Besides, that would just compound the potential error. Better to move on and hope that no one had heard the dwarf's outburst. Because his statement was exactly the kind that got people's attention—meaning they started asking "what plan?" and "who are those guys?" and "should I call security and report them?"

Not surprisingly, that last one was Cole's least favorite.

They reached the basement without incident, and pushed open the matching door to exit the stairwell onto a hall much narrower, plainer, and more glaringly lit than its surface counterpart. Clearly this was the part of the building housing those departments and rooms no one liked to visit.

Which was perfect for them.

The door they wanted read "*Archives*" on a small, plain plaque. Cole had to bite back the urge to giggle when he realized there wasn't even a thumbprint scanner or retinal scanner on the door. Just the standard keypad. He plugged his diagnostic tool into the pad's service port and had the code in a matter of seconds. The door gave a cheery little *beep* as he pushed it open.

"Wow," Alaric whispered as he and Doc followed Cole inside and shut the door behind them. "What a dump! People really used all this stuff back then?"

Cole felt much the same way as he studied their surroundings. It was a large room, stretching away to the left and the right, and filling it was row upon row of heavy metal shelves. Stacked upon those shelves were not only filing boxes but pieces of art and other objects, ranging from vases and sculptures to umbrellas, hats, and even some sort of folding game table. Evidently the archives also doubled as all-purpose storage.

The one thing he didn't see was any sort of computer. The archiving appeared to revolve around the numbers written on the side of each box and tagged onto each object, and printed on labels pasted onto the shelves themselves.

"Right, fan out," he told the others. "We're looking for that form, so check boxes marked 2040, 2044, and 2050. Hopefully it's in one of those. If we're in luck, all the art donation records are kept in one place, but if they just shoved all the forms of all sorts from that year in together, well—" he shrugged, "—we've got our work cut out for us."

Alaric muttered something about Luddites, but stomped off toward a row of shelves to start searching. Doc grinned and headed in the opposite direction, leaving Cole to wander the aisles directly in front of him.

He found himself in an area that seemed to be mostly items either waiting to go on display, that had already been displayed and taken down to make room for others, or perhaps that needed to be cleaned or repaired. He wasn't really sure. What he did know was that he wasn't looking at files—the shelves here were crammed with pottery shards and old framed photographs and medals and necklaces and license plates and bronze busts, like he was wandering a curiosity shop instead of a government archive. Each item was neatly labeled, though, all in the same boring typeface whether the labels were fresh, new, and white or old, peeling, and yellowed. It was a strange juxtaposition.

Cole stopped at one, a life-sized bronze bust of a man that struck a chord in him. The man was lean but handsome, or at least arresting, with a sharp-planed face and intense eyes over a long, narrow, slightly beaked nose. His long hair was swept back, held in place by a headband that appeared to be made of intricate beadwork, the bust capturing even that little detail, and a leather cord was visible around his neck, leading down to a medallion that sat just above the point where the bust tapered down to its base.

A round, flat medallion with something like a crystal shard at its center.

"What the—? Doc! Doc! Alaric! Come see this!" Cole found himself shouting, and quickly lowered his voice, hoping the room was at least partially soundproofed.

A second later, his two confederates were at his side. "What?" Doc demanded, then saw what Cole had been looking at. The dwarf spotted the medallion right away. "Well, I'll be!"

he exclaimed. "Don't that just beat all! No wonder they had so much security on it!"

Cole stared down at his friend. "What do you mean?" he demanded. "Who is this?"

In answer, Doc pointed at the label, which Cole hadn't actually bothered to read yet. In its clear, plain type it stated: "*Bust of Daniel Howling Coyote, cast c. 2025. Donated 2058 by private collector.*"

"Whoa." That was Alaric. "So that thing you stole, it was *his*? Daniel Howling Coyote's? Holy drek." He had his deck on him, of course, and swiveled it around now to capture an image of the bust before slinging the deck back under his arm again.

"Yeah." Cole continued to stare at the bust, his heart and head both pounding fit to burst. Daniel Howling Coyote. Founder of the NAN. Master of the Great Ghost Dance. The man who had singlehandedly changed the face of the continent, maybe even the world. Cole had heard stories, of course—everyone had—but he'd never even seen pictures of the man, at least not up close. He vaguely remembered something about Howling Coyote disappearing years ago. And now it was as if Cole was staring him right in the eye.

It was eerie.

Doc laughed. "Looks a little like you, if you squint enough," he said, then grinned. "Only, y'know, a whole lot prettier."

"Gee, thanks," Cole replied. Sure, maybe there were some similarities, but that just meant he had some tribal blood in him. Which he'd guessed the first time Doc had shown him a mirror.

Alaric cleared his throat. "Well, that makes this a whole lot more interesting," he offered, waving what looked like an ancient data stick. "'Cause just before you shouted, I'd found the box of these old thumb drives holding donation records from 2036 to 2054. And look what was packed away in this one." He tapped a few keys on his deck and angled the device so they could all see the page it displayed. It was a donation form for one "genuine Native American talisman from the early days of the Native American Nation." But the date listed wasn't 2044, or 2050, or even 2040.

It was 2035.

And the donor wasn't one Raphael Stillwater. It was a Donald Harriman Clearmont.

DHC.

"I know what you're thinking," Doc accused, but there wasn't any vehemence in his voice. "I see it too. Still, why would Daniel Howling Coyote donate his own talisman—but lie about who it was from?"

"And then go back and change the name to make it even harder to trace," Cole pointed out. "Unless the point was to hide it so nobody'd find it. In which case, changing the name and the date makes sense—neither of those would lead back to him."

"And the statue?" Doc asked, but he was already shaking his head. "Poor bastard. Went to all that trouble, and then somebody donates a bust that shows him, clear as day, wearing the same damn amulet. That's rough."

Cole nodded. "Anybody seeing the bust and the amulet both on display would've known right away who it belonged to," he agreed. "But the people in charge obviously knew, too. They might have changed the name and date later, to hide it better. And they put in all that extra security so nobody'd be able to walk off with the damn thing."

"Yeah, 'cept you went and did 'xactly that." Doc probably hadn't meant it as an accusation, but it still came out sounding an awful lot like one. It was one Cole couldn't argue with, though. They had stolen it. And if they'd known whose it was— they still would have stolen it. That's what they did. They might have asked more money for it, though.

And they might've been a lot more cautious when handing it off.

Too late for that now.

"We need to get out of here," Cole said, forcing himself back to the present, and to the fact that they were standing in a government building they'd accessed illegally. He took the thumb drive from Alaric and slid it into one of his many pockets. The bust they obviously couldn't do anything about, but he tore off the label and took that as well.

If anyone else came looking for a connection, he saw no reason to make it easy for them.

# THIRTEEN

They made it out of the building without any trouble, crossing paths with only two actual employees, neither of whom bothered to do much more than grunt and nod as they stiff-walked past. Apparently the night shift was kept plenty busy here.

Even so, Cole didn't say anything until they'd navigated the underground border crossings back to the UCAS and safely returned to Doc's place. Then, while the others were dropping into chairs with groans of relief, he pivoted and headed toward the door again. "Back in a bit," he said over his shoulder.

"Whoa, there!" For an older guy, Doc was still pretty spry—he was across the room and blocking the door before Cole could reach the handle. "Where the heck d'you think you're goin'? It's late, we're all wrung out, and we just broke into—and back outta—a government building! Time to unwind, grab a brew, and then sleep it off, son. Not go wander back out looking for more trouble."

Cole sighed. "I need to find out what the NAN knows," he answered, tensing slightly for the explosion he fully expected to follow.

To his surprise, Doc didn't blow up at him. Instead the shaggy old dwarf considered that statement carefully before finally nodding. "Yeah, I get that," he said. "You figure if anyone's gonna know what Howling Coyote was up to with that doohickey, it'd be them." Still, he shook his head. "But no reason that can't wait till morning."

"There is a reason," Cole insisted. "A good one. Where'm I going to go to check up on the NAN, specifically any operations they're running out of Denver?"

Doc frowned, but it was Alaric, still sprawled across a couch, who called out, "Council Hall, yeah?"

Cole pointed at the elf. "Exactly. That's where their council reps and high-level operatives are based, so at least it's a place to start. And when's the best time to go if I don't want to draw a lot of attention?"

"Middle of the night," the decker answered again. He then made a big show of hauling his deck out in front of him and checking the time, despite the fact that Cole was sure he had an optical display as well. "Which—hey, now—it happens to be right now!" His grin was back, and he was clearly enjoying himself now that they weren't in any danger.

Doc wasn't convinced, however. "So, what, you're fixing to break into their offices right now?"

Cole smirked down at him. "I don't think filling out a form or asking to speak to a supervisor is the way to go here, do you?"

If anything, the snark just made Doc's brow furrow even more. "Maybe not," he conceded grudgingly, folding thick arms across his barrel chest. Even though he spent most of his time at a desk or a worktable, Doc was no pushover. "And maybe you're right—breaking in to get a peek at their files could give us a clue as to what we need next. But let me ask you something, Mr. Smart Guy. You're an expert on breaking into places, right?"

Cole lifted his chin. "I like to think so," he agreed proudly.

"So when you're planning to bust into a place, what's the first thing you do?" Doc glared up at him, daring him to answer. "Hm? What do you do?"

Cole ground his teeth together—at least half of them were fake, too, but even he couldn't tell which were which anymore—but finally grated out an answer. "I case the joint," he admitted.

"Oh yeah?" Now it was Doc's turn to feign surprise. "What a good idea! I can see why you've never got caught, you're so clever like that. So when was it you cased these offices, again?"

This time Cole didn't bother to reply. He didn't have to. His sharp stare said it all.

Doc reached out a stubby-fingered hand and pushed Cole back a step, gently but firmly. "Go get some rest," he ordered, somewhere between a stern parent and a concerned doctor.

"That office'll still be there in the morning, and from what you said earlier, I'm guessing you'll attract a lot less attention if you go wandering by it in the middle of the day when there's a whole mess of other people around than if you try skulking around on your own in the dead of night. Am I right?"

Cole wanted to argue, but knew the canny old dwarf had him beat. "Yeah, you're right," he said, shoulders slumping as he acknowledged he wouldn't be going back out tonight, and as his body reminded him it had already been an eventful evening and he was still healing.

"Fine. I'll go first thing in the morning." Doc raised an eyebrow, and Cole held both hands out palm up, acknowledging defeat. "Just to see what it looks like. Nothing else—yet. Happy?"

"Ecstatic," Doc answered with a harrumph, but Cole thought he glimpsed a smug smile beneath all those whiskers. Then the fatigue really kicked in, and all Cole could see was the path to his cot, which lay warm and waiting.

His dreams were strange flashes of color and light and sound, and the sense of rapid motion mixed with the wide-open feel of being outdoors, but Cole still woke refreshed. Doc had been right, he admitted when he rose and headed to the shower. If he'd gone back out last night like he'd planned, he'd have been seriously off his game, way too easy to spot and catch if anyone had been watching and waiting. This was the smarter plan.

He just didn't like being told what to do, was all. Even when whoever told him was right.

Doc sat at what passed for a kitchen table, meaning it was only partially covered in gadgets and gizmos and wires and tools. He was sipping from a large mug of soykaf, with a second untouched cup across from him. Clearly he'd heard Cole getting up.

"Morning," Cole said, sinking into the empty chair and gratefully lifting the cup. The aroma woke him from his daze, and that first sip did the rest, the hot, fresh 'kaf burning a welcome path down his throat to his stomach even as the caffeine rose straight to his brain, kicking his mind and his senses into proper motion at last.

They sat there for a while, neither saying anything, enjoying their soykaf. Alaric was nowhere to be seen, and Cole guessed the elf had left after he'd wandered off to bed. If this had been a regular job, he'd have told the decker to stay here so they were all in one place, but there was nothing regular about this, and it wasn't exactly a job anyway, so if he wanted to sleep in his own bed, Cole didn't see any reason to argue.

"Still planning your little scouting mission?" Doc finally asked.

"Yeah." Cole set his empty cup on the table and leaned back, stretching. "Might as well. I need to know what I'm getting myself into, and if there's even a snowball's chance I can find something useful at Council Hall, and a way for me to get to it without getting myself shot, I'll take it."

Doc didn't try to talk him out of it. "Just watch your back," was all the dwarf said. "A piece like that, coming from who it did, I can see why somebody didn't want any of you talking about it. And if they find you again, they'll try to finish the job."

"I know." Cole mustered a small smile. "But they don't know where I am or what I'm doing. They probably think I've left Denver already, looking for someplace they can't find me." He frowned. "Heck, that's probably what I should be doing."

Doc studied him. "But you won't." It wasn't a question.

"No, I won't," Cole agreed, rising to his feet. "But I will be careful. Promise."

He headed out before his friend could try imposing any more strictures.

The Denver Council Hall was a large, handsome stone building in the Hub that Cole suspected dated back to well before the NAN itself, and had been merely co-opted by the coalition after the Treaty of Denver. The seals of the various Native American Nations were displayed prominently above the door, alongside those of the UCAS and the CAS, and in the plaza out front was a bronze statue of none other than Daniel Howling Coyote—with a bare neck, no amulet in sight. Cole shivered as he studied the statue from a little café across the plaza. It was like the man was following him.

He'd chosen this spot because he had a good view of the building, not just its front entrance, but most of its right side.

He didn't see any doors along there, though if there were any service doors or loading bays, they'd be in back. Still, this at least let him gauge the external security, both electronic and living.

And it was top-notch. Cameras doing sweeps of the entrance and the space before it, with others set up at intervals just below the roof, all the way around. What looked like motion-detectors spaced out against the building on its side, set high enough that a squirrel wouldn't set them off but a crouching person would. Security guards stood by the front doors, and he caught one of them mouthing something at one point, which almost certainly meant he was fitted with a throat mic and reporting in, probably to someone at a main console inside watching all the feeds. This wouldn't be any easy place to break into, at least not during regular business hours.

Finishing his coffee, Cole rose to his feet and casually strolled across the plaza, giving the statue a wide berth as he did. Enough people were milling about here that, if he kept moving and didn't actually approach the front doors, he should be able to at least get a closer look at the entrance without drawing attention to himself. If he was lucky, he'd get a look at the door locks, maybe even a glimpse of an alarm keypad inside—if he knew the make and model, it would be a lot easier to prepare some sort of counter or probe ahead of time. Then he could circle around to the back. He wouldn't cut across the grass beside the building; that would be too obvious and would set off those motion-detectors. Instead, he'd go all the way around the block and look for an alley leading back to it. There would certainly have been one when the building was first constructed and they needed a way to make unobtrusive deliveries. He'd see what things looked like from there. Maybe he'd—

Cole's musings about protocols and entry points shattered like a dropped pane of glass as a small group of people pushed through the front doors and exited the building. The two men in front were big and bulky, clearly bodyguards, as were the two in back. But the ones who had destroyed his train of thought were the pair in the middle.

One was a man, not terribly tall or particularly built, but he had a long stride, a mane of long, straight, silver hair, and though he was wearing shades, Cole knew the man had cool blue-gray eyes—and that one of them had a red pinprick at its center.

Mr. Steely-eyed Sniper.

The other was a woman. Short, blade-thin, possessing a face composed entirely of sharp edges and angles. With her glossy black hair and glittering eyes, she reminded Cole of a bird of prey, poised and ready to pounce. That image only intensified when she gestured in response to something Mr. Sniper said, and Cole saw that her nails were long and lacquered a deep red, so they looked like nothing so much as bloody talons. Even though he was too far away to hear her clearly, Cole knew what she would sound like—her voice would be sharp enough to carve through stone.

It was the woman on the phone. The client. And judging by the lapel pin he spotted, she worked for the Pueblo Corporate Council. Which meant she was NAN.

And she was heading straight for him.

Cole knew if he froze he'd call attention to himself. Likewise, if he suddenly turned and bolted, the change of motion and direction would catch their eyes. Instead he did a quick mental check of his surroundings, calling on what he'd seen already and remembered but hadn't consciously considered yet. The statue was behind him—no good, he couldn't duck behind it without being blatant. The council building was behind them, and he couldn't skirt them to get to it—that would also be so obvious it would be like sending up a flare.

But there were other people around. Including several nearby. Two, young and possibly students, were just a few paces behind him.

Cole let his pace slow—not to a complete stop, but half his previous speed—and drifted to the right. The students didn't notice; they were busy talking animatedly about something as their own steps overtook him. That put them directly between him and the NAN group. As soon as the pair was alongside him, Cole increased his pace slightly to match them, so he could keep using them as a shield. He didn't turn toward the sniper or the woman, but kept them in his peripheral vision.

They were busy talking, and didn't even glance at the students—or the man walking along just beyond them.

*Whew.*

Cole stayed with the students until they reached the far end of the plaza, then peeled off, walking briskly down the street there and turning at the first corner. He took several more random twists and turns, all while moving as fast as he dared without looking suspicious, before he could finally catch his breath.

That had been too close!

He took a few minutes to calm down, getting his racing heart back under control, then started back toward Doc's, careful to take a roundabout path and to make several sudden reversals and switches to fake out anyone who might be following him. Not that he thought he'd been spotted, but it was always best to be careful. Especially now.

He'd just been handed another big piece of the puzzle that was this job. The only thing was, it wasn't a piece he'd been expecting, and at least for now he had no idea where it could fit.

Cole was starting to wonder if he even knew what this puzzle would show when it was all assembled.

# FOURTEEN

"Say that again," Alaric demanded. The wiry elf was quivering so hard Cole thought he might vibrate right through the floor.

"I saw him," Cole repeated. "The sniper. He was at Council Hall. With a woman I'm pretty sure is the one I spoke to. The client."

But the decker ignored that last part. "You saw *him*," he echoed instead, fists clenched. "The guy who shot you. The one who killed my brother. He's here, in Denver, and you know where he is."

Too late, Cole realized where Alaric's attention was. "I know where he was," he answered carefully. "I don't know where he is now. And even if I did, he had four other goons with him. There's no way we're getting anywhere near him."

"Oh, I'll find a way to get near him," the decker promised. He was pounding his fists against his legs now. "There are ways. An elevator fails, a security laser malfunctions, a heating system overloads—there are lots of ways. I'll get close enough, don't worry about that." He was already in motion, heading straight for the door, when Cole thought to stop him.

Fortunately, Doc was a lot quicker on the uptake, and on his feet.

"Now, hold on there," he warned, planting himself in Alaric's path just as he had Cole's the night before. "This's soundin' real familiar, ain't it? One'a you young pups all ready to dive in headfirst without even lookin' around, and me having to haul you back by the scruff of your neck." He leveled a stern gaze at Alaric, and followed it up with a finger pointed right at him. "Back up and sit down," he warned, his voice low, and the elf hastened to obey.

"Look," Cole said once Alaric was safely seated again, leaning forward in his own chair so he could speak to the elf more easily. "I get it, I do. Rodrick and Tish were my friends, and Lorelei—well, Lorelei was something...more. I want to get revenge just like you."

"So why didn't you?" Alaric demanded, his eyes wide, his face flushed. "You were right there, why didn't you take him out?"

"Because I'm pretty sure if I died trying to avenge them, my friends would all laugh in my face," Cole snapped. "They'd much rather I lived, and you too, and if we're going to get revenge they'd want us to walk away after. And trust me, if I'd gone anywhere near him on that plaza, I wouldn't be sitting here now. I'd be so messed up even Doc couldn't put me back together again."

He waited a second for that to sink in. "We're going to get him," he promised after he felt the elf had calmed down enough to listen. "We are. But we've got to be smart about this. We've got to have some kind of leverage. Then we'll demand the money they promised us, and Mr. Sniper as part of the package. Okay?"

Alaric scowled, but nodded.

"Great." Cole let out his breath and slumped back. "So now let's talk about this new wrinkle. I figured I'd find something about Howling Coyote and his amulet over there. I didn't expect to find the woman who hired us to steal it—and the guy she had take us out after. I never would've thought the NAN, whether it's just the PCC or all of the nations together, was behind this."

"They've got the money and the people to put something like this together," Doc pointed out, still standing, arms crossed, in front of the door just in case. "And it makes sense they'd want the thing if it was his." He frowned, jutting his beard forward. "Heck, he was Ute, if I recall. And the PCC absorbed them, so they've got even more claim to anything of his than most."

Cole frowned and tapped a finger against the arm of his chair. "Maybe," he conceded, "but why would they need to go through all this in the first place? Howling Coyote was one of them, the *first* of them, the guy who started the NAN. Why'd they hide his talisman and then decide to steal it back? Unless someone on the, what, tribal council decided to hide it, and the others only just found out?"

But Alaric was shaking his head. "You're thinking too much," the decker warned, which would have been funny coming from someone who thought his way through computer programs for a living, except that he'd already proven he could be a jump-first-think-later hothead. "We know Howling Coyote hid the thing there, right?"

Doc and Cole both nodded. "Pretty sure, yeah," Cole agreed.

"And now we know the NAN—or at least the PCC—stole it back."

"Hired us to steal it for them, but sure."

"So," Alaric said, scrubbing at his face with one hand, then shoving his hair back where it had flopped forward, "what if that's two separate things? He hid it, they stole it back?"

"You're saying he hid it from *them*," Cole said slowly, starting to see where the elf was going. "And that's why he changed the name and date, so they couldn't find it?"

"It makes sense," Doc agreed, tugging thoughtfully at his mustache. "He donated it in 2035, right? You young'uns weren't around yet, but I was, and I remember. That was the year Tír Tairngire broke away from the NAN, declared itself a sovereign state." His eyes were as grim as his voice. "It was also when Daniel Howling Coyote disappeared."

"Disappeared?" Cole asked, though he felt like he did know this story already, or ought to.

"Sure, he was head of the Tribal Council, wasn't he? But then Aztlan broke away, and a year later Tír Tairngire did, too. Howling Coyote stepped down—I don't recall anyone blaming him, but maybe they did it in private, or maybe he blamed himself. Either way, he left the council and just vanished. There'd be sightings of him all over the country, sometimes in two different cities at the same time, but nothing anyone could prove. He turned into a ghost."

"And before he did," Cole added, rising to his feet and starting to pace, which always helped him think, "he came here and hid his amulet by donating it to the Public Works building. Somewhere nobody'd think to look for it. And nobody did—until us."

Doc waved a finger at him. "Don't go blamin' yourself," he warned. "First off, they'd've just gotten some other thief to nick it for them. Second, you didn't go looking for it. You didn't find it. They did. They hired you 'cause they'd already found it. They just weren't willing to get themselves shot or electrocuted or chopped up or whatever it would've done to them if they'd tried themselves. So instead, they hired locals to do the work for them—"

"To die," Cole cut in. "They hired us 'cause they knew they'd kill us after, and they were okay with that." He clenched his fists. "I'm not."

Alaric nodded eagerly beside him, the fight rekindled in his eyes. But Doc reached out, placed one gnarled hand on each of their shoulders, and pushed both of them down into their seats. "Settle down, you two," the shaggy dwarf warned. "You already know we ain't just stormin' their offices. What would that do besides get us all filled full of holes? We need to think of a way to hurt 'em, a way to get through to 'em. Like Cole said, they'll come to us."

Cole nodded, starting to cool down a bit. Alaric was still all wound up, shaking from eagerness to go out and attack the entire NAN on behalf of one fallen elf, but slowly he subsided as well.

"You're right," Cole told his dwarf friend once they were all calm, at least on the surface. "Every time we argue about what we're doing next, we're not honoring their memory. We have to come up with a plan, and then stick to it."

"Okay," Alaric finally agreed. "I get it. Just us against trained guards, guards would win. And by win, I mean shoot us dead. So we've gotta, what, sneak past the guards into the inner site so we can find and nab this amulet? Then get the hell back out. All without anybody seeing us or sensing anything weird."

Cole smiled. "Exactly." He hopped back to his feet. "We'll need more men," he started, beginning to pace, "enough to take out their guards, or at least hold them off while we locate and grab the thing again. Then we get out, let them know we have it, and tell them what we want." He smiled again, though he knew from the few times he'd dared mirrors that it wasn't a pretty sight. "A whole truckload of money, and Mr. Sniper's head on a stick."

"Yeah!" Alaric held out his hand, fingers curled up, and Cole bumped fists with him.

Only Doc was still scowling. "You wanna get your hands on it," he started, "that's fine. But why do it here, where you've got not only their guards, but the city's, too. Why not wait?"

"Wait for what?" Cole demanded, stopping in front of the dwarf and towering over him. "What do you know that we don't?"

"You got a few years?" the dwarf shot back. "But for this— think about it. It was right in plain sight, anybody could've seen it—but nobody went into this building much anymore. Perfect cover. Then the PCC finds out it's there, they hire you to go get it for them. When you come out and demand money, they jump you, kill everybody else, let you live, and take the amulet. So where do they go with it?"

Cole's first response was "someplace warm," but he didn't say that. Instead he thought about it long and hard. He was still thinking when Doc cut in.

"It's gotta be one of the most important items from one of the most important times to be alive," he pointed out. "Especially to them. And it's been hidden away in an office building. Now they've got it back, where do they go?"

"They take it back to their offices where they can keep an eye on it," Cole mused. "But you're right, it's not safe here either, and besides, it's too important to sit in any office, even theirs, and especially here in the FRFZ, where alliances are always shifting and everybody's gunning for everybody else..."

He snapped his fingers. "So they take it home. If the PCC's doing this alone, they take it to Santa Fe. But if it's the whole NAN working together—and something this big, it could be, 'cause if it's not and the other tribes find out, that's war— then they're gonna want to ship it back to the NAN's home. Cheyenne, where the Sovereign Tribal Council meets. That's where they'd want to keep it—it's got the best security, plus it's the seat of their power." He grinned at Doc. "And the easiest time to steal something is when it's on the way from one place to another."

Doc nodded. "Yep."

"Okay." Cole paused in his pacing. "So we follow them when they take it out of here. They might have already, but I'm betting both Sniper and Sharp Lady are going to be guarding it when they go, and they're still here, so it is, too. We hit them somewhere on the road, when they're most vulnerable." He met Alaric's eyes and nodded sharply. "And if those two go down in the process, well, all the better."

The elf grinned, but for once it wasn't wild and free. This one was dark and dangerous. "That's what I'm talking about," he replied, pounding one fist against his chest.

Cole nodded again. The puzzle pieces had come together, at least enough that he could see the outline again. And act accordingly.

They had the start of a plan.

Now they just needed to figure out how best to carry it out.

# FIFTEEN

Cole didn't sleep well that night. In addition to the now-familiar nightmares of a glowing red eye and a malicious wind, he also had bloody visions of him, Doc, and Alaric tracking the amulet's progress out of Denver, swooping down to steal it—and getting gunned down before they could lift a finger.

He woke up gasping, drenched in sweat, and tried desperately to discount those visions as nothing more than the normal before-a-job anxiety, but he knew they were more than that.

They were a hint of what was waiting for him and his friends if they pursued this.

At least, if they tried to pursue it on their own.

"We need help," he told the other two when the decker stopped by an hour later so they could discuss their plan. "Somebody who can fight. Otherwise, we're doomed before we start."

Doc bristled. "I can fight!" he insisted, patting the pistol at his side, a big, bulky piece that was probably as old as he was. But Alaric was already nodding.

"I'm not much good in a fight," the elf admitted. "Give me a system to crack, I'm gold, but put me in a room with people punching each other or out where people are shooting, and I'm in trouble."

"Same here," Cole admitted without hesitation. He knew all too well he wasn't the combative type, and it was more than just a lack of armament. His temperament was better suited to sneaking and running than to standing and shooting. "And Doc, I'm not saying you can't handle yourself, but that's not going to be enough for this. Especially if somebody gets hurt, or I need you to build something—or disable something I can't crack and Alaric can't hack. We need a heavy on this job. Somebody to watch our backs while we take care of the rest."

Doc was still scowling, but finally he nodded. "Yeah, all right," he agreed, tugging at his mustache. "You got somebody in mind?"

That was the problem—Cole didn't. He knew a few gangers, of course, and even a few street samurais, but knowing their faces and being able to nod hello without getting shivved or sliced wasn't the same as asking them along on this job. Especially since it led out of the city, had an indeterminate timeframe and destination, and came with an unclear payoff. He also needed somebody he could trust, at least enough to make sure they all came back alive.

Then an idea popped into his head. "There might be somebody who can help." It wasn't a great idea—hell, it might not even qualify as a *good* idea—but it was the only one he had short of putting up want ads, and they had neither the time nor the resources to field those. "I need to pay someone a visit."

"Who?" Doc asked, his eyes narrowed.

Cole sighed, but knew the dwarf would have to find out sooner or later. "Jen Yubi."

He'd braced himself for the response, so he barely flinched when Doc exploded from his seat. "Jen Yubi? Head of the Mercy? Are you insane?" The stocky inventor's shaggy hair was all standing up like he'd been electrocuted, just from the force of his reaction. "She'll tear you to bits!"

Alaric was studying the two of them like they were both nuts. "You want to go to the Mercy for help?" he asked slowly, like he was trying to be sure he'd heard correctly. "Doesn't that seem a little...counterintuitive?"

"Maybe," Cole admitted, rising slowly to his feet. "But it's the only idea I've got."

"Do they owe you or something?" the decker asked as Cole turned and headed toward the door.

"Not even close," he heard Doc reply with a snort. "More like the other way 'round."

Cole missed whatever Alaric said next as the door shut behind him, but he could guess. And they were both right, it was crazy.

At the moment, though, crazy was about all he had left.

It wasn't hard to find the Mercy. You just went over to the CAS sector, stepped into Chinatown, and then to the part that was the Mercy's territory—delineated by the Chinese symbols for the word "mercy" scrawled in white paint on the corner of every building and every street sign—and wandered around until one of them found you. In this case, that only took a few minutes. One second Cole was crossing a street by himself, and the next there was a shadow looming over him from his right, blocking out the sun.

Cole glanced up, and had to fight not to gasp. It was Hazard.

Tanya "Hazard" Shan was the Mercy's chief enforcer—if by "enforcer" you meant "the person they sent when they wanted to inflict maximum damage." Standing well over two meters tall, she was a solid mass of muscle mixed with steel, both arms made of twisted metal cords similar to Cole's own—except that, where his were for extending his reach, hers were for punching through walls. And the people hiding behind them. Piercings and tattoos adorned her brows, ears, nose, and lips, and her tusks were capped with metal, as were the ends of her long, curling horns. Tied around her forehead just below those horns and also around her bare right biceps were broad silk bands, white with the Mercy symbols painted in blood red.

She peered down at him, her eyes seeming small as always amid the gristle and bone and metal that was her face, and grinned.

"Cole Danvers," she rasped, the words grating out like boulders dragged uphill. "Must be my lucky day. Come to pay your debt?"

"Something like that," Cole answered, doing his best not to shake too much. He didn't try to quell his fear entirely, though. Hazard liked scaring people, and he'd rather keep her happy than piss her off. "I need to talk to Yubi."

"'Course you do." Her right hand closed on his upper arm, the fingers wrapping all the way around, and she nearly yanked his arm from its socket as she turned and dragged him with her. "I'll take you to her."

"Great." Cole had been wondering since he'd left if Doc and Alaric might be right, that this was an incredibly stupid idea. But it was too late to do anything about it now, so he tried to keep as calm as he could and hastened his pace to keep up with Hazard's ground-eating strides. Things would go a lot better if he at least arrived in one piece.

The Mercy controlled part of Denver's Chinatown, of course, but their influence extended beyond that, and so Cole wasn't completely surprised when Hazard guided him into a neighboring business district, and then to a small but sleek office building, its front all steel and glass.

"New digs?" he asked as she pushed him toward the entrance, following close behind so he couldn't run even if he wanted to.

"Yeah, we're moving up in the world." The troll enforcer smirked as she shoved him into the slick, marble-floored lobby. There was a row of elevators along one side, but she ignored them—they didn't look like they'd been designed to handle someone of her stature—and instead directed Cole toward a set of stairs behind the door at the far end. "To the top," she instructed, and he didn't ask any more questions, saving his breath for the ten-story climb ahead.

Hazard set a punishing pace, shoving him every time he flagged, and Cole was panting by the time they reached the top. With one of her trademark smirks, she shouldered him aside to slam the door open, then reached back to drag him through and sling him ahead and onto the floor. Cole hit hard and lay there for a second, trying to put his wits back together, but a cool, low voice interrupted him.

"Well, well," the voice said in a steely purr like a satisfied cat crossed with a hungry snake. "Cole Danvers. I'd heard you were dead."

Cole glanced up and met Jen Yubi's eyes. "I heard that too," he said, mustering his best smile. "Guess they were wrong."

If the Mercy's leader was amused, it didn't show in her narrowed gaze or her tight-lipped frown. "And coming so close to your demise must have made you decide to put all your worldly affairs in order," she mused aloud, steepling her long-fingered hands in front of her, the lacquered tips of her front nails just grazing her lower lip. "Which is why you are here, to repay your debt to me?"

"Uh, something like that." Cole tried to push himself to his feet, but Hazard's boot came down on his back and pinned him to the floor like a trapped rat. After a second of reflexively resisting, he gave up and lay flat. There was no way he could fight the troll's strength, and he didn't need her riled up. Besides, he suspected her boss would enjoy seeing him like this.

Sure enough, now Jen Yubi's lips did curl upward, if only a little. "Explain," was all she said. Cole had heard that her own street name—back when she had been one of the Mercy's enforcers before rising to the top of the organization—had been Iceblood. With her snow-white hair, glacial blue glare, and cold, sharp beauty, he could easily see why. He wasn't sure if it'd be worse facing her or Hazard in a fight, and had no desire to find out.

"I was going to repay you—" he started, and gasped as the boot still on his back ground down a little harder, forcing the air from his lungs. "That job, the one you thought I got killed on?" he managed to wheeze out. "It was a big score. I was going to pay you back from that."

"But?" If she had any concern over his chest being staved in before he could finish talking, she didn't show it.

"We were double-crossed," he whispered, the best he could do now. "They killed the others, thought they killed me too. Took the thing and left me for dead."

"And you came here so we could finish the job?" Hazard growled far above him. "Considerate of you."

"I'm going to steal it back," Cole said, struggling to get the words out. "Make them pay. But...I need...help." The last word was barely audible, and he collapsed, his vision starting to go black as the last of his air left him. For a second he lay there, sure that this was the end, but then Jen Yubi must have gestured, because suddenly the boot was gone and he was gasping in air, shuddering as his lungs reinflated and his vision and mind cleared.

When he finally had enough strength back to lift his head, the Mercy's leader was watching him. "You want us to help you rob the people who stole from you, so you can then extort from them the money you need to repay us?" she summarized, her face as unreadable as ever.

Cole nodded, not sure he was able to speak again yet.

Her eyes bored into him before losing focus as she considered. "What was stolen, and by whom?" she asked at last.

"An amulet," Cole answered, knowing that lying to her now would be fatal. "It belonged to Daniel Howling Coyote himself. The NAN—" it was easier to just assume it was the entire nation, rather than worrying about it only being the PCC or some coalition within the whole, and easier to explain it that way, too, "—hired me to steal it from where it was being kept, then killed the rest of my crew and took it from us." He propped himself up on his elbows and tugged his shirt up to show the bandages still wrapped around his chest. "Almost did me in too, but they didn't count on my mods. Saved my life, barely."

Jen Yubi nodded, but not at him, and the next thing Cole knew a hand the size of his head grabbed his arm again and yanked him to his feet. "Something of Howling Coyote's," the Mercy's leader said softly, "would indeed have great value. And the NAN would pay much to retrieve it." She studied him. "You need muscle."

It wasn't a question, but Cole nodded anyway.

"I will send Hazard with you. She will take care of any border crossings and make sure you succeed. You will repay what you owe, and then that amount again."

Cole knew she wanted him to gulp in shock, but he'd expected something like this. And, to be honest, he was fine with it. This wasn't about the money for him, not anymore. If it settled his debt with the Mercy once and for all, he was good with that. Besides, he might be able to take the NAN for enough to still have a tidy sum left over, even after the Mercy's extortion. So he just nodded and smiled, though he was still a little shaky.

"Done," he agreed, and that actually stole a short, sharp chirp of laughter from her, which he considered a win on his part. Usually no one could elicit a response from Jen Yubi.

She waved a hand, and Hazard hauled him back toward the door. For the first time Cole actually saw the room they were in. It was the entire top floor, end to end and wall to wall. Jen Yubi was seated in a large, handsome chair atop a short platform at the far end, directly opposite the stairs. A handful of other Mercy gangers were sprawled on couches against one side wall, and four others were playing some sort of elaborate tile game around a square wooden table on the other side. It was a large, impressive space, and gave the impression of a medieval throne room, which Cole was sure was the point.

He only had a few seconds to take that in, of course, since Hazard wasn't exactly letting him stand around admiring the architecture. As the big troll shoved him toward the stairs again, she thrust a card into his hand. It had the Mercy's symbol on one side, and an LTG number scrawled on the other.

"Call when we leave," she ordered. "Now go." With a hard push, she nearly sent him tumbling down the stairs head over heels.

"Got it," he choked out, just barely getting his feet under him in time. "Thanks." Then he hurried down, still not quite able to believe his luck. That had gone far better than he'd dared hope—he was leaving not only alive but mostly unharmed, and he'd have the muscle he needed. Plus with the Mercy handling their exit from Denver, he wouldn't have to worry about bribing guards or sneaking through—they had arrangements already in place for such things.

Now he just had to explain to Doc and Alaric that a troll gang enforcer would be joining them on their trek. Considering the interview he'd just survived, Cole figured that would be a piece of cake.

# SIXTEEN

Both the dwarf and decker took the news a lot better than Cole had thought. Which wasn't to say that they were pleased, exactly, but at least they didn't throw up their hands and walk out.

"A troll would be handy if we got into a fight," Doc agreed carefully, pushing back from the table to rub a hand over his face. "And if there's one thing the Mercy're good at, it's fightin'. 'Course, what's to say she won't just kill us and take the amulet for herself, assuming we do manage to get hold of it?"

"That's not going to happen," Cole assured him. "You know that. They've got a code." Which was true, as far as it went. Like most of the stronger gangs, the Mercy stuck to their deals. It was getting them to even talk terms with you that was usually the hard part—mostly they took what they wanted or, if they were inclined to discuss anything, they simply told you what the terms would be, like Jen Yubi had just done to him. They wouldn't renege, though. A gang was only as good as its reputation, and that was made up of two things: how scary they were, and how well they kept their word. Even the scariest gang didn't last if they constantly double-crossed people, because sooner or later all those they'd wronged and all those who expected to be wronged would band together to take them down. The Mercy was too smart to risk that.

"Okay, we need to pack and be ready to head out," Cole continued, switching gears. "They could go at any time, and we want to be right behind them."

He, Doc, and Alaric had been taking turns watching Council Hall all day. Alaric had also managed to tap their communications—he couldn't get into their secure systems without both being inside the building and possibly alerting them, but he'd set a passive tap on the PCC offices' outgoing lines, so he'd know any time they sent a message or made a call. They figured something as major as taking the amulet out of Denver would require a lot of security, a great deal of planning, and therefore a whole lot of phone calls and messages. So far there hadn't been that level of activity, and Cole had seen the Sharp Woman that morning. That meant the amulet was almost certainly still there as well.

Alaric nodded, his hair flopping in response. "I brought that bike," he stated, "and Doc said it shouldn't take more'n another day to get it roadworthy again. I've got some clothes, my deck and other gear, and a few things for the road, but they'll all fit in the saddlebags, so I can be good to go in another day, maybe two."

But Doc was frowning. "We're still missin' something," he declared. "Somethin' big."

"What?" The elf shot a scowl his way. "You said it wasn't too bad, that it was mostly okay, just needed a few tweaks!" They'd all agreed that motorbikes were the way to go—Cole had the one he'd taken from Mace's place, while Doc had a bike he'd built himself exactly to his own size and specifications. Alaric didn't own anything like that, but Doc had promised he could repair any old junker they brought him, so the decker had gone out and found a wreck for cheap.

Now the dwarf inventor waved away Alaric's whine. "The bike's fine," he snapped, "almost ready, I'll have it done for you tomorrow, maybe even tonight. That's not what I meant." He turned his sharp little eyes toward Cole. "We're missin' something, I mean. Something we need with us. Or someone."

Cole shook his head. "I know what you're going to say," he stated, flinging his hands up as if to ward off a blow. "And the answer is no. We're not going there."

"We need one," Doc insisted. "Otherwise, from what you told me about before, we're pretty much screwed afore we even start."

Alaric was watching the exchange, his head swiveling back and forth between them like he was at a Thunderheads game. "What do we need?" he asked, but then he stopped, and his face went pale. "Oh. Right."

"Exactly," Cole said, pointing at the stricken elf. "That's exactly it. I'm not doing that again."

Because he knew precisely what Doc was talking about. They had muscle now. They had stealth and speed. They had medicine and gadgets and repairs. They had computers. The one thing they were really missing—

—was magic.

But Cole had watched Rodrick's head explode out there in the mountains. Alaric's brother. Because the mage was always the first one targeted, the biggest threat, and so the one taken out first. He couldn't bear the thought of hiring on a new mage, knowing full well that, if things went south, that mage would be the first to die.

Doc wasn't backing down, though. "I get that," he insisted, his mustache bristling, "but make sense. We *can't* do this without one. Hell, you may not even be able to hold the damn thing without a mage present! You said Rodrick told you it was some potent juju—what're a grease monkey, a hacker, and a thief gonna do if it turns out that magic's woken up some, and it don't want to be touched? Or moved?" He wagged a finger at Cole. "It's magic, so we gotta have some magic ourselves. Otherwise, there's no freakin' point in even goin' after it."

Cole opened his mouth to argue the point—surely, with all their skills and talents, they didn't absolutely need a mage?— when Alaric surprised them both by cutting him off. "Doc's right," he said quietly, placing both hands flat on the table in front of him, palms down, fingers splayed. "Sure, we could die from this, but we could die tomorrow anyway, and then we'd never have done anything exciting, anything worth writing down. Or we can take the chance and go after this thing, but we can't fight magic without some magic of our own."

Looking back and forth between his two companions, Cole could see he was beat two to one. And while there was still a chance they could pull this off without one, he had to admit that bringing in a mage could be the deciding factor. He couldn't let some lingering guilt make his choice for him, especially if that choice put them and the job at risk.

"All right, fine," he said after a moment. "You're right. We need a mage."

Alaric whooped and threw a fist into the air, pumping it over his head like he'd just won something, and Cole couldn't help but smile a little at the young elf's enthusiasm. The reaction also further convinced him that this was the right choice.

After all, if Alaric didn't feel bad about the idea of essentially replacing his own brother, why should Cole?

"I guess that means we've gotta find us a mage," he mused once the decker had calmed down. "I don't suppose either of you know anyone?"

"Well, not know, exactly," Alaric offered, looking a little sheepish, "but I might know *of* a guy."

"Oh?" The elf now had both Cole's and Doc's full attention, and squirmed a little under their scrutiny, but after a second he continued.

"I saw this guy posting on one of the job boards this morning," he said, pulling out his ever-present deck and calling up a screen. He clicked over to a forum Cole recognized—it was a popular place to post if you were looking for work or needed to hire someone. He'd never used it himself—his kind of work wasn't really the sort you wanted to advertise about, all word of mouth and private posts and in-person meetings— but he knew other people, ones with slightly more aboveboard professions or needs, who found it helpful.

While he'd been musing about this, Alaric had been scrolling down. Apparently he'd found the post he wanted, because now he clicked something and turned the deck so Doc and Cole could both read what he'd pulled up:

*Looking for work. Human male, shaman of many years, practiced at casting and dispelling, summoning and exorcising, conjuring and shielding. Formerly with the Pueblo Corporate Council, references available upon request.*

A contact number followed.

"Wait, you wanna hire some mage who used to be with *the NAN* so we can use 'em against the NAN?" Doc protested. "That's crazy! What's to stop him just runnin' to them and spillin' his guts 'bout everything we're doing?"

But Cole put a hand on the dwarf's shoulder, urging his friend to calm down. "Actually, this might be perfect," he said slowly. "The NAN's all about family and loyalty and stuff, right? So if you're part of one of their tribes, why would you leave? He didn't say 'one of the NAN' or 'worked with them,' he said 'formerly with them.' To me that sounds like he was one of them and now he's not. And that probably didn't end well." He grinned. "And anybody who hates the NAN, right now they're good in my book."

Alaric nodded enthusiastically. "And he'd know how they operate," he pointed out eagerly. "He could help us figure out their command structure, their protocols, what they're gonna do next, stuff like that." The young decker was clearly thrilled that Cole thought his idea had merit.

Doc still didn't look too happy, but finally he sighed. "Yeah, could be useful," he admitted. "Still don't mean I'd trust him, though."

"You don't have to," Cole promised. "And I might not like him once I meet him. But if we're gonna have a mage, and we don't know anyone else ourselves, this sounds like it might be our best bet."

He nodded to Alaric. "Send him a message, set up a meeting as soon as possible. Somewhere in a different sector, say Sioux, and neutral, okay? A coffee house or bar, someplace with other people." He wasn't about to go blindly trusting somebody he'd never met, either.

"You got it." The decker pulled up a reply window and quickly started typing. Only a minute later, he had a reply. "He says he can meet in an hour, at the Smokehouse," Alaric read off. "Yes or no?"

Cole knew where the Smokehouse was, and even though it was in the next sector over it was barely twenty minutes away, plus the bar was a decent-sized place with good lighting and the kind of booths you could hold private conversations in.

"Yeah, say yes," he replied. "Tell him I'll be the one with the metal arms and the black headband." He grabbed a black cloth off the table and tied it around his forehead. That should mark him well enough for this guy to find him.

Now it was just a matter of seeing what this guy was like, if he was the real deal or not, and if Cole thought he could be trusted, at least enough to hire him for this job.

The man who presented himself at Cole's booth was so short and stocky Cole wondered if he might actually be an unusually tall dwarf. He was also completely bald; his ruddy scalp was covered in an elaborate tattoo, the thick, broad strokes extending across his forehead, over one eye, and onto his cheek. Not only rings and studs but cylinders pierced his ears, and several piercings adorned his bushy brows, fleshy nostrils, and thin lips as well. The stranger looked startled when he saw Cole, then nodded and held out a thick, callused hand.

"Goyathlay Seevers," he declared. His handshake was firm and dry, and he released Cole's hand soon enough to not make it awkward, but late enough to show that he wasn't timid about contact.

"Cole Danvers," Cole replied, and gestured at the seat opposite him. Goyathlay—Cole was already trying to wrap his brain around how to pronounce that properly, and hoped not to tangle his tongue too much the first time he tried it out loud—slid into the booth without additional prompting. He was wearing a red robe, Cole noted, but it was short and belted at the waist, and below that the man had on what looked to be buckskin leggings, fringed along the side. A bone-and-bead choker and beaded moccasins completed the picture, along with the fringed leather bag slung over his shoulder. If the man wasn't an actual Native shaman, he certainly did a good job presenting himself as such.

"So you used to be with the PCC?" Cole asked once Goyathlay had seated himself. A waitress approached, but Cole prevented her from getting too close by tapping the side of his beer with two fingers. She nodded and retreated, the sign of a good server, and he returned his attention to his new companion in time to see the man scowl fiercely.

"I did," he agreed, almost spitting the words onto the table. "Born into the Zuni, trained from the time I could walk to follow my grandfather's footsteps as a shaman. I came into my power early, and strong, and served my tribe and the PCC and the NAN well—for all the good it did me."

"What happened?" Cole felt a slight twinge of guilt at bringing up what was obviously a painful subject. But he had to know, and there was no way the shaman hadn't expected this, not when he mentioned his connection to them in his post.

Goyathlay's face twisted still further. "'Inadequate performance,'" he quoted, using his fingers to emphasize that those were their words, not his.

The waitress appeared silently and set two fresh beers on the table, and Cole slid one across to the shaman, who grabbed it and chugged down half the contents in a single long swig.

"In other words," he explained once he'd lowered the bottle again, "I disagreed with something the tribal elders had planned, and had the balls to call them on it. I was overruled, and did what they wanted, but under protest. It blew up in their faces, just like I said it would, and they needed someone to blame. That was me."

He finished the beer and set the empty on the table with a heavy thud. "Kicked me out of the tribe entirely. But they couldn't strip the magic away—it wasn't theirs to give or take. That comes from Raven, and to Raven I remain true."

Cole considered. If the shaman was lying, he was very convincing. His hatred for the NAN certainly looked genuine. That was definitely something Cole could use—a man like that would jump at the chance to screw them out of their prize. The next question, of course, was whether the man could be useful in other ways. Specifically, magical ones.

"I hate to ask this," he started, "but—"

"Can I show you something to prove I'm not just faking it with the robes and the marks and the rest?" Goyathlay laughed and cupped his hands around the beer bottle before him. His eyes closed for a second, and when they reopened they had turned a milky white and glowed faintly. That same glow rose around his hands, and then between them the bottle began to shift, its form melting and reflowing. After a few seconds the shaman blinked, his eyes reverting to their normal dark gaze, and moved his hands away from the delicate glass vase that now graced their table.

"Very pretty," Cole acknowledged, reaching over and lifting the vase to study it. It was cool to the touch, its sides and edges perfectly smooth. "I hope you can do more than recycle old bottles, though. That won't be much help in a fight."

The shaman laughed again. "Trust me, boy, you want me on your side in a battle." He leaned forward and lowered his voice, a thunderous expression settling onto his face. "I can boil the blood of your enemies. I can knock arrows and bullets out of the air. I can rain down birds and hail and lightning. I can split the ground beneath their feet." He sat back, the darkness fading, to be replaced by a more jovial expression. "Yes, I can help in a fight."

Cole chose to believe him. The man had power, clearly, and the way he'd spoken—it hadn't seemed like an idle boast. "All right," he said easily, pushing the untouched second beer toward Goyathlay. "Good." He smiled as the shaman accepted the bottle and tipped it toward him before taking a sip. "So let me tell you what we're doing, and why."

"He's in," Cole told Doc and Alaric when he returned an hour later. "And you were right, I think he'll be useful. He's got his own grudge against the NAN, so he's just as eager to take them down a peg as we are."

"Good," the decker replied, "because I picked up a whole burst of messages right after you left. Most of 'em I couldn't read, but a few were dumb enough to talk or text over an open line. Soldiers, getting ready to move out with a convoy first thing tomorrow. Full escort, guarding something mega-important. Heading for Cheyenne."

Cole felt a burst of excitement in his chest, like a small starburst. He'd been right. They were taking the amulet to the Sovereign Tribal Council.

"I'll let Hazard and Goyathlay know," he promised. He grinned at his two friends, starting to feel the thrill of the hunt. "We leave at dawn."

# SEVENTEEN

"*This* is your team?" Hazard demanded as she stomped into the garage, ducking to clear the doorway. "A musty old hairball and a blue-topped geek? No wonder you needed help."

The big troll was dressed the same as Cole'd seen her last time, in sturdy leathers thick enough to serve as armor, now including a long black duster with the Mercy's sign painted across the back. A heavy pistol, big enough that anyone else would need two hands just to lift it, was strapped to one thigh, a nasty-looking short-handled throwing axe to the other. A sword and a shotgun were crossed at her back, their straps crisscrossing her chest and adorned with heavy metal globes Cole guessed were grenades. She looked ready to fight a war all on her own.

In the interest of moving things along, and not starting this job with a fight, he ignored her comment and quickly introduced her to the others. "Doc Cragtop, Alaric Kaine, Hazard." He leveled his best "play nice" glare at her, but the troll didn't even seem to notice. "You bring a bike?"

"In the alley," she replied, jerking her head back behind her. Cole started to ask whether it would be safe out there, but stopped himself. Who in their right mind would mess with a troll's ride? Especially one marked by the Mercy?

Besides, he wasn't entirely sure any bike big enough to fit her would have fit through the door.

"We're just waiting on—" he started to say, but the bang of the door slamming open cut him off. There was Goyathlay, a heavy sheepskin coat over his robes and a pair of saddlebags slung over his shoulder.

"I am here," he declared, sidling in to get past Hazard, who hadn't moved more than a pace from the door. "We may begin."

"Goyathlay Seevers," Cole said, "meet Hazard, Doc, and Alaric." He studied the shaman. "Where's your bike?"

The shaman shook his head and fluttered one hand in the air. "A holy man does not need such contrivances," he declared. "I will walk, as I have walked much of this land already."

"Walk?" That was Doc. "You can't walk, you bloomin' idiot! We're all on bikes! We'd leave you in our dust!"

"Good," Hazard commented, peering down at the shaman with obvious distaste. "Better to leave him behind. He looks and smells like them." Cole assumed she meant the NAN.

"He used to be one of them," he agreed. "But he's not anymore. Now he's working with us. And we need him, so he's gonna have to keep up."

Cole turned to Doc. "Any chance you've got a spare bike tucked away in here somewhere?" They weren't at Doc's place, but at a garage he used for some of his side projects. It was only a few blocks from his home, but this way he could also meet with potential clients and still be able to trust that they didn't know where he lived. Alaric had suggested they meet Hazard and Goyathlay here, and it had seemed like a smart idea. Especially with Hazard—no sense telling the Mercy where to find them if they could avoid it.

Doc grunted, and muttered something under his breath, but stomped off toward the back of the garage. A cacophony of clattering and banging and slamming and cursing arose from that direction, followed by the cough and sputter, and then finally the purr of an engine. When Doc returned, he was wheeling a heavy motorcycle that had clearly been extensively chopped, its front wheel extending well forward and its body angling down away from that to the seat, which was barely higher than the rear wheel it butted up against. All of its struts and pistons were matte black, and its body was covered in rust-red primer, but it seemed functional.

"Not pretty," the dwarf declared, stopping the bike in front of the shaman and shoving it at him, "but it's solid and it runs."

The shaman looked like he was about to argue, so Cole cut him off. "It's this or you don't go," he stated. "You want to get back at the NAN, you have to be able to keep up."

Goyathlay studied him only a second before nodding. He tossed his saddlebags onto the bike so they lay across the rear fender, then bent down and began buckling the sides into place so they covered the rear wheel but wouldn't interfere with it. Within a few minutes he'd straightened up, nodded, and climbed onto the bike.

Cole had spent the time grabbing his own bike, the big beast he'd inherited from Mace. Alaric was already astride his, which Doc had finally finished repairing last night. Doc had wheeled his out from the back as well, and was seated and ready to go—his was a touring style, with elongated handlebars so he could sit back comfortably, his feet in rests well above the ground, and still steer the bike without a problem. Alaric's and Cole's were more along the lines of cruisers.

Hazard nodded and ducked back out through the door, and the rest of them followed, wheeling their bikes outside. Doc was the first one out, and he burst out laughing. "You call that a bike?" Cole heard him say. "More like a small, open-air tank!"

"Tank works for me," Hazard growled back, and Cole hurried forward, cutting past Alaric and the shaman. He had the feeling he'd better hurry if he didn't want his muscle and his medic-inventor getting into a fight before they'd even left the city!

Edging out into the alley, Cole got his first look at Hazard's "bike," and he could see why Doc was laughing. It wasn't really a motorcycle at all—it was an all-terrain vehicle, with four hefty wheels spaced evenly around its sturdy metal frame. It looked to have armor plating, and what seemed like unnecessary pipes and coils and tubes. And it was easily five feet tall.

Then again, considering Hazard's height and bulk, Cole could see why she'd need something that big. And with that many wheels to disperse her weight.

"Looks good," was all he said, earning him a glare from the dwarf and a smug look from the troll. "As long as it can keep up."

Hazard patted the side of the thing. "It'll keep up."

By this time Alaric and Goyathlay had joined them, and Doc scurried past them to shut and lock the garage. Once he was done and back to his bike, Cole nodded. "We know they're making for Cheyenne," he said, "which means they've got to be heading due north. So that's what we're doing, too." But he'd only just started to turn his bike toward the mouth of the alley when Hazard spoke up.

"Bad idea," the troll enforcer warned in her usual harsh tone. "We need to go northeast."

"Now why the hell would we wanna do that?" Doc demanded, glaring up at her. "That's gonna take us out of our way, and we won't be able to tail them. If they turn off, we'd have no idea."

"I will know where they go," Goyathlay declared smugly. "I can sense the emanations of the talisman Cole Danvers spoke of. It is very potent, and it calls to me. Wherever it goes, I can follow."

"That's swell," Doc replied, "but I still say we need to dog their steps every inch of the way, just in case. If we can't see 'em, we could lose 'em, and then we're sunk."

"And if they see us, they'll come after us," Hazard warned. "Then I've gotta kill 'em all." She shrugged. "Fine by me, but you might not survive it." She didn't say it like a threat—more like she was just reminding them of the possibility—but when something like that was delivered by a troll nearly three meters tall, it still came out ominous.

Alaric bristled. "Listen, lady," he said, "you do your job, we'll do ours. Long as you keep us safe, we'll handle the rest."

Hazard half-rose from her seat so she could loom over him, even though the elf was on the other side of the alley. "Yeah? You gonna handle me too, blue boy?" She sneered down at him. "Like to see you try."

"Plug in somewhere and then we'll see who's in charge and who's just large," he shot back. "Come on!"

"All right, enough!" Cole insisted, stepping between them and putting his hands out as if that would somehow hold them both back. "Knock it off!" He waited until they'd both calmed down, checking the shaman and the dwarf to make sure they weren't fixing to jump into the fray as well. "Hazard is right. We can't let them see us or notice us in any way. We need to be able to sneak up on them and take the amulet before they even know we're there. So we'll head northeast instead." He called up the maps in his head. "They'll probably take 76 to 25," he explained, referring to the old highway designations most people still used to navigate. "We can take 76 to 85. We'll parallel them, but we'll have twenty to thirty klicks between us. That's enough that the mountains'll provide some cover."

He glanced at Havoc. "You can get us through the checkpoints there?" She nodded. Good enough. He flicked the ignition on his bike and it roared to life. "Let's go."

Nobody argued this time, though he did hear some grumbling behind him as he exited the alley and headed north.

*I hope this isn't what it's going to be like the whole way,* Cole thought as he rode, seeing the others slowly pop up in his rearview and then speed up so they were following him in a staggered line, with Hazard bringing up the rear. *Otherwise the NAN won't have to worry about us much—we'll be too busy tearing into each other to give them any real trouble!*

# EIGHTEEN

They were well into Sioux territory and nearly to the Outer Boundary when Cole realized they were being followed. It was just a quick blur of motion to the side as they passed through an intersection, but at the next block Cole saw it again. Then he tilted his head to the left and, at the next crossing, there it was again. Something small and fast and running parallel to them on both sides.

Like motorcycles.

He deliberately slowed so the others, who had been riding in a loose diamond formation behind him, caught up. "We've got a problem," he said, trying to keep his voice down but having to speak up over the rumble of the engines—he didn't quite trust comms to be audible while riding. "We've got company."

Doc, Alaric, and Goyathlay all looked surprised. Hazard just nodded. "Huns," she rumbled. "They won't try anything."

The others stared at her. "The Huns?" Alaric finally managed to sputter. "We're in their territory?" The big troll shrugged like that was no big deal, which only seemed to make the elf angrier. "You knew we were crossing into Hun territory, and you didn't say anything?"

"They won't try anything," she repeated confidently. "Wouldn't dare."

Doc snorted. "Why, because we've got you with us?"

She didn't reply, just stared down at him, arms crossed.

That didn't stop him, however. "You may be a big deal in the Mercy, but you're not there right now, sister. And you're definitely not enough to take out the Huns all on your own."

Still she didn't reply, and finally Cole stepped in to end the silent staredown. "Look, we need to keep moving," he pointed out. "There isn't a whole lot we can do about the Huns right now. Maybe they're just checking to make sure who's passing through their area, and once they see we're headed out of town and not looking for trouble they'll leave us alone." The words didn't sound all that convincing even to him, but the others slowly nodded one by one, and a minute later he was leading the way down the street again. This time he kept glancing to the sides, watching for those motorcycles, and he made sure the pistol he'd kept from Mace's armory was close to hand.

They'd gone only two more blocks before, with a blitz of sound and motion, the Huns closed in.

This part of Denver was more industrial, which was good at least because it meant there weren't as many random people around. It was largely factories and warehouses out here, and early enough that most workers were still on their way in, so the streets were quiet.

Of course, that also meant there wouldn't be any witnesses to whatever went down here.

A half-dozen bikes roared at them from all directions. For a second it looked like they were going to charge straight into Cole and his team, but at the last second the lead bike braked, its wheels locking up and spinning it sideways. It skidded a few feet, tires squealing on the asphalt, and came to a halt barely a meter from Cole's front tire. All around them, the other bikes had done the same, causing an ear-splitting racket, and when their heads stopped ringing Cole and the others were surrounded. It was a neat trick, very impressive, and showed clearly that the Huns' reputation for being skilled bikers was no exaggeration.

Unfortunately, the other half of their rep was that they were prone to violence. And that they didn't like trespassers.

"Wrong part of town, Mercy-girl," the Hun directly in front of Cole called out. He was human but as big as an ork, with a long, forked black beard. Like the rest of his gang he wore black leathers studded with spikes, and his helmet was also spiked and had a thick fur band around its base. Resting across his handlebars was a heavy shotgun that had been melded with a battle-axe. The rest of his gang had a similar mix of ancient nomad and modern biker attire and weaponry, which made them look even more fierce and dangerous than just regular leathers and guns would have. "This is Hun turf, and you gotta pay to pass."

Cole held up his hands, palms out and fingers spread. "We aren't looking for any trouble," he declared, making sure he could be heard by all of them. "We're just heading out of the city."

"That's fine, you can get the hell out," one of the other Huns, a powerful-looking woman with short, blindingly white hair replied. "Soon as you pay the toll."

That got laughs from several of her friends, and Cole felt a chill steal down his spine. He had the sinking feeling that whatever coin he and the others could scare up wouldn't even come close to matching the "toll" they had in mind.

A gasp from one of the Huns startled him, and he looked up to see that the biker was staring—but not at Cole. Rather, at something behind him.

Cole glanced back over his shoulder and his heart began to beat triple-time. Goyathlay had started muttering, the shaman's eyes going that pale, glowing white again. But if the shaman hoped to take the gang members by surprise, he had failed spectacularly.

"Hey, knock that off!" the lead Hun ordered, hand reaching for his weapon, but the shaman continued his chanting. "I mean it," the Hun warned. "You try anything, and you're toast!"

"Goyathlay, don't," Cole urged, but the shaman ignored him as well. The chanting continued, and then suddenly he stopped, sat bolt upright, and spread his hands wide.

A whistling sound began overhead, and a flock of dark birds descended from nowhere, swooping and circling and spinning around the shaman until he was lost from sight. Everyone ducked, the Huns cursing, but the birds stayed in their tight spiral and didn't seem interested in going after the gang at all. A second later the birds—crows, some part of Cole said—rose and dispersed, flapping away with loud caws, still ignoring everyone else and making for the open sky instead.

And Goyathlay was gone as well, his motorcycle now standing empty in their midst.

For a second, everyone could only stare at the space where the shaman had been. Then the lead Hun laughed. "Well, guess he decided to turn back," he said, still chuckling, and a chorus of laughs and insults sprang up to echo him. "As for the rest of you," he went on, the humor vanishing from his tone in an instant and fading from his gang a second later as they all fell deadly quiet, "time to pay up."

Cole started to say something, but Hazard got there before him. "Fine," the big troll announced. "I'll pay." Her hands tightened on her handlebars, and the engine revved. Cole wondered if she was planning to charge the Huns.

She hit a button hidden in the rubber of her handlebar grips, and several of the tubes Cole had noticed earlier irised open.

And fired, with a deafening bellow like an angry dragon.

The lead Hun was blown clear off his bike by the force of the gunshots that struck his chest. Several bullets hit the bike itself, piercing its side and its tank, and a second later the bike exploded. At the same time, other tubes had fired to either side and even behind Hazard, taking out three more Huns at once.

When the smoke cleared, only two of the Huns were still intact and astride their bikes. They were staring open-mouthed at the carnage that had descended upon them and their friends.

Hazard, for her part, leaning back on her seat, grinning broadly, her metal-capped tusks gleaming in the early light. "Did I pay enough?" she said in her usual gravelly tones. "Or do you need more?"

That had been directed at the two remaining Huns, and after a second one of them came out of her daze enough to shake her head. It was the white-blonde who'd first mentioned the toll. "Fine," she managed to gasp out, although she looked like she was ready to fall over herself. "You can go. This time."

Hazard nodded curtly and gunned her engine again. Then she plowed forward—Cole barely managed to scoot to the side before she barreled past him—and right over the remains of the lead Hun and his blackened, smoking bike. With a shrug and one last, quick glance back at the last two gang members, Cole reached out, extending his right arm, and grabbed the handlebars of Goyathlay's abandoned bike. Better not to leave it behind, in case the shaman reappeared. Doc and Alaric clearly understood what he had planned and moved to either side of the riderless vehicle, pinning it between them and shepherding it along. With a nod of thanks Cole released his hold on it, faced forward again, and followed in Hazard's wake, though he went around the wreckage rather than through it. Doc and Alaric brought up the rear with the shaman's bike.

They rode in silence for three blocks before Doc burst out, "What the hell did you think you were doing back there?"

It was obvious his question was directed toward Hazard, and the troll replied. "Clearing our path." She sounded pleased with herself, and a grin still tugged at her thick lips.

"You nearly got us all killed!" Doc insisted. "That your idea of keeping us safe?"

She shrugged. "You're safe, aren't you?"

"It was reckless," Cole agreed, though without Doc's vehemence. "But it did work. You could have warned us, though."

Hazard only grunted. "Would've warned them, too. Had to be a surprise."

"Yeah, I guess it did." He eyed her ATV again, reconsidering what he'd thought were useless attachments. "How'd you know you wouldn't hit any of us, though?" It looked like all the weapons had fixed positions, so there was no way she could've aimed.

The troll's grin only widened. "Figured it was worth the risk," she said, and laughed.

That brought more grumbles from Doc, and plenty of dark looks from Alaric, but neither of them argued further. It had worked, after all, and they were all fine.

All except their shaman, who'd vanished in a flock of birds.

Just as Cole was thinking that, however, someone stepped out from behind a building they were approaching and into the street ahead of them.

It was Goyathlay.

Cole skidded to a halt, as did Doc and Alaric. Hazard didn't slow down, though. "Hazard!" Cole shouted, and at the last second she braked, making the shaman jump back to avoid being flattened. Cole thought he heard Alaric snicker at that, but let it go.

"Where the hell have you *been?*" he demanded instead, focusing all of his ire on their reappeared shaman. "We get in trouble and you disappear on us? You told me you were good in a fight!"

"I am," the tattooed man replied as he sidestepped Hazard and took his bike back from Cole. "But this was not my fight. I thought it best to make myself scarce instead, remove the temptation from them and distract them at the same time."

Cole started to yell again, then stopped himself. The shaman's showy disappearance had distracted the Huns, right enough. And maybe it had given Hazard the time she needed to better position her ATV so she could take out their leader. But had that really been Goyathlay's plan? Or had he just cut and run to save his own skin?

Either way, there wasn't a lot Cole could do about it now. He could fire the shaman, of course, but then they'd be without magic again, and he knew that was a bad idea. Plus they'd been counting on him to track the amulet. So they needed him. And it seemed, from his serene expression as he reseated himself, that Goyathlay knew it.

"Fine," Cole told him. "But next time, talk to me before you do something like that." He switched his glare to Hazard. "Same goes for you. We can't just all go off doing whatever we want whenever we want, without discussing it. That's now how a team works."

"This is a team?" Hazard asked. She snorted. "Huh. Coulda fooled me."

Looking around at the others, Cole was forced to agree. A more hodge-podge assortment of individuals he'd never seen. But he knew they'd have to learn to be a team, or they'd never get that amulet back.

Hell, if they couldn't learn to work together, they probably wouldn't even survive!

It was with heavy thoughts like those that he took the lead again, guiding them down the last few streets toward the city's edge—and the uncertainties that lay beyond.

# NINTEEN

"It has moved."

Cole twisted around to study Goyathlay. The shaman was sitting bolt upright on his bike, head raised like a dog catching a scent. Indeed, for a second it seemed that his eyes were closed and Cole worried that he'd have to grab his bike to keep him from crashing, but then the tattooed man blinked and regained control of the bike before it could veer off course.

"What're you talking about?" Cole demanded. He had to raise his voice to be heard over the rush of the wind and the roar of the engines. His pulse pounded in time to the thrum of the wheels over the road. They'd been out of Denver for an hour, everyone keeping mercifully quiet as they rode, and so Goyathlay's sudden pronouncement had taken them all by surprise.

"The amulet," the shaman answered. "It has moved."

Behind him, Doc snorted. "'Course it's moved, you idjit," he snapped. "It's on the move, same as us. That's why we're chasing after it." The way his bike cradled him, his feet well off the ground, reminded Cole of a baby in its crib, all swaddled and warm.

But the shaman was shaking his head. "No, it has moved off course," he stated, his words clear and strong and unhurried. "It is now traveling west." He gestured in that direction.

"West?" Alaric said. "That doesn't even make sense! Cheyenne's straight north from here!"

"Nonetheless," Goyathlay said calmly, "the amulet is now headed west."

Colt held up his hand and the entire procession ground to a halt. He wheeled his bike around so he could confront the shaman face to face. "How sure are you?" he demanded.

"I am certain," Goyathlay replied. "Its power calls to me, like the roar of an approaching storm. But it is also receding, the distance between us increasing with each passing second."

Cole chewed on his lip and considered that, and the road, and his companions. He scanned the horizon, but there was no sign of the NAN convoy—they had deliberately stayed back far enough to not be noticed, but that meant they couldn't see the NAN trucks either, and right now he cursed that decision. Had they really turned off, or was Goyathlay mistaken? The shaman claimed he could feel the amulet, but what if he was wrong—or simply lying? If they turned off west as he suggested, and he was wrong, they'd never catch up again. But if he was right and they didn't follow, they could lose the amulet completely. It came down to what he believed, where he felt the amulet was now.

"We go west," he said finally, and Doc and Alaric groaned.

"Seriously, you're buying this?" Alaric gestured at the shaman in their midst. "How do we know he's feeling anything besides saddle sores from riding? He could be making all of this up. Or he could still be with the NAN, and they told him to lead us away so they could get the amulet back safely."

Goyathlay glared at the blue-haired elf, eyes starting to glow faintly. "How dare you?" he practically spat at the decker. "They threw me out! Called me unfit! I would never work for them! Never!"

"Okay, okay." Alaric reared back. "Geez. Sorry."

That decided Cole. "We go west," he repeated. He called up the maps in his head and projected them into his left eye. "They must have split off onto 40," he said once he'd studied the intersecting lines of the area's highway system. "We're coming up on 35—if we take it west, it'll loop us around to 40 as well." He looked a little closer. "Ah, or we can take 34, which is just north of 40. That'll work—we can do exactly what we were planning to do here, stay close but hidden until we're ready to bridge the gap."

Doc frowned. "Still doesn't make any sense," the dwarf insisted. "Why would they turn off when they can just head straight there?"

"I don't know," Cole agreed. "But Goyathlay says that's what they did, and I believe him. So we go after them." He scrubbed at his chin with one hand. "Once we hit 34 we can pick up speed, try to spot them on 40. We'll have the high ground."

"What if we don't see them?" Alaric demanded.

Cole shrugged. "Then he was wrong, and we hurry back this way and hotfoot it toward Cheyenne, hoping to make up whatever time we lost." He glanced at the shaman again. "But I don't think he's wrong."

Hazard hadn't said a thing through all of this, but now she gunned her engine and bolted forward, continuing the way they'd come—but also toward the intersection with 35. "Keep up," she growled over he shoulder as her ATV barreled ahead. "We can't let them get away."

Doc and Alaric both studied Cole for a second, but he was already taking off after the troll. After a moment, his two friends followed him. The shaman brought up the rear without a word.

"All right, one point for the shaman," Doc admitted a few hours later. They'd taken the loop around onto the westbound 34, then raced ahead as fast as they could along the winding mountain road. Now they were pulled off to the side, and Doc handed his binoculars to Alaric.

Cole sat on his motorcycle beside them, but he didn't need to wait for a turn with Doc's optics. He had his own. Which was how he was already staring at the road below and south of them—and the small string of dark figures gliding along it at a decent but not breakneck speed. With his vision enhanced, he could easily make out the NAN trucks—and the black Jeep up in front.

They'd done it! They'd beaten the NAN here! Now they just had to wait for the right moment to attack, grab the amulet, and get back to somewhere safe.

Though he still wondered why they'd decided to detour and take the amulet out this way in the first place. There wasn't much out here, just a handful of small towns. They'd already passed through one and seen signs for several others, but if those were anything like that first one, these towns were barely worthy of the name. They were little more than a collection of shacks and huts and perhaps one or two larger buildings, all grouped together around a central square or on either side of a narrow, old road. As far as he could see, there wasn't anything worth visiting out this way, much less someplace that merited a trip with such a powerful artifact.

But the NAN crew showed no sign of slowing, and so the chase—and the hunt—continued.

"This is ridiculous," Doc commented two days later. They'd continued to head initially a little north and then almost directly west, keeping the NAN convoy in sight below them. "Where the hell are they going?"

Several more towns had appeared and disappeared along or around the highway, and they'd ridden through the Arapaho National Forest as well. They'd eaten most of the food they'd brought with them—it was only an hour and change to Cheyenne, after all, so they hadn't thought to pack much more than a few drinks and snacks for the road. They'd have to do something about that soon.

Twice they'd encountered other people, once on the way through a town and once out on the open road, but both times it had been a band of thugs rather than the NAN. The first time, Hazard had moved to the front, her lips pulling back in a fierce snarl, and the gang of youths had backed off, letting her and the others pass through safely. The second group had been larger and bolder, and hadn't backed down at all, even when Hazard had waved her new toy, the shotgun-axe she'd taken from the dead Hun leader. Instead they'd blocked the entire highway, forcing Cole and the others to come to a stop long enough to deal with them.

"There's a toll," one of the youths, a dark-skinned girl, elven judging by the sharp beauty, the large, slanted eyes, and the gracefully pointed ears declared, gliding her bike forward a few feet. "For so many of you, it's going to have to be—"

Cole had thought that, after seeing Rodrick's head explode, he couldn't be surprised or sickened. Especially not by something of a similar ilk. But when the girl's head burst apart, showering her surroundings with a deluge of smoke and blood and brains, even he jumped. He craned his neck and stared at Hazard. The big troll had her back to him, but he could still see the smoking shotgun-axe in her hands.

"Anyone else?" Hazard asked loudly, pumping the shotgun to eject the spent casing and advance another.

"You crazy bitch," one of the other youths snarled, nudging his bike forward. "We're gonna—"

This time Cole expected it, and had wheeled his bike back almost out of spatter range.

"Anyone else?" Hazard repeated, her voice husky but deceptively calm as she ratcheted another shell into place, her gaze sweeping the remaining assortment of teens ahead as if already zeroing in on her next target.

This time the gang did back away—two members lighter, but perhaps a little wiser. Hazard stayed at the ready, shotgun-axe in one hand, bike's handlebars in the other as Cole led the way past the traumatized gang members. The remaining gangers just watched them go, clearly seething, but not willing to risk any more of their number by closing that distance again.

Cole hit the gas as soon as he was clear of the gang, and the others did the same, staying close behind him as he sped away. All of them stayed nervously alert for the next few hours, until they were fairly certain they must have passed the boundaries of whatever territory that gang had claimed. Cole was once again glad he'd thought to bring some muscle with them. He might not find Hazard the easiest person to talk to, and obviously the others agreed with him, but there was no question that without her they'd either have been turned back before ever leaving the city proper or have been carved to pieces by one of the gangs they'd encountered.

And Goyathlay had proven himself as well, by detecting the amulet's changed course even from such a distance. Without him they'd have lost the route entirely, and forfeited any hope of stealing the amulet back. Yes, he'd cut and run during that encounter with the Huns, but one mistake didn't mean he was hopeless. And he'd made a point of sticking close to the rest of them since, and not vanishing when the new gang had shown up. Cole hoped that meant the shaman wouldn't take off again, and was trying to make amends for before.

Cole knew he could count on Doc, who was his oldest friend. The same was becoming true for Alaric. Cole was sure he could trust them to have his back, both against stupid suggestions within their group and against more serious threats from beyond. But they wouldn't coddle him, either. Neither of them hesitated before letting Cole know he was doing something incredibly wrong—or, on rare occasions, that he'd done something right.

Cole felt his lips curl up in a small smile. They were hardly a cohesive team yet, but it was starting to look like they had all the necessary parts, at least.

Now it was just a matter of getting each part to work with the others.

# TWENTY

The first thing they saw upon pulling up at the outskirts of the little town were the flames.

"What the hell's going on here?" Cole muttered as he watched red and gold flickers dancing against the night sky somewhere up ahead. Judging by the shadows they were casting upon buildings, the flames had to be monstrous, at least three meters high, and three meters or more across. Was the town burning?

But although he could hear a babble of voices in front of them as well, there were no panicked screams or shouts of pain. Instead he heard shouts and laughs and—singing?

"Slowly," he warned, and applied only enough throttle for his bike to creep forward at no faster than a brisk walking pace. He didn't like strangeness or surprises, and wasn't about to go charging into a situation unprepared if he could avoid it.

"Where are we?" Alaric asked as they slowly glided down the town's one street toward the odd juxtaposition of merriment and destruction.

"Dinosaur," Cole replied absently, trying to watch in every direction at once. The town wasn't very big, and most of its buildings looked to be constructed along this single road or just behind it. They all appeared to be old, weathered wood, and were only one story tall except for a saloon and a hotel facing each other near the town center. He knew that was what those establishments were because the flames were now near enough that he could easily read the signs in the blaze of shifting light.

"This is Dinosaur?" Goyathlay said behind him, and Cole looked back at the shaman. The tattooed former NAN man was studying their surroundings with open curiosity, but didn't look terribly worried about his safety or that of the group. He rode casually with one hand on the handlebars and one resting on his hip and the fringed leather bag there. "Interesting."

"Why's that?" Doc demanded, but anything the shaman meant to say vanished as a silhouette suddenly appeared mere centimeters ahead of Cole's front tire.

"Hello!" The man—for now they could see it was a man, tall and heavy-set with bushy brown hair and matching sideburns—called out over the squeal of brakes. "Welcome to Dinosaur!" He thrust a bottle toward them.

Cole accepted the bottle, which proved to be a made of heavy green glass and bore no label. It was still corked, but he was able to extract that without any real difficulty. At once a whiff of cherries, oak, chocolate, and other elements enveloped him, all with another rich aroma he couldn't identify wrapped around them.

Although he was hardly an expert on the subject, Cole guessed it had to be wine.

"Thanks," he replied, and raised the bottle to the man. "So, what's all this about?" he asked, gesturing toward the fire and the people singing and dancing around it.

"It's our annual harvest celebration," their new benefactor answered, blinking owlishly at them. "We light the last of the previous year's leavings and pray to the gods that, in exchange, they grant us a bountiful harvest next year as well."

Doc scowled at the man. "So what if last year sucked?" he asked bluntly. "Or it did okay, but not well enough to leave you anything for that prayer?"

"That hardly seems likely," the stranger protested. "We always have enough. More than enough this past year, even before the late additions." Someone danced by, a young woman with long blond hair flowing free behind her, and handed him another bottle. "Ah, thank you," he called after her. He raised the bottle and saluted them with it. "Cheers!" Then he took a long swallow, loudly smacking his lips afterward.

Cole wanted to reply, to say something snappy in response, but it was late and he was tired and there was a full bottle of wine in his hands. So he did what any smart person would do—

—he raised his own bottle and drank directly from it.

It was indeed wine, the droplets he saw possessing a deep crimson hue, velvety on the tongue but smooth the rest of the way down, and Cole felt his body heating up as the alcohol began to bleed through his system. His heart raced, his head pounded, and it felt like someone had locked him inside an oven in the act of warming up. "Don't drink it!" he shouted even as Doc, who had taken the bottle from him just seconds before, raised it to his own lips.

Doc raised an eyebrow, but it was clear the shaggy dwarf inventor wasn't about to hand the container back over. Not without examining it himself. He took a hefty swig—and promptly spat it out, just missing Alaric, who was seated beside him. "Holy drek!" the dwarf declared, rubbing one forearm across his mouth as if that would somehow dispel the last traces of that foul flavor. "What in the hells is that?"

A massive hand reached out, and Hazard took the bottle from Doc and brought it close to her right eye. Then she lowered the bottle to her nose and took a long whiff. "Fortified," she declared finally. "Good for explosions and getting drunk fast and not a whole hell of a lot else."

Cole considered this new information. "So what you're saying is someone doctored this wine? Before or after it was made? Because I'd like to know if we have to watch out for foul play from the locals, just so we know how belligerent they're likely to be."

"Probably before," Doc replied. "Unless you saw any holes in the cork—even then, that's fine for injecting a small something but not for packing the whole bottle full of extra kick."

Cole nodded. So either the stranger—who had drifted off while they'd been examining the wine—had deliberately handed them an altered bottle of wine, or someone had handed him an altered bottle without him realizing it.

Accepting the bottle back but not drinking from it again, Cole searched the crowd dancing in a ring around the fire, which he could now see occupied the center of a wide, open town square. After a minute he spotted the same stranger from before. "Hey!" he called, leaving his bike with the others and then dodging stumbling, laughing people as he headed toward the man.

When he finally caught up to the stranger, Cole noticed two things: The stranger was already very drunk and the fire was even bigger than he'd guessed, roaring three to four meters high and perhaps fifteen meters around. It was easily the biggest deliberate fire he'd ever seen, and rivaled the only other fire he'd seen close to this size, which had been when an old warehouse had caught and gone up in a blaze before anyone could arrive to extinguish it. That conflagration had nearly taken most of the surrounding buildings with it, and there were still singe marks for several blocks around the blackened hulk of its remains.

"Hi!" the stranger shouted at him as Cole stepped up to confront the man. He was wearing a huge, sloppy grin across his face. "Want to join us?"

"Do you guys usually get this drunk?" Cole asked, reaching out to steady the other man as he nearly faceplanted—over absolutely nothing.

"Never," the stranger replied, struggling to regain his feet but unable to do so. "We're typically a dry county, wine and beer are allowed on Sundays, but that's all. And never during the festival."

"But you're drinking now," Cole argued, and the bushy-haired man glanced around, eyes wide, as if he had only just realized this about himself.

After a second the stranger nodded. "I am," he agreed with all the ponderous slowness of someone well and truly intoxicated. "In fact, I believe I may be drunk."

Cole sighed. "So where did the alcohol come from?" he asked, leaning in to make sure the other man could hear him over the celebration and the crackling of the fire.

The stranger grinned. "We were having dinner when this man approached us. He was all bundled up as if he were made of nothing but clothing. He wished us a happy harvest festival, and then offered us a pile of dry plant stalks and old leaves and vines, and a case of this same wine. I decided it would be very rude not to at least toast him with the wine he had just gifted us with, and that's exactly what we did." He shrugged, exhausted. "But now it's late and I can't feel my toes. Or my fingers. Or my nose."

Cole studied the other man, frowning as he put the pieces together. "So this stranger shows up, hands you some wine on the night of your big festival, you all drink it, and now you're all drunk?" he recounted slowly. "Do you usually make the fire this big?" He gestured behind them at the inferno towering overhead.

"Hm?" The other man glanced back over his shoulder, then did a double-take and looked again. "No," he admitted slowly, carefully shaping the word. "That is . . . quite a bit larger than normal." Now he was frowning. "The past harvest was good, but it wasn't that good. I don't know why the flames are so high." He winced and pulled back. "Or so very hot." It was true—Cole could feel the heat crisping his skin even where he stood, like the fire was sucking all the moisture from the air and from him personally.

"Okay, thanks." As he turned to rejoin the others, Cole stopped. "Oh, did you guys see a convoy pass through here?" he asked with what he hoped was a casual air, before realizing that he didn't have to worry about that right now. This gentleman probably wouldn't remember a bit of their conversation anyway.

"A convoy?" The man paused, eyes screwed tight for a second, clearly trying to marshal his failing brain back into function. "Oh! Yes!" His eyes popped open again and wavered before finally fixing on Cole. "Big trucks. Lots of men. Passed through here. It was just after that stranger brought us the wine. They didn't stop to celebrate with us." He looked almost ready to cry, and hit Cole with the sad but hopeful expression of a small child denied one toy but spotting another. "But you'll stay and celebrate, won't you? It's the highlight of our year!"

Cole tried not to think about that, or feel the surge of pity racing through him at the thought that this normally tame and sober little bonfire was the high point of the entire town's year, as he started backing away. "We can stay for a little bit," he offered carefully, "but we do need to get back on the road before long."

Especially since it was clear the NAN hadn't dawdled. And had deliberately made it so that these townsfolk wouldn't remember their presence.

"Really? That's great!" the other man's whole face lit up, and he turned toward the rest of the locals and the giant mass of flames they were still ringing. "They said they'll stay and celebrate!" he shouted, and although those nearest cheered, it was obvious that his words were swallowed up by the night and the breeze and the hungry, noisy fire.

Breeze?

Cole froze where he was and lifted his head. Yes, there was a breeze, stirring the now-stiflingly hot air. And causing those same flames to lick out farther and farther, as if they were eager to extend their grasp.

He picked up the pace, pushing past oblivious celebrants to reach his companions.

"The NAN came through here earlier tonight," he reported quickly as soon as he had reached his bike again. "They've got to be the ones who gave him the doctored wine. They wanted everyone here so blitzed they would barely even see the convoy, much less remember it. Not sure why—they didn't bother doing that anywhere else." He frowned. "I think they did something to the fire, too."

The others, who had been lounging against or near their bikes or crouching down in order to get their legs working again, now climbed back onto their respective vehicles. "The amulet has changed course yet again," Goyathlay declared, face raised to the stiffening breeze, eyes closed as it caressed his tattooed face. "I cannot be sure which direction yet, however." He lifted his hands as well, palms upward, and held that position.

"We need to get after them quick as we can," Doc pointed out, already ensconced in his bike again. "They might be pulling a fast one, and using this little campout party as cover."

Cole nodded, but even as he reached for his own bike he hesitated. "The wind—" he started, the breeze growing even as his concerns escalated. "It's getting stronger." The others just stood there, staring at him without speaking. "The fire's already out of control," he tried again. "If the wind picks up anymore, those flames could jump from the bonfire to the buildings. They're all wood."

Still everyone stared. After a moment, when he didn't elaborate further, Hazard shrugged. "So?" she asked in that rough voice of hers.

Cole wasn't surprised to hear such lack of concern from her, and the shaman was still lost in his own world, but his eyes widened when Doc and Alaric both nodded. What, now they agreed with the troll, of all times?

"This whole town could go up in flames," he pointed out, and this time it was Doc who responded.

"Sucks for them," the dwarf agreed, "but so what? It ain't our problem."

"It'd be their own fault," Alaric agreed, his blue hair shining almost silver in the light of the fire beyond. "They lit a big fire and then got drunk around it. Stupid. But we've got a job to do, we can't stick around to babysit a bunch of idiots."

Cole tried again. "You heard the guy," he said, aware he was practically pleading now. The wind had grown strong enough that it actually buffeted him, knocking him back half a step. "They don't normally act this way. The NAN did this. We can't let them kill this town."

"Why not?" Hazard asked. "Means nothing to us. We can't let it slow us down."

Doc and Alaric were both nodding—the first time they had ever agreed with Hazard about anything—and Cole saw he wasn't going to be able to sway any of them.

Then Goyathlay opened his eyes again. "I agree with Cole," he stated. "We should remain and help this town as much as we can."

"Too bad," Hazard replied. "We're going." There was a challenge in her tone, clearly daring the shaman to disagree with her. "Where's our target now?"

"South," the shaman declared after a moment, slumping slightly but clearly seeing that he and Cole were outnumbered. "The amulet now wends its way south."

As usual, it was Doc who questioned this first. "What?" he demanded, twisting to glare at the shaman. Cole suspected it was only because they were more than arm's length away that the dwarf didn't grab the tattooed man by the collar and yank him forward until their noses brushed. "South? Why the hell would it be heading south? Cheyenne is north of here, and east! That doesn't even make any sense!"

The shaman scowled but held his ground. "I know what I sensed," he insisted proudly. "It has turned south."

Alaric was shaking his head. "Can't believe I'm backing this guy," he admitted, "but he was right about it going west. We know the NAN was here. And northeast would just mean they'd turned around and were going back the way we came, in which case why'd they come all the way out to Dinosaur in the first place? So—" he sighed like he wanted to stop the words spilling from his mouth, "—I think we gotta trust Goyaguy and go south."

"Goyathlay," the shaman corrected, but without any apparent rancor. "Goy-ath-lay."

Doc continued to glare at the shaman, but finally nodded. "Fine," he snapped. "Let's move, then."

Hazard started her engine, and the big ATV rumbled forward, Doc and Alaric falling in behind her and the shaman taking up a position after them. For a moment Cole didn't move, still stunned by how easily his friends had decided to leave this town to its fate, but finally he turned his bike and rejoined their little convoy. It felt strange to not be leading the group for once.

The only two ways to go south from their present position were to cut through the town square or to reverse course and then detour around the entire town. Clearly the first course was faster, so it was no surprise that Hazard led them that way, straight toward the raging bonfire and then to the left. They drove so close to the blaze that Cole was sure his hair had singed, and all of his exposed skin felt seared. The wind was raging about them now, whipping the fire into a crazed maelstrom of incendiary limbs that reached out randomly to touch trees and railings. The people were still dancing and singing, seemingly oblivious to the danger growing in their midst, though Cole thought they were several paces back from where they had been. When he found himself passing the bushy-haired man who had greeted them, he couldn't help stopping his bike in front of the poor fellow, blocking him from the rest of the celebrants.

"You need to get everyone out of here!" Cole warned, forced to shout to be heard over the wind and the fire and the partiers. "It's not safe!"

"We're fine, thanks," the man replied, his words clearly even more slurred and his movements sloppier and more erratic than just ten minutes before. "We've got it under control."

Even as he said that, one of the tongues of flame danced out far enough to finally reach the roof of one of the buildings looking out onto the square. In an instant smaller flames licked the shingles and tiles, and Cole could see them spreading. By the time he'd drawn breath to yell, the entire roof was ablaze.

"Fire!" he shouted, but the locals who heard him just laughed and nodded, gesturing to the center of their ring. "No, over there!" he tried again, pointing toward the building, where the inferno was now crawling down the walls—and reaching out to the buildings on either side, where only narrow alleys separated them. "You have to put that out!"

But no one listened. Even the bushy-haired man had somehow slipped around him and rejoined the celebration, and the townsfolk were once again a whirling, singing mass surrounding the conflagration at their center, never even stopping to notice that it was now spreading behind them as well.

A hand reached out and grabbed Cole by the shoulder, almost yanking him off his bike. It was Doc. "We need to get moving, son," the dwarf warned, and under his heavy mustache Cole thought the dwarf was frowning sadly rather than scowling. "Come on."

"We can't just leave them," Cole insisted, trying to shake the hand free, but Doc had a strong grip. "They'll all die if we don't do something!"

That first building was now completely engulfed, its burning wooden structure forming a mirror image of the original blaze, and the fire had now extended to both of its neighbors as well. If the flames made it all the way around, the villagers would be trapped.

"We'll die with 'em if we don't move now!" Doc snapped, the sharpness of his tone surprising Cole enough that he stopped and listened to what his friend was saying.

Doc was right, Cole realized. Their way out was rapidly closing as well. And there wasn't much they could to help at this point, either. Both fires were now far beyond anyone's ability to extinguish them.

Briefly Cole considered knocking people out and dragging them away by main force, but quickly abandoned the idea. There were too many villagers for that to work—even if he saved two, the rest would surely perish. And of course the longer they delayed, the bigger the NAN's lead.

Which was why he finally nodded and allowed Doc to lead him away, past the burning buildings, to where the others were waiting.

But the whole way out of town, he kept glancing back over his shoulder. The two fires had merged by now, forming a single enormous wall of flame that reached high into the night sky. The wind was whipping past so strongly he had to blink his eyes rapidly to see, and all of Dinosaur appeared to be just a single large, writhing blur of yellows and oranges and reds.

He thought he could hear where the singing had turned to screams, but then the shriek of the wind mercifully tore the sounds away.

# TWENTY-ONE

By the time they finally stopped, pulling off the highway into a little stand of trees, the sun was already beginning to peek over the horizon. But Cole thought he could still discern a glow to the north, where the town of Dinosaur burned. He doubted anyone had escaped. His dreams that night were of wind and fire mingled together, dancing and laughing mixed with glares and silent hatred, and he awoke almost as tired as when he'd lain down.

Their travels for the next few days were plagued with harsh winds and scattered clouds that occasionally let loose bursts of cold rain, leaving them all drenched and miserable, their leathers creaking, hair dripping, tires slipping on the slick asphalt. Cole didn't mind. The weather matched his mood, and the guilt still eating away at him.

They were in the Uncompahgre National Forest, and had paused to stretch their legs, clear their heads, and empty their bladders when a big hand descended on Cole's shoulder. Glancing back and up, he found himself matching stares with Hazard.

"Let it go," the horned enforcer rumbled down at him. "It'll tear you apart if you don't." For once she didn't sound belligerent or vicious or even angry. If anything, Cole thought he detected a hint of sadness in her tone, and in her eyes. That, and a surprising empathy. Like she had been through this herself.

It wasn't the same, though. "You did...whatever you did because you had to," he guessed. "You did it to survive. I didn't do anything, but I could have. I could've stayed. I could've helped."

"Could you?" He didn't think she was mocking him—it sounded like a genuine question. "How many could you have saved, really?" Even her language had altered, he realized. Her grammar was more complete, her vocabulary more complex— it was like speaking to a whole different person. Or just talking to the real person behind the façade she'd constructed, the person hidden by the mask of a cold-blooded killer. "One?" she continued. "Two? Five? Assuming they didn't fight back and drag you down with them?"

"I know I couldn't have saved everybody," he admitted, staring down at his hands to avoid meeting her eyes again. "But I could've tried. That would've been something. Instead, I let Doc lead me away, and I didn't do anything to stop him."

She grunted. "He was looking out for you. If you'd stayed, you'd be dead now, too."

"Yeah." He shrugged. "I get that. But that doesn't make me feel any less crappy for not trying harder. Or at all."

"Sure." This time she was the one who shrugged, the motion like a massive wave rippling through her tall, brawny form. "You'll feel that way for a long while yet. The thing to do is tuck it away somewhere, so it's still there but not right on top. Like when you stub your toe and it hurts like hell, but you've got to keep moving so you just push the pain out of the way. It's still there, but you're not letting it stop you. Same thing."

Now Cole did risk peering up at her again. But Hazard wasn't looking at him anymore. Her head was up, her eyes staring out and away somewhere, at some memory she still carried with her. And her face said the pain still remained, no matter how deeply she'd buried it.

Still, she was right, he knew. If he let it, the guilt would cripple him completely. He had to tamp it down, bottle it up, use it to push him forward instead of letting it hold him back. There was nothing he could do for the people of Dinosaur now, but there was no reason to let them take him with them.

"Message received," he assured the troll. "I'll get it under control." If nothing else, it gave him more reason to hate the NAN and to want revenge against them—not just for his friends now, but for that sad, doomed little town as well.

"Good." She gave him one last look of understanding, then grinned and slapped him on the back hard enough to make him stumble, the guise of the careless killer dropping back over her like a steel-plated shroud. "'Cause otherwise I'd have to knock you out and drag you around by your heels. Pretty sure you'd hate that a whole lot more."

She sauntered off toward the bushes to take care of business, and Cole watched her until she'd disappeared into the foliage. He never would have guessed there was a real person under all that armor and bravado, or that she would be the one to pull him out of his funk.

His sleep that night was not perfect by any stretch, but it was deeper and more restful than it had been since they'd left Dinosaur behind. And the next morning he woke to a sunny sky and a calm, cool day.

"Kinda reminds me of the good ol' days," Doc stated, leaning back. The skies had been clearer the last few days, and they had found a spot to set up camp for tonight, their bikes ringed protectively around them, a small fire burning at the center, the flames adding a burst of color as well as warmth to the pleasant chill of the evening.

"What, back in the Stone Ages?" Alaric retorted, and the others laughed even as the dwarf glared. "Sorry," the decker offered after a second, hands up in surrender. "Couldn't resist."

"Fraggin' whipper-snapper," Doc shot back, but Cole could see he was actually smiling under that mustache. "But no, back when I was still young, I used to go gallivanting about, just like we're doin' now. Things were still a little different then, not as locked down, a lot more chaos and a lot more danger—but more opportunity, too, if you had the guts to go for it."

"You saying we don't have guts?" Hazard demanded, but the troll didn't rise to her feet or reach for a weapon, and her tone was more lazy than truly offended.

"You? More'n I can measure," the inventor replied, sounding surprisingly sincere, and Hazard grunted, evidently not sure how to handle a compliment. "You'd have done just fine back then. You all would've," he added, glancing around at the rest of them. "That's part a' why it feels like the old days to me, I guess. Here we are, outside the city, setting our own course, following our own rules,." He chuckled. "Wasn't sure I still had that in me, after all this time."

"So talk," Hazard challenged, propping herself up on her elbows to see him more clearly. "Tell us about one of those times. Old-timer." But she was grinning as she threw in that last crack, and Doc didn't take offense. Instead he nodded, chuckling himself, and launched into a tale that might or might not've been entirely true, about a time he and some friends had raided a supply train on its way to Denver and wound up cursed as a result.

"That was barely a curse at all," Goyathlay protested when the story was done. "Now, you wish to hear of a true curse, let me tell you . . ." And he broke into a tale of his own, about when he had been young and had made the mistake of angering a senior shaman, who had hexed him in retaliation, and forced him to go through a series of excruciating trials to overcome the spell.

When he was done, Hazard laughed. "You call those trials?" she asked, and proceeded to tell about her early days as an enforcer, before she'd even joined the Mercy. Then Alaric recounted some early escapades of his own, back when he was first learning how to deck and barely survived, and Cole told about some nearly disastrous jobs he'd pulled shortly after Doc had put him back together.

It was a pleasant evening, all in all, the five of them talking late into the night, and when he woke up the next morning Cole felt that things had shifted somehow. Before, they had been people thrown together by circumstance, just assembled for a job. Now it felt more like an actual group, a team. Maybe even friends, though he hesitated to suggest that out loud. Whatever it was, everyone seemed to feel it—tempers were less frayed, requests were more civil, teamwork was quicker and easier, help was offered freely. All that certainly made their trek more enjoyable, and if it also meant a better chance of success, he'd take it, no question.

"What the hell is that?" Hazard demanded, one hand going to the gun at her side.

The road had dipped down even as the general terrain had risen, and now they were riding through a wide defile, long rock walls looming on either side. Hazard was watching one of those walls, up near its top. Cole followed her gaze, and had to wince as light stabbed down at him. It was like he'd looked directly at the sun—except that he was facing west and it was still before noon, so the sun was on his other side.

Everyone studied the strange light, which multiplied as they rode until an entire constellation glowed down at them from the cliffs up above. "Are we under attack?" Alaric asked, ducking lower on his bike, though with that sort of elevation anyone up there would have a clear shot at all of them regardless. In fact, Cole realized with a chill, if those were people, they were sitting ducks.

But Doc chuckled. "Huh, I heard tales, but never thought I'd see 'em myself," he muttered, rubbing his jaw through the beard. "Might haveta stop and take a closer look in a bit here."

"A closer look at what?" Alaric asked. "What are those things?"

"Dead meat," Hazard answered, drawing her pistol and aiming it at one of the lights. But Doc was already shaking his head.

"You can shoot all you want," the dwarf told her, "and you'll hit 'em, too—not like they can move outta the way or anything. But they ain't dangerous, so you'd be wastin' your ammo for nothing. Best leave 'em be."

"You still haven't said what they are," Cole pointed out. "What're we looking at here, Doc?" He'd already tried enhancing his vision to get a better view, but the light was simply too bright, it overwhelmed even his strongest filters, leaving behind nothing but a blurry afterimage and several glaring spots.

"They call 'em the Fairy Lights o' San Juan," Doc answered, "on account o' we're right near that San Juan forest. But there's nothing fey, or even magic about 'em." He laughed again. "They're solar panels, is what they are."

"Solar panels?" But now that he'd heard that, and looking up at them again, it made sense. They were blinding to the west because the sun was to the east and the panels were reflecting that. "What're they doing all the way out here?"

"Providing power to Denver, Colorado Springs, Pueblo, and every other city around here," Doc replied. "There's panels all through here, I heard, where the forests end and the desert starts. Lots and lots of 'em, all sucking up that sunlight and converting it to electricity and sending it on to all the towns and cities. Without the Fairy Lights, story said, all those places would've gone dark inside a month, at least back when they were first set up."

That made sense too, Cole thought. Denver alone required massive amounts of power every single day. Solar power was plentiful and free, and out here was the perfect place to put panels. Then you just had to run cables back to the city, or at least to some kind of junction box. It was smart.

They saw the glow of more panels throughout the day, and a few times even the panels themselves, when the sun had shifted overhead and so the panels were no longer reflecting down into the canyon. That was what they were traveling through now—the cliffs on either side had grown higher, the floor around the highway deeper, the sky overhead narrowing to a thin crack between the cliffs.

A crack that seemed to be darkening as well, even though it was only a short while past noon.

Something shifted to his side, and Cole turned to see Goyathlay shiver. "Something wrong?" he asked the shaman.

"The weather grows angry," the tattooed shaman answered, drawing his coat more tightly around his shoulders. "It has sensed us, and does not want us here." As if summoned by his words, the wind began to pick up noticeably, a sharp, wet breeze tugging at their clothes and hair and hands. Cole had to struggle to keep control of his bike, as the wind tried yanking that from his control as well. The others were doing the same—only Hazard seemed unperturbed, but it would take a hurricane to shift her.

"Can you talk to it?" Alaric asked. He gestured aimlessly. "I don't know, tell it we're just passing through, and don't want any trouble?"

The shaman sneered at him. "Do you not think I have tried? It does not care what we say, it does not like us. And it is far too powerful for me to control or even appease."

Doc angled his bike to come in close on Cole's left side. "We maybe got a problem," the dwarf said, speaking just loud enough to be heard over the wind. "This canyon's nice for shade and avoidin' pryin' eyes, but there's no real way outta here if that storm hits. And it sure looks like it's gonna."

Cole studied the visible sky and had to agree—the clouds overhead were nearly black now, casting a gloom over the little group as they blocked out the last of the sun.

"Maybe we can find an overhang," Alaric suggested, riding on Doc's other side. "Wait it out there."

But Cole understood why Doc was so worried. "It's not the rain he's worried about," he explained to the elf. "It's the flooding. There's no dirt down here, nothing to absorb water, so it'll just pool. And nowhere for it to go except forward, same as us. If the storm hits hard enough, this whole canyon will flood—with us in it."

"Oh." The elven decker was turning a shade of green that went nicely with the blue of his hair, but Cole doubted he cared about that right now. "So we can't get out of it, then?"

They'd all gathered in a tight little clump now, and everyone studied the cliffs around them. But after a few minutes they'd all evidently reached the same conclusion.

"Too smooth," Hazard rumbled, reaching out to glide one heavily callused hand down the nearest cliff face. "No good purchase."

"Too high, too," Alaric agreed. "I'm not exactly an expert, but I'm guessing a climb like that'd be tough for anyone, even an experienced climber." He turned to face the others. "And there's no guarantee whatever's up top is any better."

Thunder crackled overhead, following their progress but illustrating how much of a distance remained, and as the rain began to fall in big, heavy drops, Cole knew that whatever they were going to do to protect against possible flash flooding, they had better figure it out now. They were rapidly running out of time.

"Can we block the water somehow?" he asked, but guessed the answer from the frown on Doc's face.

"Nowhere to block it," the dwarf replied. The rain had started in earnest now, pelting them with its thick, heavy showers that struck like an old velvet curtain, weighing you down at once.

"And nowhere we can take cover," Cole added, giving the cliffs and the valley floor some thought as well. There wasn't any dirt here; it was all solid stone, way too sturdy for them to knock out handholds or shelters or anything else. They were stuck down here, with the storm increasing intensity every second.

"Maybe we can gun it, and get out of here and onto level ground before it gets too bad," Alaric shouted, the wind and rain clawing his words away almost as soon as he uttered them.

But they still heard, and Cole nodded. Right now it looked like their only chance to get out of this intact—water was already beginning to pool along the bases of the cliffs, and from there to dribble across and add to the layer slowly starting to coat the highway. Obviously when the authorities had constructed this road, they hadn't worried about the risk of heavy rain, which was a rarity in this part of the state. It was just Cole's and his friends' luck—or lack thereof—that they had to face it now.

Revving the engine, Cole raced forward, the others falling into line behind him. But as the rain increased, the road got slicker and slicker, and his wheels began to slip more and more. After hydroplaning on a wet patch and very nearly wiping out, Cole was forced to slow back down.

"No good!" he shouted over his shoulder. "We can't outrun it!"

"So we dig in!" Hazard hollered back, her voice loud enough to be heard clearly even through the increasing deluge. "Let it wear itself out!"

She turned and brought her ATV right up against the western cliff face, shutting off the engine. The others pulled their bikes up against hers like puppies snuggling up against their mother for warmth, so close their handlebars overlapped each other and the edges of the ATV's frame. Then they sat there, curled up on their individual bikes, soaked through and shivering and cursing the strange storm that had appeared as if just to plague them.

"Try talking to it again!" Cole shouted at Goyathlay.

The shaman scowled but obediently dipped his head, his eyes glowing. After a moment, however, he shook his head. "Its temper is up," he explained, yelling to make himself heard. "It will not listen, nor will it stop until it chooses!"

They were huddled there—Cole couldn't say for how long, it could have been mere minutes but it felt far longer—when he felt something tugging at his boot. He glanced down. It was water, and not just from above. The puddles at the cliff's base had joined together to become a steady rivulet that was now at least a third of a meter deep.

"We've got to move!" he warned the others, leaning in so his head was almost touching each of theirs in turn. He pointed down to indicate the water. Goyathlay and Doc nodded, but Hazard and Alaric looked confused.

"So what?" Alaric argued. "It's just some water. We're good where we are."

"We're not!" Cole hollered back. "It's almost deep enough to carry off bikes and cars and whatever else it finds. Trust me, we can't let it catch us when it hits that level." He wasn't even sure how he knew that, but he was absolutely certain of it right to his bones.

Fortunately, Doc and Goyathlay backed him up, and finally the other two agreed to follow their lead. But if they couldn't stay still, and they couldn't ride out and they couldn't climb, what could they do?

Doc shivered, all of his hair plastered to his head so he looked like an incredibly grouchy otter. "Sure wouldn't mind the heat from those fairy lights right about now," he groused, blowing his wet mustache out of his mouth.

Cole started to agree, then stopped. Maybe— "I've got an idea," he declared.

Since they were all close together already, it was easy enough to put their heads together, literally and figuratively. Cole quickly explained what he was thinking, the idea taking on form and definition even as he spoke.

"We need to stop the rain," he said, "otherwise we're done. But even with that over, we've got the flash flood to deal with. Those panels, they store up heat and light, right?" When Doc nodded, he continued, "So if we can angle them down this way and release all that heat, they could dry up this water, maybe?" He had no idea if that even made any sense, but trying it seemed better than nothing.

Doc frowned, but it was his thinking frown, not his disapproving one. "Flash fry a flash flood?" he said. "Yeah, could work. Maybe. Worth a shot, anyway. If I can get up to those things, I can probably redirect 'em."

"They're all programmed," Alaric piped in. "Get me to a main junction or even a control panel and I can fix that, rig all of 'em to release in a burst."

Cole nodded. "Goyathlay, can you try again to shut down this storm? We really need the rain to go away and the sun to come back."

The shaman considered, then nodded. "I will entreat the spirits," he replied. "Now that they have had their moment, perhaps they will be willing to listen to reason once more."

"What about me?" Hazard asked. "What'm I doing in all this?" The big troll actually sounded eager, and anxious to be involved.

For a second, Cole didn't have an answer. Then it hit him. "Doc and Alaric need to get up there fast," he replied, waving up at the top of the cliff. "Climbing's going to take too long, and it's too risky. Can you toss them up there?"

The enforcer grinned, showing her fangs and tusks to full advantage. "Like a cannon," she promised.

But now Alaric had a question. "What're you gonna do?"

Cole smiled. "Something boring but necessary." He reached out, extending his hand, and grabbed Alaric's handlebar, even though they were on opposite sides of Hazard's ATV. "I'm going to make sure our bikes don't wash away before the rest of you can work your magic." He glanced from face to face. "So, are we gonna do this?" He read the acquiescence in each gaze. "Right, then. Let's get to work."

Goyathlay immediately assumed what Cole had already started thinking of as his meditative position, head back, spine straight, hands out, eyes closed, mumbling chants under his breath. Doc fumbled with his saddlebags and pulled out several tools, sticking them into his belt, and Alaric grabbed his deck, which had been slung over his back the whole trip in its waterproof, bulletproof, shockproof case. Then Hazard reached out and scooped Doc up in one of her huge hands.

"Ready?" the troll rumbled.

Doc gulped. "As I'll ever be."

Hazard nodded and cocked back her arm. "Go!" she shouted, hurling him forward and up. Doc hit the side of the cliff about halfway up, scrabbling for purchase and slid a heartstopping several centimeters before finding something to grip. But from there he could dig in, and Cole watched as his old friend scrambled up the rain-slicked rock without pause, reaching the top in a matter of seconds. A minute later a rope dropped down, the laced metal threads only a few millimeters in diameter but strong enough to support even Hazard and long enough to reach them on their bikes.

Alaric grabbed the end and wrapped it around himself, tying it tight, then nodded to Hazard, who snatched him and tossed him at the cliffside without giving him time to reconsider. He also landed more than halfway up, and started to slide back down immediately, but Doc was ready and pulled the rope taut, catching Alaric before he could freefall and hauling him up. A minute later, they were both atop the cliff and by blinking away water Cole could just make them out as they ducked behind one of the solar panels and got to work.

He'd been busy through all this himself, extending his arms and threading them through all of the bikes so that it was a single big knot with himself at the center. A good thing, too, because the wind was buffeting them hard from the top and the water was tugging at them from below, but Cole had a firm grip now, and none of the bikes could pull loose. Either the current took them all together or it didn't take any of them, and their combined mass was enough to keep them still anchored. For now.

The rain was starting to lessen, the clouds lightening from black to slate gray, but it wasn't enough. "Clear the storm!" Cole shouted at Goyathlay, who nodded, but otherwise didn't react. "Clear it now!" The shaman's mumbling increased, and took on a slightly frantic pitch, but still the storm lingered, dumping sheet after sheet of water on their heads.

"Get rid of it!" Cole screamed, feeling the stream now engulf his trailing foot and the bike's wheels start to float. *"Now!"* His own vision was starting to strobe as he gulped in air, his heart going like a bellows, and his head felt as if it were splitting at the seams.

And finally the shaman's spirits must have answered, because a mighty gale whistled through the valley, nearly dragging Cole from his bike despite his grip—but it also tore the storm loose and tossed it aside like so much refuse, leaving only blue sky in its wake.

"Nice one," Cole managed as he regained both his breath and his seat, and Goyathlay nodded, slumping onto his own bike and leaning forward to rest his head on the handlebars.

That was one threat down, but there was still the burgeoning near-river to contend with. Fortunately, Doc and Alaric hadn't been idle. With the rain gone and the wind dying down, Cole clearly heard a series of loud clangs and rusty grating noises as the solar panels all suddenly swiveled as one, aiming their shiny surfaces down toward the valley.

"Look out below!" Doc hollered.

And then it was like someone had switched on the sun and aimed it straight at them.

Cole felt the intense heat burst across him, shoving the moisture off his clothes and skin and hair and drying them in an instant. Steam wafted up from him and all around him, and he thought he smelled the odor of cooked flesh rising from himself, Goyathlay, and Hazard. But even more steam was billowing up all around him as the river was heated, its volume evaporating in massive chunks all up and down the valley.

In a matter of minutes, it had been reduced enough that Cole's feet now swung in air, and were toasty warm and dry to boot.

Ten minutes later, the water was barely lapping at his bike's tires.

Ten minutes after that, the entire highway was bone dry, as was the valley floor all the way to the cliffs.

The duo up top gave it another minute just to be safe, then the barrage of heat ended as swiftly as it had begun. Alaric came sliding down the rope a few seconds later, then Doc came down as well, carrying the now-detached rope with him. Cole had disentangled himself by the time they touched down. He felt slightly dizzy and realized he must be badly dehydrated—he had been sweating heavily in the intense heat, but then the sweat had evaporated, leaving his skin dry and his whole body parched. They would need to replenish their liquids, and quickly. Still, that seemed a small enough price to pay.

"Nice one!" he said, and saw that everyone else has the same huge grin he knew he was sporting. They'd done it! He wasn't entirely sure how, but they'd faced the craziest weather he'd ever seen, and they'd survived!

"Good plan," Hazard said, clapping him on the back. The others all chimed in as well, and for a second Cole didn't feel any more guilt or anger or even fear. He and his team had worked together and saved each other, and right now that was all that mattered.

# TWENTY-TWO

When the canyon finally ended, the cliffs to either side slowly diminishing until they were little more than low hills, Cole saw they were now headed east.

"This is good," Goyathlay assured him. "The amulet travels this same road."

Cole still couldn't make any sense of that. They'd gone north from Denver, then west, then south, and now east. Were they simply racing along the state's perimeter? To what end? But for now it was enough to know that they were still on the right path.

Then came the breakdown.

It happened a few days after they'd passed Pagosa Springs. The sun was high overhead, the sky was crystal clear for a change, without the wind that had been dogging them along most of their journey, and the road was smooth and wide and gently curving through hills and valleys. Then they hit a detour, the regular road evidently closed for repairs. Following the signs, the road abruptly narrowed as it descended, becoming more of a trail as it arced up over and through rises, the ground becoming more uneven so that they were jostling and bouncing their way across rocky terrain.

At first Cole thought one of the others had coughed. And again. He twisted around, trying to figure out who it was and if they were all right, and saw Hazard was grimacing like she was in pain. Then he heard the sound again, and realized it was coming not from her but from her ATV.

"Everything okay?" he called back, but even as he spoke black smoke began billowing from the front grille of her vehicle. She hit a bump and sailed into the air, seeming to pick up even more speed in the process, and Alaric had to slam on his brakes in order to avoid getting crushed by her larger vehicle as it slammed back down hard and careened forward.

"Hey!" the decker yelped, but forgot his consternation when he saw what was going on. "You all right?"

The big troll didn't answer, but that was because she was visibly wrestling her bike, trying to force it to the side with brute strength. Doc spotted the problem at once.

"Her engine's shot!" he shouted. "Put it in neutral!"

"Trying!" Hazard yelled back, but whatever she was doing didn't appear to be helping. Plus they were on a steep slope at the moment—coasting to a stop probably wouldn't work anyway.

"Hit the brakes!" Cole added, but then saw that her foot was already stomping down on the brake pedal.

"Not the rear brakes! Use the front!" Doc hollered, but he was too far behind the troll for her to hear him. "We gotta do something!" he yelled at Cole. "She don't slow it down somehow, she's either gonna flip over or slam into a wall, and either way she'll hit like a freight train!" Cole could hear the part his friend had left unvoiced—even someone as tough as Hazard might not survive an impact like that.

They had to come up with something, and fast.

Reaching into his saddlebag, Cole yanked out his magnetic grapples, and the ropes he used with them. "Hold me steady," he called, and Alaric complied, the elven decker pulling up alongside and steadying his bike so Cole could lift his hands free.

"Catch," he hollered to Hazard, knotting the rope to a grapple before tossing it to her. Even in her current panic she caught it one-handed. "Stick it on somewhere it'll stay," he instructed, and waited until she'd done so before throwing the second one to her. Then he waved Alaric off and gestured for Doc to pull closer. "Wrap this around your handlebars," he ordered, passing his friend one of the ropes, but the dwarf shook his head.

"'Round the front fork," he corrected, demonstrating as he spoke. "We'll get better pull that way, and it won't yank our own bikes to the side." Then he was peeling off to the side so he was flanking Hazard on her right.

Cole followed Doc's suggestion and looped the remaining rope around his bike's front shaft, making sure it was knotted good and tight. Then he put himself on Hazard's left. At a nod from Doc, he hit the brakes, his bike screeching to a stop.

Hazard's ATV shot past them—until she hit the end of the ropes, both woven cords pulling taut. Cole felt his bike sliding forward, and spun it around, gunning the engine. The tires screamed, and the smell of burning rubber rose around him, but at least he wasn't being tugged any more, his bike's push countering the pull from Hazard's.

And, as the grapples held fast, the force from his bike and Doc's started to slow Hazard's ATV down. She had weight on her side, and momentum, but they had actual acceleration on theirs.

"Squeeze the brakes!" Doc shouted to her. "The handlebars!" She nodded and complied, and that seemed to help as well. But it still wasn't enough.

Then a strong wind rose from nowhere, directly in front of them and pushing hard, adding to Cole and Doc's drive and slamming Hazard back. Her ATV finally ground to a halt, and the wind faded away again just as Cole and Doc shut off their own bikes, leaving the highway quiet except for their panting.

Hazard took a minute to catch her breath again, mopping sweat from her face, but when she'd recovered she looked over at each of the others in turn. "Thanks."

Cole nodded. "I think our friend here did most of the heavy lifting," he admitted, gesturing toward Goyathlay. The shaman merely shrugged. "But you're welcome."

Doc was already off his bike and headed toward the ATV, his stumpy little legs working overtime. "Let's see what the heck's goin' on under that hood," he practically growled, and Hazard hopped off and backed away to give him space. She almost looked intimidated by him, which was pretty funny considering she was easily twice his height and weight. Still, Cole understood. When he was pissed off, Doc wasn't someone you wanted to mess with.

In a matter of minutes he had the ATV opened up and was poking around inside. "Who the hell built this Frankenstein's monster?" he demanded, his words muffled as they echoed from within the chassis.

"Shubai," Hazard replied, which made sense. Hurricane Shubai was the Mercy's best gunsmith, and he was known to tinker with bikes and other toys from time to time. Only this time it sounded like he hadn't done the best job.

"Well, he's an idiot," Doc confirmed, finally hauling himself back out. There was engine grease and machine oil smeared on his forehead, and streaked through his hair and beard. "Leastways, he was when he built this monstrosity."

Hazard had the good grace to shrug and look down, evidently embarrassed. "He'd never built anything that could hold a troll," she said after a second. "Wasn't sure of the best way to go about it. Tried making a regular bike my size first, but it was so heavy even I couldn't pick it back up when it toppled. Finally came up with this instead."

Doc sighed. "I get what he was doing," he said, some of the vitriol leaking away. "And it makes sense, far as it goes. Four wheels to distribute weight, lets you have a nice wide seat, but needs a monster engine to pull all of it along. Plus integrated weapons systems, those guns you're so fond of using to clear a path. Which is fine, except—" here he aimed a kick at the ATV, which still had a few wisps escaping it, "—he didn't account for the increased heat, both from the engine struggling to handle the load and from the weapons sending signals back and forth even when they're supposedly off. Not a huge drain, more like a constant little trickle. No problem if you're just bopping around the city for an hour or two, but pulling a road trip like this, constant use for days on end? Heats the whole thing right past its breaking point. Boils away the engine oil, which leaves your gears high and dry. Strips the hell out of 'em. That just makes everything heat up more, trying to keep up without any lube. Eventually something gets thrown or stuck or jammed, and this—" he waved at the sidelined vehicle, "—is what's left when the smoke clears. Looks to me like it was your throttle cable that started it. It got stuck, forcing your engine to rev up and redline, and then everything went kablooey."

"Can you fix it?" Alaric asked. Unlike Cole, the elf looked like he'd followed that entire explanation without a problem.

"No, I can't fix it!" Doc snapped. "You see a machine shop out here? Or a garage? I'd have to rip out all the damaged bits, rebuild the engine, then put in heat sinks so this same thing wouldn't happen again. Take me at least a week, maybe more. Time we don't have, tools and equipment we don't have, neither." He hit the ATV with a scowl so fierce Cole was surprised the thing didn't crumple in embarrassment. "Should strip the thing and start over from the ground up, but don't have time for that either, 'course."

Cole sighed. "So what can we do?" It was abundantly clear Hazard couldn't ride with any of them. She was simply too big. They couldn't even give her one of their bikes and double up because Cole was sure none of their bikes could handle the weight. And the last thing they needed right now was another broken vehicle.

Doc was busy thinking, tugging at his beard as he paced a rough perimeter around the ATV. "We ain't far from Antonito," he said finally. "I know a guy there, runs a tavern, trades info and weapons. He can get me the parts I need to put something new together—might not be pretty, but it'll run and it'll carry her." That last was said with a nod at Hazard, who managed to look slightly embarrassed for her size. "Gonna have to walk it until then, though. No other choice. No way we can drag this deadweight along." His glare at the ruined ATV made it clear he was referring to the vehicle, though, and not its owner.

The big troll's chin came up. "I can handle that," she stated. She turned back to the ruin that had been her vehicle. "Let me just grab my saddlebags and we can get going."

Surprisingly, it was Alaric who intercepted her. "I'll take some of them," the decker offered, skipping in between the troll and her ATV. "No point you having to lug them on your shoulders when we've still got perfectly good bikes ourselves."

Cole nodded. "I'll take some, too," he agreed. He weighed more than the elf, but his bike was also bigger and could carry more. Besides, it was only to Antonito.

"Same here," Doc chimed in, and even Goyathlay grunted an agreement. Hazard just stared at them a minute, tusked jaw working like she wanted to speak but wasn't sure what to say. Finally she just nodded and stepped around Alaric to the ATV, hauling a saddlebag from its side—and passing it to the elf without a word.

It took them an hour or so to get everything situated, distributing the troll's belongings so no one bike was too badly weighed down.

At one point during the process Goyathlay closed his eyes for a bit and, when he reopened them, informed the others there was a small stream nearby. The shaman then hiked over there and brought back full canteens of ice-cold mountain water for everyone.

When they were finally able to get moving again a few hours later, everyone was sweaty but satisfied. Hazard was on foot but unencumbered save for her personal weapons and gear, and the others all knew without saying that they wouldn't push the big troll past her limits—if it took them a day or two longer to reach Antonito, so be it. As long as they all got there in one piece, that was what mattered.

"Once we're there, I'll see what I can rustle up," Doc told them as he settled onto his bike. "Should be able to figure something out."

"Sounds like a plan." Cole smiled. "And maybe, just maybe, while we're there we'll have time to sleep in a real bed, and eat something somebody else prepared for a change."

They all laughed, and when they set out they were all in a much better mood. Funny how mechanical failure and near-death could do that to you, he thought as they rode, now at a more sedate pace. Funny how it bonded you, too. Hazard was no longer just some muscle they'd hired to watch their backs. After she'd tried to help Cole get past what happened at Dinosaur, the others had started to accept her more. And now, judging by the way they'd all jumped to save her, he was confident she truly was one of the pack.

So for that alone, he was grateful the NAN was apparently taking the scenic route to Cheyenne.

Even if he still didn't understand why they were doing it.

# TWENTY-THREE

Cole had never thought of himself as a snob, but as they pulled in he found himself wondering exactly how small a place had to be before it could no longer lay claim to the word "town." Because whatever that cutoff was, he was sure Antonito had to be clinging right to the edge, if not already falling off. There was only a handful of buildings he could see, all of them bellied up to either side of the highway, all of them at least a few decades old and definitely showing their age, all of them what a guidebook might describe as "charmingly rustic" and anyone else would call "crudely built by hand with whatever raw materials could be found," and none of them more than two stories tall. A handful of smaller structures were scattered back behind, most of them barely more than crude shacks, and most of them far enough back that he wasn't sure whether they were counted as part of the town or just individual homes that happened to be in the general vicinity.

At least Doc's friend's place was easy enough to find—The Watering Hole was one of the bigger buildings here, and its weathered wooden sign hung from the long porch right in front of the double doors, swaying in the breeze.

"Looks cozy," Alaric commented as they pulled up the hitching posts lining the porch's front lip. "If by 'cozy' you mean 'crazy people live all the way out here and probably slaughter anyone who passes through, just for fun, then wears their faces as hats.'" He shuddered. "Just how good a friend is this guy, Doc? You sure he isn't just playing you?"

"Not a chance," Doc replied, switching off his bike and clambering from the seat. "I've known Jake longer'n you've been alive, and I'd trust him with my life."

"Yeah, but do you trust him with mine?" Hazard muttered, but none of the others caught the remark, and Cole decided to let it slide. He did keep his eyes open, however, as they crossed the porch and pushed the doors open to step inside.

He found himself in a large room, probably taking up almost the entirety of the tavern's footprint, so wide it seemed low even though the ceilings were tall enough that Hazard could stand and not have to worry about clearance. The floor was wood plank that looked like it had probably been rough once but had been worn smooth by countless feet stomping back and forth over many long years. The walls were corrugated tin below and cracking plaster above, and despite the windows across the front and the recessed lights spaced all across the whole place was half-covered in shadow. Between that, the illusory low ceiling, and the warmth, it felt like a giant man-made cave.

That was not helped by the fact that only two patrons appeared to be hibernating. One was slumped over a table in the far corner, drunk or dead or just asleep. The other sat at the bar, drooping like a week-old flower. The only other person in here was a burly man with a shaved head, tattoos, and biker leathers who came around the bar as they took a few hesitant paces from the door, slinging a dish towel over one shoulder as he waved them over.

"Howdy, strangers," he told them, sounding a bit like an old cartoon Cole had caught once. "What's your poison?" Then he caught sight of Doc, and his face, which had been round and unassuming, even pleasant, hardened into a mask. "Get out," he stated, his voice gone cold and flat. "We don't serve your kind here."

"My *kind*?" Doc pushed his hat back so he could peer up at the man, scowling beneath his mustache. "And what kind's that? Smarter 'n you?" He made a show of glancing around. "Guess that's why you ain't got too much business, hm?"

*This is his friend?* Cole thought. He was about to cut in when the man glowered down at Doc, opened his mouth to speak—and burst out laughing.

"Frag, Doc!" he howled, tears streaming down his face. "I never can win 'gainst you!" He scooped the dwarf up in a bear hug, pounding him on the back. "It's sure good to see you! How long's it been?"

Doc was grinning too, and Cole relaxed. "Ten years, maybe?" The inventor replied once the man had put him back on his feet. "You know me—I like to stay put."

"I do know that," the man agreed. "Which has me wondering what all this is about, you showing up here with your own little gang of sorts." He held out his hand to Cole, who was closest. "Jake."

"Cole." They shook. "That's Alaric, Goyathlay, and Hazard." Each of them nodded as he gestured toward them. "Nice to meet you."

"Same here." Jake led the way back over to the bar, slipping around behind it as they each claimed seats along its polished, dark wood length. Hazard settled for dropping into a cross-legged position on the floor. "What can I get you?"

"Beers all around," Doc replied, saving the rest of them the trouble of ordering. "And a little help. Nothing dangerous, just need some parts and some workspace. I've gotta build—or restore'd be better—a new bike. A big one."

Jake frowned, but it looked more thoughtful than upset. "Sure, no problem," he agreed easily. "I've got an old shed out back, I use it for projects, and there's some parts scattered around it. But you'd be better off just squatting at Sparrow's— she was the town rigger, 'fore..." This time the scowl seemed genuine, nor did it fade right away. "Anyway, she left, and that place's just sitting there. It'll have what you need. Plus she had a pretty decent-size junkyard out back, kept collecting new castoffs out on the highways. Should be you can find something usable in all that drek."

Doc was rubbing his hands together, his eyebrows almost twitching from excitement. "That'll do, yeah," he agreed, trying for nonchalant and failing miserably. The others all laughed, and Cole decided that perhaps Antonito wouldn't be so bad after all. If nothing else, he'd have a day or two to stretch his legs while Doc worked, a day or two where he didn't wind up riding eight hours or more each day, and that he was definitely looking forward to.

As if thoughts of riding had summoned them, he heard the sound of engines approaching outside. More motorcycles, he thought. But heavier, throatier. Modded out?

The sound reached the rest of them, too, and Hazard was on her feet in an instant. "Trap!" she shouted, one hand diving into her coat to yank out a massive pistol, the other already groping for Jake. "You set us up!"

The tavern owner backed away a step, bumping into the shelves along the wall, causing glasses to rattle over his shoulder and above his head. "I didn't," he assured them, his voice staying level despite everything. "Just wait here a minute, okay? And don't let them see you." Reaching under the bar he retrieved an impressive assault shotgun and, slinging that over his shoulder by its strap, he brushed past them all, heading for the front doors.

None of them said anything. They didn't have to. Instead, after exchanging a quick glance, Cole stalked silently toward the front, followed by the others. They spread out, each sidling up to one of the large windows there and positioning themselves so they could peer out without being seen themselves. It helped that the windows were heavily tinted to the outside, Cole remembered, but there was no point in being careless.

A small gang had pulled up outside the bar. Cole didn't recognize any of them, but certainly knew the type—young, tough, cocky, convinced that they were the biggest thing around. And their bikes were the same, big and flashy, built to let the whole world know they were in control. Their leader—a lean, muscular elf with emerald spikes of hair and matching silver spikes on the shoulders of her leather jacket, the arches of her black boots, and the curves of her knuckledusters—was sneering something at Jake, who was clearly not having any of it, standing defiantly with his legs apart, arms crossed over his chest. Until one of the other gang members moved and suddenly the shotgun was up and in Jake's hands and the gang was all backing away. There were taunts and jeers, but they gathered themselves and rode off without attempting to come inside. A moment later, Jake returned.

"Guessing you saw all that," he stated, reclaiming his place behind the bar. "Nothing to worry about. Just some local color."

"Looked like more than that," Hazard retorted, leaning on the bar until it creaked. "Looked like a gang asserting control, claiming territory." She grinned, showing her capped teeth. "Believe me, I know."

"I've got it under control," Jake insisted. "Now, here's where the garage is." Grabbing a napkin, he sketched out a simple map. They let themselves be distracted, but Cole caught Doc's eye, and after a second the inventor nodded.

Looked like they'd have something to keep them busy here in Antonito after all.

The garage was perfect. At least, Doc seemed to think so. All Cole saw was a battered old one-story building, a pair of massive doors set across the front big enough for even a heavily-armored truck to squeeze through, a smaller door off to the side leading into a tiny office, and the interior almost entirely taken up by the mechanics' bay, complete with dugouts and hydraulic lifts and long benches along the walls crammed with equipment and old parts. But the dwarf let out a happy sigh when they'd picked the office door lock and let themselves in, his eyes agleam as he started roaming the place, selecting this and that from what looked like random piles everywhere.

Still, Cole had slept worse places. It was dry, at least, no leaks in the flat roof, and the office was dusty but clean, equipped with a sturdy little metal desk surrounded by tall metal filing cabinets, a squeaky high-backed wooden desk chair, and a handful of folding chairs in front of it. The workbenches in the bay could be cleared to use as makeshift beds, and there was plenty of space to fit their bikes inside. "It'll do," he agreed.

"Dibs on the desk," Alaric called, dropping into the desk chair with a groan and a small explosion of dust and kicking his feet up onto the desk. "So, those guys at the bar..." he started, leaning back, hands behind his head.

"Yeah." Hazard perched on the desk itself, which at least was sturdy enough to hold her. "Like I said, definitely looking to take control. Of Jake's."

Cole nodded. "Agreed. Question is, what do we do about it? Or do we just stay out of it?"

"Teach them the error of their ways," Goyathlay offered. "I do not like bullies."

"Me either," Alaric said. "And Jake's sorta our host, right? Means we should be looking out for him while we're here. Plus he's a friend of Doc's."

Hazard shook her head, her capped tusks gleaming even in the room's dim light. "Won't work," she argued. "I got no problem beating on 'em, and I'm all for paying Jake back for taking us in—" she glanced around at the garage, as if to illustrate the point that "taking them in" was debatable, "—but we just stomp them, they'll just come back angry. We put 'em down—" her quick, bloodthirsty grin showed she had no objection to that course of action, but it vanished just as quickly, "—somebody else'll take their place. Nature abhors a vacuum. Just the way it is."

Cole considered that. He was sure the big troll was right—she knew more about gang behavior than the rest of them combined, but even he could see that those guys weren't going to just back down, and taking them out might solve the problem in the short-term, but it wouldn't fix the bigger issue. "Jake's place is the only decent spot here," he commented, thinking aloud. "So anybody looking to hold this area's going to need to own it. And he's gonna keep fending people off until somebody gets lucky." He sighed, leaning against the doorframe. "Problem is, how do we stop that?"

This time when Hazard grinned it didn't look like violence personified. More like...mischief. And a bit of trouble. "I've got an idea," she said slowly, ducking her head a little. Was she embarrassed? Concerned they wouldn't take her seriously? But they'd been on the road together for a while now, had fought alongside one another, and so when she started to explain, hesitantly at first but with growing enthusiasm, they all listened.

After she'd finished, the room was silent. Finally, Alaric spoke. "That's just plain nuts," he said, kicking his feet to the floor and straightening with a snap, sitting with his elbows on the desk, hands steepled like an odd blue businessman, looking dead serious save for the huge grin threatening to break free from his face. "When do we start?"

"Why is it," Cole muttered, "that every time I break into someplace, trouble seems to follow?"

*"'Cause you're good at your job?"* Alaric offered over the comms.

*"Or really bad at it,"* Hazard countered.

"Thank you, that's super-helpful from both of you," Cole told them, but left it at that. His friends might be able to laugh and joke, but that's because they were tucked away behind some bushes a good thirty meters away.

He was a little bit closer to the action. As in, right on top of it. Literally.

He held himself still, arms splayed, hands grasping supports to either side, body suspended by the rope he'd played out from where he'd tied it around the roof joist. And beneath him were the punks he'd seen at Jake's earlier. Nearly a dozen of them, all lounging about, drinking, laughing, playing cards and dice and darts, napping, sharpening knives and cleaning guns—all the things you might expect a gang to do back at its home base.

The problem being, Hazard's plan required them to infiltrate the place. And of course Cole was the one they'd all looked at to handle that aspect.

Still, he had to admit that this was one of things he was genuinely good at.

It didn't hurt that these idiots clearly thought no one would ever possibly dare to come after them. They hadn't bothered to alarm the skylights and upper windows beyond simple motion detectors and lock sensors, and they hadn't thought to look up once.

Cole certainly didn't mind. He enjoyed dumb, careless targets.

But he wasn't going to be able to do much if they caught him at it. And there was no way he was landing in the midst of all that, not without ending his life rapidly and violently, as a sort of awkward half-metal punching bag. Instead he released the grip with his left hand and reeled in with his right, swinging himself toward that side of the simple, one-story building, toward what looked like a small office. Fortunately this whole place looked like it had been a warehouse or factory before becoming the gang's lair, and the interior walls didn't reach all the way to the high ceiling. They stopped about eight feet up, high enough to provide privacy, but low enough to allow airflow—and burglar passage. Once he reached that next wall, Cole was able to extend his left arm, catch the wall past that, and drag himself along that way, playing out more rope as he went. A few minutes later he'd reached the office.

It was indeed an office, and no one was in it right now, which certainly helped. Cole hooked one of his grapples to the beam overhead, right onto the exposed junction box there, and looped his rope around that so that he could descend straight down into this new room. The space was not all that large, about the same size as the mechanic's office, and it was dominated by a single big wooden desk, with chairs scattered all around. A pair of decks covered most of the desk's broad, scarred surface, and Cole grinned. *Perfect!*

Lowering himself down slowly to avoid spinning and bumping into anything, Cole landed just behind the deck. As soon as his feet touched the ground he pulled out the data stick Alaric had given him.

"I'm in," he reported softly. "Alaric, looking to plug this in now."

*"Go for it,"* the decker replied. *"No special treatment, just plug it in and get out of there."*

Cole examined the bigger of the two decks—he didn't know much about the hardware but figured when in doubt, go for bigger and shinier—and found the input port. He slid the datastick into it. "Got it," he declared quietly.

*"Right, hold on."* He could hear Alaric typing and a tiny indicator light on the deck turned from red to green. *"Okay, I'm in. Planting that in three, two, one—now!"* More typing through the comms. *"Okay, we're good—yank it and run!"*

Cole wasn't about to run—that would just make everything worse if something did go wrong. Instead he calmly, carefully extracted the datastick, tucked it back away, and then used the ropes to haul himself back up into the roof beams. From there it was easy enough to retrace his steps up to and through the skylight, and then down from the roof and into the grass where the others waited.

"All good?" he asked, handing Alaric back his thumb drive.

"Oh, yeah," the decker agreed. "Let's go."

They ducked back through the brush to where their bikes were waiting. Then they headed toward Sparrow's. "Goyathlay reported in while you were inside," Alaric added as they rode. "He raided Jake's stockpiles and a few abandoned shops and found what we need, or close enough."

Cole nodded at that, pleased. In the morning, it would be time for Phase Two.

Doc took one look at them and shook his head. "I even wanna know?" he asked, scratching at his whiskered cheek.

"Maybe not," Cole admitted easily. They hadn't bothered to fill the dwarven inventor in on their plan, mainly because he'd spent all of the previous day roaming the junkyard out back. That was why they hadn't included him, too. The whole reason for their stay here was to give him time to find something Hazard could ride. Dragging him into this mess would only distract him. Meanwhile, it kept the rest of them out of his hair. And, if everything went well, it would help his friend out, too.

If it all went well.

"Well, whatever," Doc decided finally, shrugging. "Just don't blame me if it blows up in your faces." Then he stomped out into the bay, grumbling something about people with too much time on their hands.

Once he was gone, Cole looked around at the others. "We ready?" They all nodded. "Okay, then." He took a deep breath, sighed, took another. "Let's do this."

This time they didn't bother with stealth. Quite the opposite. They drove over to Jake's—Hazard walked—and then arrayed themselves at one of the larger tables, right by the window. "What're you up to?" Jake asked, frowning at them.

"Just relaxing a bit," Alaric told him, leaning back in his chair.

"Nothing to worry about," Hazard agreed.

"Looking for ways to pass the time," Goyathlay added.

Cole pulled out a deck of cards and began to shuffle it. "Can we get a few beers?"

An hour or two later, halfway through yet another card game, they heard the sound they'd been waiting for—that of motorcycles, deliberately loud.

"Don't bother," Cole told Jake as the bar owner reached for his shotgun. "Just stay where you are, keep calm, and let me do the talking." The other man's eyes narrowed, and Cole sighed. "Look, trust me on this, okay?"

Finally, Jake nodded and, picking up a glass and scooping up a hand towel, began to polish it.

After a few minutes, the bike sounds cut off abruptly. That sudden silence was quickly broken by the noise of several booted feet hitting the ground, then clomping on the front porch, then the slam of the front doors. Cole waited until the footsteps stopped before glancing up from his hand.

There were five of them today, though he knew there were actually a few more than that in total. This time the green-spiked elf had an orc, a dwarf, and two humans flanking her as she strutted in. She quickly scanned the place, her eyes passing over the handful of other customers, flicking a glare at Jake, and then coming to rest on Cole's table. Even from across the room he could see her eyes widen just a little, though she controlled herself well. The second human, a short but broad woman with dark skin and pale hair, did not have the same level of restraint. She practically squealed upon seeing them, and leaned in to whisper in the elf's ear.

Showtime.

"You must be Nightshade," he drawled, rising slowly to his feet and giving her his best disdainful glance. "The reports pegged you as slightly taller."

He saw her lips twitch, a sharp retort starting to form before her brain caught with what she'd just heard. They mouthed "report," then, though no sound emerged.

"We appreciate entrepreneurship," Cole continued, nodding at her and her pack as if they were teens who had just opened their own business delivering ammo door-to-door. Then he let a sharper tone enter his voice. "Provided it knows its limits." He speared the gang leader with his best killer glare. "Do you?"

The dwarf and the orc both snarled, in almost perfect unison—and their inarticulate protests cut short abruptly as Hazard slid in front of them. Under any circumstances the troll was intimidating. Now, in black combat gear head-to-toe, a massive gun dangling from its strap below one arm and an equally large knife below the other, wraparound mirrored shades hiding her eyes, a completely blank expression replacing her usual predatory grin, she was Death personified. Cold, calm, collected, and completely deadly.

As befit an enforcer for the NAN.

The elf stared at Hazard, at Goyathlay—clearly a shaman—at Alaric, and then turned back to Cole. "We do," she agreed, her voice quavering only slightly. "Sorry. You don't have to worry about us."

"Glad to hear it." Cole favored her with as condescending a smile as he could muster. "It would be a shame to waste such promise." He turned away, then, deliberately showing her his back as he moved back over to the table and sat, picking up the deck and starting to shuffle again. A moment passed, and then the elf backed away, motioning for her gang members to join her as they vacated the bar, doing their best to look like they weren't puppies running home with their tails between their legs.

Jake waited until the sound of their engines had faded in the distance before blurting out, "What the blazes was that?"

Cole grinned at the bar owner, no longer forced to play "cold and collected." "That was us convincing them to leave you alone—for good," he explained. "They won't be back."

"Because you threatened them?" Jake didn't sound convinced.

"Us?" Alaric put on an exaggerated tone. "We didn't do anything. The NAN, on the other hand—they might have had something to say about it."

Jake looked back and forth between them all, a growing look of horror on his face. "You told them you were NAN?"

"We never said that," Cole pointed out. He shrugged. "Not our fault if they jumped to conclusions."

Alaric snorted. "'Course, that doc I had you insert into their system might've helped."

Cole laughed with him, as did Hazard and even Goyathlay. It had been a clever plan, actually. As Hazard had pointed out, beating up the gang would only slow things down. They'd had to convince them that someone bigger and badder was moving in, or was actually already here. So Alaric had doctored some files to make it look like the NAN were actually stakeholders in The Watering Hole. When the gang had found them sitting here, dressed in their borrowed tactical gear, clearly professionals showing a vested interest in the bar, they had simply put two and two together. And no matter how big and bad they thought they were, the gang knew better than to mess with the NAN. They'd steer clear of Jake's place from now on. Nor would they dare to try calling the NAN for confirmation, since that would just be an insult.

"Good plan," Cole told Hazard, who ducked her head and shrugged to hide the smile peeling back her lips. To save her any further embarrassment, he shuffled and cut and then started to deal out cards. "Now, who's in?"

A day later, Doc unveiled a success of his own. "Ta-da!" he declared, whisking a dropcloth off the thing he'd been working on the last two days straight.

All of them stared, unable to find words.

"It's beautiful," Hazard whispered finally. "What the hell is it?"

"That," Doc told her, practically beaming, "is a real-deal Honda Valkyrie."

"What?" Cole burst out. "No way!"

He'd seen Valkyries plenty of times before—they'd been popular a few years back, especially among the larger metahumans. But those bikes had a completely encased back wheel, the seat back sloping down over the rear and all along the sides, a curved windshield covering the handlebars and, if you bent down enough, the driver's head.

The thing before them now was completely different. It was massive, with no windshield at all, the rear tire fully exposed, as were the front forks, which ran all the way up to the handlebars. It had a massive engine, also visible, with a wide, flat grille just behind the front wheel and pipes just behind that on both sides, above and below. It *was* beautiful, Hazard was right, but in a big, powerful, dangerous sort of way, and nothing like anything he'd seen before.

Meanwhile Doc was laughing at him. "Not the modern variety, idjit," the inventor told him. "This is a classic! An EVO6, from back in the early 2000s." He rubbed his hands together. "We're lucky I spotted the frame out there! And managed to piece it together." He nodded to Hazard. "Give it a try."

Gingerly, the big  troll stepped up beside the heavy bike. Then, slinging one leg over it, she settled onto the seat. Almost immediately a look of bliss appeared on her face. "It's nice," she said dreamily, hands going automatically to the handlebars. "I love it." It did seem big enough to work for her, and now she wouldn't have any trouble keeping up with everyone else.

"Awesome work, Doc," Cole told his oldest friend, clapping on the back. "Get some sleep, everybody. We hit the road again first thing in the morning."

It had been a fun few days, relaxing but also exciting. Now it was time to pick up the trail back up and resume the hunt.

He just hoped their delay wouldn't cost them in the end.

# TWENTY-FOUR

The sun was just disappearing, stealing the last dregs of dusk with it, when Goyathlay sat upright on his bike. "Something is amiss," the tattooed shaman pronounced.

"What'd we miss?" Alaric asked, waking from the semi-daze he'd been in. They'd all gotten very good at zoning out while riding, alert enough to watch the road and react to any dangers while letting their minds drift at the same time.

"Nothing," Hazard growled from her position at the group's rear. "He says something's wrong."

Cole glanced around, having only just come out of a road-haze himself. "Let's make camp," he suggested. "Give Goyathlay a chance to figure out what'd going on. Then if we need to course-correct or something, we can do that in the morning."

Without a word they all pulled off the road. Finding a patch of ground wide enough and flat enough for them to park their bikes was easy enough—the entire area was flat as a week-old pancake, and just as dry. No signs of water nearby, so they each took sparing sips from their canteens, careful not to overdo it. They hadn't passed a village or town or even another traveler for the past day or more, so if they ran out of water now, they'd be in real trouble.

The nights had turned chilly, especially out here without any sort of cover, so Alaric and Cole lit a fire, using wood they'd collected at the last few stops. Then they heated some water for coffee and soup, and everyone crouched around the small circle. Goyathlay joined them, but the shaman didn't look at any of them or say anything beyond his muttered prayers and entreaties.

"Any idea where we are?" Hazard asked as they dug into their meager dinner.

Cole frowned. "Near Campo, I think," he replied after a second, consulting the atlas images stored in his headware. "Southeast corner of Colorado."

"So we've hit northwest, southwest, and now southeast?" Doc asked, sipping his cup of soup. "Let me guess, we're gonna do northeast next, collect the whole set?"

Cole sighed. "No idea," he admitted. "I still have no idea why the NAN didn't just take the darn thing right back to Cheyenne. But they didn't, and as long as they're riding around with it, we're gonna follow them."

"I thought the whole point was to steal the amulet while they're on the road with it," Alaric commented. "So why haven't we yet? We don't we just sneak up on them first thing tomorrow and snatch it before they're even awake yet?"

Surprisingly, it was Hazard who answered. "'Cause we don't know how many they've got guarding it," the big enforcer pointed out, "or what they're packing, or what other surprises they got tucked away. We go charging in without checking all that out, we'll wind up dead in a ditch and they'll stroll back to Cheyenne and anywhere else they like, easy as you please."

Cole didn't have anything to add to that, so he stayed quiet. But even though she was right, so was Alaric. They'd come out here to steal the talisman, and that was going to be a lot easier to do while it was still on the road. Which meant they had to stop trailing along behind and start making things happen. "We'll scout it out tomorrow, see if we can catch a glimpse of them up ahead," he announced, rubbing at his face. "Once we know what we're facing, we can come up with a proper plan to snatch the thing."

Everyone else grunted or nodded, and Cole felt the mood lighten. It was nice having a plan, even if it wasn't any more complicated than "grab them, grab their stuff." And clearly the rest of his people had been wanting to ask the same questions, but hadn't want to disturb him. Now they'd heard him answer, and that seemed to calm most of them.

Cole just hoped the dawn would bring him an equally wonderful and calm and productive idea on exactly what to do next. Because the two things his admittedly vague plans lacked up until the night before were a clear starting point and a clear plan of exactly how things would unfold next.

Cole woke to a scream.

He was already sitting up and reaching for his boots when he heard it again. It was a person screaming, not an animal, and it was nearby. Very near. Their fire had dwindled but not yet gone out, and in its remaining glow Cole did a quick headcount. Hazard was up and had her gun in her hand. Doc was blinking but not really awake. Goyathlay was peering about.

But where was Alaric?

"Alaric?" Cole called, getting to his feet and staggering a few steps, his legs no more awake yet than the rest of him. "Where are you?"

He'd worried there'd be no response, but after a second the blue-haired decker shouted "Here!"

Cole couldn't see him, but he sounded no more than ten to twenty meters away. There was something odd about the elf's reply, though, something about the sound itself that put Cole on edge.

"Call out again," Cole instructed, and this time he was able to isolate a direction. He hoped. He started walking that way, moving carefully with nothing but a flashlight to guide him, its beam barely strong enough to reveal a space a few feet in diameter. His vision was optimized for low light, of course, but not enough to combat the darkness out here in the wild, where there were no streetlights, no power grids, no high-rises. It was a new level of dark for him, and one he couldn't completely penetrate.

That was why he very nearly tumbled headfirst into the hole.

As it was, he thought the dark patch on the ground was just a shadow. It was only at the last possible second, as he began to lower his foot, that the flashlight played across the exact spot. It did nothing to brighten it, the weak beam disappearing instead as if the shadows had gobbled it up. Cole yanked himself back so hard he almost overbalanced and fell on his butt, but after wobbling a second he regained his balance and peered down what he now recognized as a deep, wide hole.

"Alaric?" he called.

"Here, I'm here," the elf answered, his words coming from within that pit. That also explained the strange timbre to them, Cole realized. It was because the words were echoing, bouncing off the sides as they worked their way up and out.

"Over here," he shouted, and the others hurried toward him. "Careful, there's a pit." He ran his flashlight's beam along the hole's edges so they could all see it properly.

"How'd you wind up down there?" Hazard wanted to know, leaning out to stare down into that darkness.

"Went to take a leak and next thing I know, I'm falling," Alaric answered. "Not sure how far down I am, or how long I've been down here. I hit my head on the way down, so maybe I passed out and don't remember?"

"You didn't pass out," Doc shouted down. "We heard you scream and came running." He sounded relieved, and Cole realized that was because if Alaric hadn't been knocked out it lessened the chance that he'd incurred any serious damage—particularly brain damage—on his way into the little makeshift prison.

"We'll have you out of there in no time," Cole promised, even though he still couldn't actually see Alaric and thus had no idea how far down he was. But they could always lower a rope down. He tried to see if he could spot the elf while Doc and Hazard and even Goyathlay did the same, all of them careful not to lean out too far over the opening.

Which is why they all squawked and yelped and screamed in surprise when the ground under their feet gave way as well, and they all plummeted into the pit.

Cole scrabbled for something, anything to hold onto, but his hands found nothing. He was flailing in empty air—and then his head collided with something much harder and the dark within swallowed him whole, even as the dark without enveloped his flesh.

He was in a cave somewhere, eyes shut as he tried to feel around him, looking for any landmark or other identifier with his other senses. At first there was nothing, but then he heard a strange whooshing sound, and felt warmth upon his fingers and traveling up his arm. Blinking his eyes open, Cole wasn't surprised to see the great ruby eye peering back at him.

It was the only illumination in this dark, dim cell, but even without words, without any other indicator, he somehow knew the eye hadn't been tricked into this space the way he had. It already resided here, and it was Cole who had tried to trick it—and failed.

Which only left brute force, he decided as he rushed for the eye, hands outstretched. It recoiled, but the tight quarters left it nowhere to go. Then Cole was upon it, grabbing that glowing red eye and squeezing as hard as he could. It fought back, and the two of them battled beneath the earth, no one around to witness their struggle. The conflict carried both of them to one side and then the other as they jockeyed for dominance, and when Cole collided with the rock wall it tore the breath from him, and then stripped away his consciousness as well.

"Uh, ow," Cole muttered, twisting around and wincing as the movement set off a chorus of protests all up and down his side. "What the hell?"

"Hell's 'bout right," a familiar voice replied. Doc!

Cole opened his eyes, squinting in the light, and saw the dwarf crouched beside him. "What—?" Cole started to ask, but broke off with a gasp as their recent activity came flooding back to him. The night. The scream. The pit. The ground giving way. He sat up, wincing again, and looked around.

At first he thought they were in a nice little room somewhere in an adobe hut or fort, the walls that warm reddish-brown that denoted baked clay. But these walls were too perfectly sealed, not a seam or joint in sight. And they rose much too high, he saw as he tilted his head back, towering at least six meters before ending in a small, roughly square opening that let in the light of the sun beaming down on them.

They were still in the pit, he realized.

And "they" meant all of them—that was the second thing that occurred to him. He, Doc, Goyathlay, and Hazard had all joined Alaric, who was sitting with his back against one of the walls.

They were all down here together.

It had been at least a few hours since they fell, because the sun was high in the sky, without a single trace of night remaining. Plus Cole felt stiff, like he'd slept in an odd position. He stood and stretched, trying to put everything back in place.

"Why didn't you stay back where it was safe?" the elf asked, though he sounded more resigned than angry, or even curious. "Then you could've just hauled me out of here."

"We did stay back," Doc snapped. "The ground was rigged. It gave out right under our feet."

That was exactly how Cole remembered it, too. He'd been careful to stay clear of the edge. They all had. But then they'd fallen in anyway.

He knew some hunters used traps, and occasionally they concealed those traps so the animals they hunted wouldn't notice the snare or pit or whatever until it was too late.

But this pit was too big and too deep for any animal except maybe a bear. And having the pit be visible but the entrance rigged to fall apart the minute enough people showed up on it—that wasn't for any animal, since they'd know to steer clear of a pit in the first place.

No, this trap had been meant for people.

And clearly it had worked.

Now the only question was, how the hell were they going to get out of it?

# TWENTY-FIVE

First things first—Cole took stock of his crew. Doc looked annoyed and grumpy, as usual, but otherwise fine. Hazard also looked angry, and the way she was cradling one hand suggested she'd already tried punching her way out at least once, but if she was well enough to manage that then she was okay. Alaric was sporting a hefty bruise on one cheek, and Cole thought he spotted a lump rising up through the elf's blue hair, but he was clearly lucid as well.

Goyathlay, however, was still lying on the bottom of the pit, limbs splayed, eyes shut but mouth open.

"Goyathlay!" Cole scrambled toward the shaman, tripping in his haste and sliding to a stop right beside the tattooed man. He pushed on the man's chest and got no response but was relieved to see that at least he was breathing. That was something.

"He's out," Doc explained unnecessarily, but then the dwarf added, "I checked him already. Pupils are responsive to light, which is a good sign. Could be just took a heavy bonk and now he's gotta sleep it off. Could be he's cracked his skull and his brain's leaking out. Not much I can do without equipment, 'cept let him sleep and hope he wakes up."

"Great." Cole rose to his feet and resisted the urge to kick or punch the wall out of sheer frustration. If the shaman had been awake, getting out of here would have been easy— Goyathlay probably could have levitated himself out of the hole and tossed a rope back down, even if he couldn't lift anyone else. How much he could carry was a moot point right now, however. They'd have to do this without the aid of magic.

Cole studied their current lodgings. The pit was roughly square, and close to seven meters on a side. Something was wrong with that measurement, however. He leaned back and stared up at the opening again. He was pretty good at estimated sizes and distances—part of the job, or maybe just one of the reasons he was so good at his job—and he was sure that the top of the pit was still only about three meters to a side.

"Yeah," Hazard said, coming up beside him with unusual stealth for someone so big. "It tapers in as it rises. Keeps you pinned down—walls're too far apart to try using two to push off. Even if you've got someone strong enough to throw a person six, seven meters straight up, they'd have to get the angle absolutely perfect or all they're doing is killing their friends by throwing them head-first into a solid stone wall."

*Ouch.* Cole tried not to wince at that mental image, but he knew the troll was right. Tapering the pit narrower as it went down made it way too easy to scale back up. Widening it on the descent, however—that was smart. Way too smart for a bunch of random backwoods hunters. No, this trap had been set by someone really good, really fast, and really ruthless.

Someone like the steely-eyed sniper. Who was still shepherding the NAN convoy to its destination, as far as Cole knew. And who had a vested interest in keeping Cole away from the convoy and its prize.

Of course, he wasn't sure how the sniper could have dug such a pit so quickly, when Cole thought they were only a few days behind the convoy at most. But perhaps they'd used magic to do it. Or explosives, or some other trick.

Or maybe this pit had always been here, and they had simply known about it and led Cole and his team right to it.

But how could the NAN have known they'd camp at this exact spot?

Well, he could worry about that later. Right now they needed to get out of this hole in the ground.

The question was, how?

Magic was out. So was Hazard just tossing one or more of them to the surface. Their bikes were all still topside, as were their packs, and therefore most of their tools. What did that leave them?

"We need to figure out a way out of here," he told the others. "Anybody have any ideas?"

Hazard grunted and shook her head, still massaging her hand. "Solid rock all the way 'round," she explained. "No way through it. Can't shoot it, neither—would just ricochet, or chip loose nice sharp shards that'd slice you up in a heartbeat."

Doc ran a stubby hand over the wall nearest him. "It's rough, but not rough enough to have any handholds," he observed. "No way to climb it without tools or handholds or both." He sighed. "If I had my supplies, I might be able to build something. Supplies and our bikes and I could have a ladder put together in a jiffy. Down here, though, all we've got is rocks, rocks, and more rocks." He kicked one near his feet, just to emphasize the point.

Goyathlay was still unconscious. But Alaric—even as Cole turned to him, the blue-haired elf rose to his feet, brushed himself off, and began pacing the perimeter of their little prison. "We just need to think our way through it," he declared, eyeing the walls and the floor and the exit. "That's all."

That drew a snort from Hazard. "Think our way through it?" she asked, staring down at the slim decker. "Seriously? What, you're gonna walk through solid rock now?"

Alaric rolled his eyes at her. "Through the problem," he explained patiently. "We've got to think our way through the problem, not literally through the rock." A grin split his rock-dust-covered face. "Though how cool would that be if we could walk through it?"

"Okay, okay," Cole cut in before Hazard could respond. He rubbed a hand over his face. "So what've you got in mind? And have you ever done something like this before?" He waved a hand at their surroundings.

Alaric laughed. "Been trapped in a pit out the middle of nowhere? No, sorry, until last night that was still on my to-do list. But the rest—" he spun in a circle, gesturing at the pit around them. "Dude, it's just another logic problem. And thinking my way out of problems is *exactly* what I do."

Cole frowned at that, but didn't argue. Besides, in a way Alaric was right. It was a logic problem. And if bouncing around for a bit would help him figure out a solution, Cole was all for it.

"How far down are we, would you say?" Alaric asked next.

"Six, seven, maybe eight meters," Cole replied, squinting up at the patch of sky again to confirm that. "Yeah, about eight."

"No way I can throw anyone that far, even with room to really wind up," Hazard commented. "In here, with those leaning walls on top of everything else? No way. Sorry."

Alaric was eyeing the big enforcer. Cole suspected it was to see whether the troll really was telling the truth about not being able to throw them that far. "Your guess is as good as mine," he finally admitted. "But there's a way out. Trust me—there's always a way." He turned to Cole again. "How long can your arms reach?"

"Three meters," Cole answered. He'd had to test that reach often enough! "I can pull myself up with one, though it's rough, but I can't push myself up with the other, not enough leverage."

"Three meters." Alaric nodded, pacing again, his gaze and thoughts both far away and oddly focused on the problem before them. "If only we had some way to cut into the rock," he muttered, trailing his fingers along the wall as he went. "Then we'd be in business."

"Well, I've got this," Doc offered. He pulled a narrow metal tube from a pocket. Pressing the tiny nub along its side caused a red light to appear at one end, and when he held that to the wall the rock sizzled and a thin slice appeared in the wide expanse. "I use it to cut into metal housings," he explained. "Or sometimes to cauterize cuts."

"Nice," Cole said, touching that spot on the wall. "Doesn't look like it goes more than an inch in, though. And at that width, we'd probably burn it out just cutting one handhold."

Doc nodded. "Yeah, figured it was worth a try, at least."

A blur shot by them. All three jumped back—and then stared at the knife embedded in the rock wall a little above their heads. They all turned to gape at Hazard, standing opposite them. She shrugged.

"Comes in handy when I gotta cut my way outta something," she explained with a smirk that showed her teeth.

Cole reached up and managed to wrench the knife free. Its blade extended a good six inches or more, and all around its edge glowed a vivid red much like Doc's small cutting tool. "Yeah, this'll work," he said, jamming it into the rock wall again in a new spot. The blade sank in as easily as if he'd been stabbing it into soft wood, and when he put pressure on it he found that it could hold his weight. "Don't suppose you've got two of them?"

But the enforcer shook her head. "Sorry."

"Naw, it's still good." He looked at Alaric. "Right, so we've got a way to cut holes in the rock. What can we do with it?"

The elf was contemplating the wall, the knife—and Cole. "You'll have to climb out and then toss a rope down," he pointed out. "You're the only one who can."

Cole nodded. He'd already figured as much himself. He was easily the most adept at climbing, plus with his arms he could cover the distance a lot more quickly. He still had one major question, though: "How'm I going to do that when I only have the one knife for a handhold?"

Alaric reached past him, having to go up on tiptoes, and by using both hands he was able to tug the knife free again. Then, a little lower down so he'd have more leverage, he used the red-edged blade to carve out a wedge in the rock. "Like that," he said when he'd finished, panting for breath as he handed Cole back the knife.

Cole considered it. He could slam the knife into the wall, then twist it to the side as he extracted it. That should give him a wedge shape or better. He'd have to basically jam his fingers into that hole in order to hold on, but if he could support himself that way he could then reach up and carve the next hole. Two, two and a half meters at most, to make sure he could get enough force to drive the knife in properly, so he'd need at least three, maybe four holes. It wasn't going to be easy, but he thought he could do it.

"All right." He took a deep breath. "Might as well get started."

"Hang on." Hazard stomped over to him and reached into one of the pockets on her long leather trenchcoat. "Here." She passed him something heavy, cold, and metallic. Cole glanced down at the curved row of thick metal circles, with a fifth and longer loop connecting them at their base. It was a set of brass knuckles, but one sized for the troll's significantly larger hand. When he looked up at her, she shrugged. "Works better than fingers," she said with a wink.

Cole tried it out. He could fit all of his fingers into the longer loop, and then jam the last of the finger loops into the wedge Alaric had carved out. The brass knuckles held much better than his fingers would have. "Thanks."

Now properly equipped, he took another breath, let it out, then reached up with one arm and planted the knife firmly into the wall almost as high up as he could get. Twisting it as he pulled it loose, he created a nice deep divot in the rock. Then, extending his other arm, he planted the end of the brass knuckles in that gap and hauled himself up. It held his weight, so he was able to set the knife a little over two meters farther up and repeat the process.

It was slow going, and he had to be very careful not to tug the brass knuckles free, drop the knife, or overextend himself and wind up without enough leverage to dig in properly. It didn't help that the walls did lean in, so he was not only reaching up each time but also out, which put excessive strain on his shoulders. But, slowly but surely, he ascended up the rock wall. The others watched him from down below, but didn't call out encouragement, which he appreciated. He needed all of his concentration not to screw this up.

Finally, after what felt like hours but couldn't have been with the sun still beating down on him, Cole reached up and stabbed the knife into the ground past the pit's edge. This time his friends did cheer as he crawled completely out and lay gasping on the surface. When he regained enough strength to lift his head, he spotted their camp only about twenty feet away, and their bikes just beyond that. "Be right back," he called down, forcing himself to his feet.

His legs felt like cold noodles, limp and rubbery, his neck and back were stiff, and his shoulders ached, but Cole managed to stagger over to the bikes. His rope was in his saddlebags, but instead of attaching it to his own bike, he tied it securely to the central frame of Hazard's instead. He knotted both lengths together, testing the knot, and then climbed onto the massive motorcycle. Its controls were standard enough, and in a few minutes he'd gotten it started and then driven it over toward the pit. He was careful to stop several yards back from the edge, just in case.

"Here," he shouted as he walked carefully back over and then tossed the rope down. "Tie it around one of you, then yell out and I'll pull you up."

A minute later, Doc hollered, "Go!" and Cole put the Valkyrie into reverse. He backed away slowly, and after several minutes a familiar bushy head appeared from the pit.

"I've had worse rides," the dwarf commented as he climbed out, quick-stepped over to Cole, and then untied the rope and tossed it back down. "Send up the shaman!" he ordered.

They brought Hazard up last, just in case her weight proved too much for them. But the ropes handled it just fine, and of course her bike was used to carrying her, though in a slightly different fashion. The sun was still up but edging toward the horizon when they all gathered on solid ground again. Even Goyathlay was finally starting to stir.

"I have seen the amulet," he declared as he sat up, rubbing his head. "It travels north. Why does my head hurt so? And why is it so bright out?"

The others laughed at him, and Cole leaned back against his bike, relieved. That could have been a great deal worse, but he still didn't understand why or how it had happened in the first place. The important thing, though, was that they'd made it out of that nasty little trap, and they'd only lost a single day.

That night he dreamed of the cave again, and the red eye. But for the first time he wasn't alone. Someone else was there with him, someone he couldn't see but who was fighting the red-eyed creature at his side. He even thought the figure said something to him, but his head was pounding too much for him to hear anything but the rush of his own blood.

# TWENTY-SIX

"Okay, what the hell are they up to now?" Doc grumbled, spitting out dirt. He lifted his head to shake debris from his hair and whiskers.

Cole shoved him back down, though as gently as he could. "We don't know," he reminded the dwarf, keeping his voice just above a whisper, "which is why we're here. So shush."

His friend grumbled and glared, but didn't make any other noises or try shifting position again. Their current perch was exposed enough, out in the searing heat of the noonday sun with only a few small patches of scrub brush for cover. The last thing they needed was to shout or wave their arms or otherwise draw the NAN's attention.

Especially since the convoy was parked in a circle a hundred meters away.

They'd ridden for several days after escaping that pit, heading north the entire time. "We really are patrolling the border, ain't we?" Doc had complained after they'd passed the town of Kit Carson, which was on level with Colorado Springs. "What's the point?"

Something had tickled the back of Cole's mind at the question, a flicker he'd felt every time he'd wondered the same thing. It was as if he knew or at least suspected an answer, but the thought remained stubbornly buried or unformed. He'd said nothing, just urged them on. It didn't matter why the NAN was driving all over the region, just that they were, and that Cole and his team were still desperately trying to catch up.

And then, just like that, they had. They'd just been passing Haxtun when Goyathlay had done his usual "I am getting a vision from the spirits" look, jolting ramrod straight, eyes wide but glazed, head back, arms outstretched. Cole had wanted to ask if he got better reception that way, but had held off, less because it seemed disrespectful than because he hadn't wanted to piss off a guy who could summon giant scorpions to infest his bedroll every night.

"The amulet is near," the shaman had announced when he'd recovered from his trance, which had happened a lot more quickly than on previous occasions. "And it slows. We are very close."

That had spurred them on, but after the first impulse they'd all accepted the need for caution. The convoy had contained a whole big mess of thugs when it had left Denver, after all. There was no reason to think they weren't just as large a group now, so charging straight in would be a terrible—and very short-lived—idea. Instead, they needed to scout ahead to figure out exactly what the NAN was up to and why, and see how they were configured.

Which was why they were currently crouching behind bushes, staring down at the convoy.

Cole still couldn't figure them out, though. Yes, the convoy had clearly stopped and set up camp. They'd found a nice, wide mesa high up in the tall hills and low mountains that made up this region, and had not only ringed their vehicles but erected tents within that protective circle. From here, crouched atop a much smaller peak some fifteen meters higher up, Cole had an excellent view of the arrangements.

The problem was, it didn't look like the NAN were up to anything other than putting down roots. And that made no sense to him.

"We've already passed Denver," he'd said the night before, an hour or more before Goyathlay's announcement, when they'd paused to stretch their legs. "If they were just out on a tour of the countryside, why not head back there now? And even if they don't want to stop in Denver, if they're still planning to go to Cheyenne, they'll need to cut west at some point, seeing as how it's right above Denver and that's almost perfectly centered in the area. But instead they're still going north like there's something up that way they've got to reach. I just don't get it."

"Baseball," Hazard had offered, and chuckled when they all turned to look at her. "You know, baseball? The game?"

"We know what it is," Doc had snapped, his already short temper frayed by the hours upon hours of riding and by the general uncertainties they faced. "But what the hell's that got to do with anything? Or did you wanna challenge them to a game, winner takes all? 'Cause if so, we're a mite short on players."

Cole had caught glimpses of baseball games on the vids, and unbidden an image had popped into his head, of the five of them attired in old-fashioned baseball jerseys and pants and shoes and hats, taking the field at some stadium. Hazard was the pitcher, up on the mound tossing a ball from hand to hand with an evil glint in her eye. Doc was the catcher, crouched down behind the plate, his wild hair jutting out from behind his mask, muttering at the batters to throw them off their game. Cole was playing infield, where his arms could snag most balls before they shot past. Alaric was on first, ready to make snap decisions about which way to throw the ball if it came to him, and Goyathlay was on third, meditating and preparing to catch any fly balls the spirits warned him were headed his way. It was an amusing image, and Cole had laughed, which had drawn strange looks from the others as well. All except Hazard, who had winked at him.

Fortunately, Alaric had stepped in. "She's talking about the bases," he'd suggested, pushing his blue hair back out of his face. "Right?" At Hazard's nod, he continued: "There's four bases, set at each point of the diamond, and you've not only got to touch each one, you've got to do it in the proper order."

Kneeling, he'd drawn a diamond in the dirt, adding a circle at each corner. Then he put another dot in the middle. "Denver, where we started." He traced a line over to the nearest corner. "This was Dinosaur." Cole shuddered as he once again heard the laughs and the screams and saw the flames dancing with glee as they consumed the town. But Alaric had already been connecting that dot to the next one. "This was that canyon where we almost drowned." He continued on to the next corner. "Here's that stupid pit I fell into." And finally he completed the diamond. "And now we're up here and almost to the last base."

"Home plate," Hazard had corrected, but without rancor. "It's called home plate. You need to cross that one to score."

"So you think this is their home plate," Cole said. "That whatever they're doing, they had to hit the other bases first, in order, and once they get to this last corner that'll be it?" He'd shaken his head, scrubbing at the hair over his forehead. "But what do they win if they do? And who're they playing against?"

Hazard had laughed again. "Last part's easy," the troll drawled. She'd waved a hand around her. "They're playing against us. And we've gotta win this. Don't know what happens if we don't, but it'll be bad, I can guarantee that."

"She's right," Doc said. "We've been a step or two behind 'em this entire way. We can't do that no more. We've gotta catch up, get out in front, cut them off before they can cross the finish line or whatever."

"So we wait until they've stopped," Alaric had suggested, "and figure out what they're doing. Then we see about getting that amulet back."

Everybody had nodded, and then they'd hopped back on their bikes and taken off again, riding as fast as they'd dared, as fast as they could go without risking wiping out, or missing the convoy and shooting past them. Goyathlay had noticed when the amulet turned off the main road to Sedgwick and Julesburg—the last two towns in this northeast corner before crossing into Wyoming—and headed instead for a small dirt road leading up into the surrounding mountains. They'd been close enough to actually see the dirt plumes from the convoy's passage, and had used those to follow more easily, right up until the ground had started to fall away on either side, leaving them on a narrow road that led into a series of mesas, peaks, and plateaus.

"We'll leave the bikes here and continue on foot," Cole had announced, braking and hopping off his bike, then leaning it against a small jumble of rocks. "That way they won't see us coming, but we can still get out of here in a hurry in case they do."

But the NAN crew hadn't spotted them, or at least hadn't reacted if they had. Goyathlay had spied this small peak near the mesa, and now here they were, crowded around its narrow tip and staring down at the convoy they'd been chasing for many long days.

Cole squinted, enhancing his vision, but even with that edge he was still too far away to make out much detail. He spotted a tall, silver-haired figure that could have been the steely-eyed sniper speaking with two other men, who immediately turned and scurried off once he was done. And he saw a smaller figure that could be the sharp-faced woman he'd spoken to on the phone, conferring with the sniper and others, so they were almost certainly in the right place.

Unfortunately, there were just as many guards in evidence as Cole had remembered.

And there was something else, too.

Something that writhed in the air, filling the space with a sharp, high keening like the scream of a striking bird, and a shimmer that distorted his view of everything beyond it. Something that made his stomach clench and his head pound and his heart race, and brought back half-remembered images from the dreams that had been haunting him every step of their journey.

"What is that?" he whispered to Goyathlay, who was stretched on his stomach beside him. The shaman sighed.

"A wind wall," he answered. "One of those below must have summoned it to form a perimeter. It will tear apart any who try to cross it without the proper codewords or gestures." His frown was so deep the lines and wrinkles looked like they might be permanently etched into his flesh. "I do not believe I can dispel it—certainly not without drawing the attention of every magician over there."

"Yeah, that wouldn't—" Cole stopped midsentence. Then he glanced over at Goyathlay. "Every magician, huh?" He smiled, and waved to catch the others' attention, then gestured back down to where they'd left the bikes. By the time they'd regathered, he was grinning so widely he could fee the skin of his cheeks stretching.

"I've got a plan," he told his team.

# TWENTY-SEVEN

Doc put the finishing touches on his latest creation, sighed, and glanced up at Cole. "You know this is crazy, right?"

Cole laughed. "Yeah, I know."

"I'm not even talkin' borderline 'hey, a little out there, but still basically okay' crazy. I'm talkin' full-on 'you've lost touch with reality if you think this's gonna work' crazy."

"Got it. Thanks for clarifying." But Cole still couldn't keep the smile from his face, which only made his friend scowl even more.

"What is wrong with you?" Doc finally burst out, rising to his feet to confront Cole face to face. Or at least face to chest. "You gotta death wish? Because I sure as hell don't!"

Smothering another laugh, Cole leaned down to meet his friend's eyes. "Look, I know this is a little nuts—" he started, holding up a hand when Doc began to sputter at his use of the word "little." "Hear me out. I know it's nuts. But that's exactly why it could work. They sure as hell won't be expecting it. And to be honest? I've done crazier stuff than this, and I'm still here."

"Which just means Lady Luck has been stringing you along, and now she's got you to bet it all on black so she can pull the rug out from under you!" Doc snapped.

Cole rested a hand on his friend's shoulder. "Have a little faith," he advised, which of course only made the dwarf snort so loudly his mustache blew out like a leaf caught in a strong wind. But when Cole held out his other hand the, inventor slapped the device into his waiting palm.

"Fine," he groused, "but if we get killed doing this, I'm blamin' you!"

"Fair enough," Cole agreed. He turned to the others, who were alternately pacing or sitting or leaning nearby. "Everybody ready? We all clear on what we're doing? Remember, stay off comms if possible—we don't know if they can pick up our signal, so let's not give them that option." Nods all around. "Right. Let's get to it." And, checking one last time to make sure his own gear was in place, he turned and began hiking back up toward the peak.

It was twilight, which Cole had always considered the perfect time for a robbery. The day shift was getting tired and wanting to go home, the night shift was still waking up and fuzzy, the light was fading overhead, the colors of the sky distorting depth perception and general visual acuity, the nighttime creatures just starting to move about and creating a blanket of sound. Everything was perfectly aligned for maximum confusion and minimum awareness, and he knew exactly how to take advantage of that.

Four of them were hunkered up there on that peak. Goyathlay was already sitting crosslegged, hands on his knees, eyes closed, starting one of his low, keening chants. Meanwhile, Alaric had his deck out and was rapidly typing in commands.

"Got 'em," the blue-haired decker declared after a few seconds, keeping his voice down so only Cole and Doc would hear him. "You were right, that was easy." It had occurred to Cole—and Alaric had confirmed it—that hacking into someone's systems in the city was tricky in part because you had to make sure you isolated their network and didn't get sucked into someone else's by mistake, or that the signal didn't bounce you somewhere else. But out here, there wasn't anyone else around. The only signal Alaric should even be able to detect would be the NAN's, for whatever electronic security they'd established.

Sometimes, bringing a transmitter with you so you had the only clear signal for miles and miles wasn't necessarily a good thing.

"How tight is it?" Cole whispered, and the elf grinned.

"Like a water drain," he answered. "They didn't bother setting up any real countermeasures—why would they, when it's not like they're carrying sensitive files or bank account info or anything like that? It's just their communications and their alarms and that's it." Even in the dusk, his eyes gleamed as he hit one last key. "And now they're all mine."

"Nice." Cole patted him on the shoulder, then glanced down to a spot at the foot of the mesa and nodded. He wasn't entirely sure his signal had been seen until a second later, when he heard the rumble of an engine. Before he'd had time to blink twice, a large, dark-clad figure on something like a motorcycle mixed with a small tank went barreling up the path onto the mesa—and headed straight for the NAN encampment.

"Hazard alert!" Hazard bellowed at the top of her lungs, the sound reverberating against the other peaks and cliffs surrounding them and echoing out over the valleys. "Drop your weapons, hand over your valuables, and cover your heads, 'cause I ain't leavin' empty-handed!"

Figures were erupting from the NAN's tents and vans, most of them also dressed dark and all of them carrying weapons. From his vantage point, Cole could see that they weren't fully conscious yet, blinking away sleep as they scanned the area, watching Hazard's charge, but also wary in case this was a diversion.

They had no idea what was coming next. But Cole did.

The NAN men didn't fire at the rapidly approaching troll, because why should they? She was on one side of the wind-wall, they were on the other, and if she kept going she'd just be driving to her death.

Except that, watching from his perch, Cole was tensed and ready. "Now!" he barked over his shoulder as Hazard closed to within fifteen meters of the wall.

And the shaman opened his eyes, the orbs glowing a pale white that was startlingly bright against the twilight sky, and cried out in a language that some part of Cole almost seemed to understand—

—and down below, a section of the wind-wall peeled away like a curtain being pulled back. Not a very big section, perhaps three meters by three meters.

The section directly in front of Hazard's bike.

With a growl that could send hardened combat vets running for their mommies, Hazard roared into the encampment. Most of the NAN men froze at the sight of this towering, horned, tusked figure racing toward them on a massive old-fashioned motorcycle, a strange-looking axe held high in one hand. After a few seconds some of them remembered themselves enough to raise their guns—

"Hit it!" Cole ordered. And, beside him, Alaric nodded and, with a little cackle of delight, pressed *Enter*.

Instantly every light and alarm in the encampment went wild. Spotlights zigzagged crazily about the mesa, flashing lights erupted at the corners and by some of the tents, klaxons blared out their harsh cry, and even automated messages shouted various instructions and commands from speakers placed around the perimeter. It was dizzying and deafening and blinding and bewildering, and the men spun about, trying to make sense of it all—

—and then Hazard was upon them.

She scattered the men like they were bowling pins, sending them flying every which way. Even though she'd already hit the brakes, her own momentum carried her past the first wave, but she wheeled around and gunned the engine again, sending her smashing into the second wave just emerging from the largest tent. She had yet to fire her shotgun or use its blade, but so far it hadn't been necessary. Just using her fists and feet and the Valkyrie's body and wheels was proving to be enough.

"Goyathlay," Cole called to the shaman behind him. "Get their attention."

The shaman didn't show any signs of having heard, but his chanting increased in both pace and volume. Down below, the wind-wall shuddered, whole swaths of it flickering in and out of existence. Several figures, men and women, came running from a smaller tent set back toward the mesa's far edge, hands raised and shouts in some other language emerging from their lips, though Cole could barely hear them through the cacophony. He knew who they were and what they were doing, though.

"Time to go," he declared, clapping Doc on the shoulder. The dwarf swallowed, for once looking more nervous than nettled, but he rose to his feet and joined Cole by the edge. Peering down, Cole lifted the new toy Doc had made for him, sighted carefully along it, then pulled the trigger.

His magnetic grapple shot forward, the rope trailing behind it as it flew straight and true, slicing down at an angle that took it just above the unstable wind-wall before plunking hard against the side of one of the NAN vans. Cole quickly anchored his end around the cluster of rocks behind him. Once that was secure he tugged the line once, twice, putting all his weight into the pull, but the grapple was good and firm.

"All right," he said, stepping back so Doc could wrap the loop around his hands. "Remember what I said."

"Yeah yeah, I got it." The dwarf gasped once, twice, then took two big steps forward and flung himself off the peak. His motion propelled the loop down the rope, and he slid rapidly along its length, keeping his legs together and up just as Cole had told him, and passing right over the wind-wall. Cole could see his friend's terrified expression, the wide, staring eyes and the gaping mouth, and also the way Doc's grip was white-knuckled on that loop. He worried that Doc wouldn't be able to make himself let go in time, but when the dwarf was only a meter or two from the van he apparently remembered himself enough to pry his hands loose. He dropped to the ground, a fall of only a couple meters, and a second later he stood and waved back up at Cole.

One down.

"Keep 'em busy," Cole told Alaric and Goyathlay before grabbing the second loop and taking a deep breath. He'd done slides like this plenty of times before, of course, but he still got that same burst of mingled terror and delight as he committed himself to the air's embrace and let himself fall with only the grapple and the rope and his own hand strength keeping his controlled plummet from becoming a disastrous and most likely fatal drop.

Then he was airborne, and he forgot to worry as the rushing air stole his breath from him and left his eyes watering and his ears ringing, the ground leaping quickly up to meet him.

Old habit made Cole keep his legs up properly, just skimming over the wind-wall, and he blinked away the tears so he could see the van and judge his approach. When he had only seconds left he let go, dropping his legs and bending his knees so he landed in an easy crouch.

"Show-off," Doc muttered beside him, but Cole could hear the relief in his old friend's gruff voice.

Cole looked around. Everywhere he turned, it was utter chaos. The NAN shamans were desperately trying to keep the wind-wall up, but of course it was nearly always easier to disrupt something than to maintain it. Goyathlay didn't care if they knew he was here, so he didn't have to worry about trying to be subtle—he was punching at the barrier with all his might, making it ripple and flicker and crumble and stall at random across its length and forcing the other shamans to keep shifting their attention back and forth trying to contain the damage. Alaric was evidently still in control of the security systems, which were blinking and blaring and flickering and occasionally shutting down completely, leaving sections of the small encampment pitch-black and dead silent for just long enough that the NAN agents would breathe a sigh of relief—right before everything started back up again. Hazard was smashing into everyone and everything she could find, keeping all the security men busy. They were shooting back now, but her natural armor and heavy leathers were enough to block most of that, and she was using other NAN as shields from the rest.

Which left Doc and Cole free to sneak across the mesa, toward a smaller tent set beside the one the shamans had been using. This one was made of a nicer material, with a silky sheen to it. The kind of tent a leader might have for herself.

And for her prize.

Cole had his pistol out and ready as he slid the tent flap open and peeked inside, but after a second he lowered the gun. "Empty," he told Doc, not bothering to whisper. It wasn't like anyone else could pick out their voices in all this tumult.

They both stepped through the opening and scanned the interior. It was clearly set up for one person, with an inflatable bed, folding desk and chair, and portable cooler. The walls were just fabric and the floor was the mesa's surface, so Cole didn't bother worrying about hidden safes. Instead he headed straight for the desk, pushing papers and maps aside, looking for a lockbox, a jewelry case, anything that could hold what he sought—

—and unearthing instead a large golden disc on a chain, with a ruby wedge set at its center like a great big red eye.

An eye that suddenly looked all too familiar.

"Careful," Doc warned, but Cole wasn't listening. He reached down and grasped the amulet, raising it up to eye level. There was a scrap of paper stuck to it, and he recognized the words scribed there, for they were ones he had recited before, what felt like a lifetime ago. "I possess the amulet," he found himself repeating again, though this time in a whisper. "Here it lies in my hand. *Kichisi Igluhica.*"

—and he gasped, staggering from the tent into the cool night air as a haze of red washed over him, filling his mind.

And then clearing away, leaving other images in its place.

# TWENTY-EIGHT

Cole fell to his knees, eyes wide, mouth open but no sound emerging, staring at the scene before him.

He was in a small cluster of buildings, all made from the same reddish clay as the ground they stood upon, all rough-hewn squares, boxy and plain but with colorful woven rugs hanging over doors and windows. There were people—more people in one place than he'd seen anywhere outside of Denver—but they weren't penned in or just standing about. They were busy, these people. Doing things. Lots of things. Some were working with their hands, beading or carving or crafting. Others were preparing food, great quantities of food, enough to feed the entire assemblage. Others were toting bedclothes and clothing in and out in large, woven baskets, some of it dirty and disheveled, some of it clean and neatly folded. Some were writing, or typing on computers. And a handful were teaching, instructing the crowd's collection of small children, who were all gathered together off to one corner.

Small children like him.

Cole knew he was one of them. He was on eye level with the other children, but in the vision it didn't feel like he was kneeling, he was simply standing on his own two feet. Even more than the question of height and perspective, however, there was an overwhelming sense of belonging. This was who he was. It was where he belonged.

It was a place and a scene Cole had never seen before. Yet it felt right, and in his heart he knew at once that it was real and true.

This was his past. The past he'd always wondered about. The past that had been nothing but a blank gray fog since the time he'd awakened on Doc's table.

This was his memory, his early life, finally coming back to him.

The scene shifted, changed. It was like watching a film in fast-forward—Cole saw the people blurring into motion, saw everyone moving at high speed, saw the surroundings change little by little, those alterations that naturally occur over years, but are so small and so incremental you barely even notice as they happen. He could see them now, taking place from start to finish: new walls going up here and there, rooms being repainted, tapestries being replaced. At one point the setting changed completely, from the adobe walls he'd first seen to more utilitarian ones of plain wood and bare metal siding. The decorations vanished, the beaded curtains and tapestries and painted vases and other signs of love and home replaced with bulletin boards and ugly posters and a prominent American flag. Everyone growing older, the elders becoming more stooped and gray, the adults growing more seamed, the children sprouting into young adults themselves.

He could feel himself growing with them. This was an abbreviation of all his youth at once, a visual conglomeration of his childhood compressed into a single rapid stream of overlapping images. It was like his brain was giving him a shorthand version of his early life, letting him get a sense of it without bogging him down by immersing him in twenty years of memories from start to finish.

Because that was how much time had passed by the time the scene slowed again, he knew. Twenty years.

Now he stood in front of many of those same people, and others who had appeared when the relocation happened. Before, Cole had simply been one of them, mixed in with the rest, barely noticed as a child except for those assigned to care for him and the others. But now they were all turned toward him, all watching him. Everyone was listening to what he had to say.

Cole couldn't hear himself. He couldn't feel his mouth moving. There were sounds, but they were blurred, indistinct, like he was listening through a heavy filter, and possibly at the wrong speed. He could feel the passion pouring out of him, however. He could feel the intensity that was keeping every gaze glued to him, that was making the entire crowd nod along, that was causing many of them to shout and cheer in reply.

And then came the violence.

It hit like a thunderclap, jolting everything into motion. Still the same place, the same scene, but now everyone was charging toward tall chain-link fences erected around the edges. Fences that were clearly electrified.

Except that, as they ran toward the fences, storm clouds gathered overhead. And then lightning lanced down, striking the fenceposts. Overloading their circuits. Sparks flew in a wide cascade like a spray of glowing water, and when they faded the fence was smoking and blackened. Dead.

The people raced to it and torn down the now-powerless links, pulling them aside and pouring out into the lands beyond.

A handful of guards tried to stop them, but they were like a collection of twigs before a flood. They were washed away by the living tide, bowled over by the sheer number of people pushing past, and most went down without a single shot fired or blow leveled.

Cole felt the exhilaration coursing through him as he led the way. He had caused this, he knew. He had orchestrated it, had set it in motion. And even more than that, he had been one of those who had summoned the storm and called down the lightning.

Somehow, that had been him.

More scenes flickered past—Cole and the rest of the crowd spilling out of that prison or camp or whatever it had been, dispersing into the countryside, only to regather later, small groups slowly trickling into several locations they had already selected. He saw himself meeting with others, mostly men and women far older than him, but who listened to him nonetheless as they pored over maps and charts and made plans.

Then Cole was up on a stage. Glancing down, he saw that he was dressed well, in full tribal regalia. In the manner of a great chieftain. Looking up again, he saw cameras pointed at him, and knew his speech was about to be broadcast all over the country, even the world. Again, he could not hear the words, did not know what he was saying, but he knew that it was major. World-changing. He knew everyone was paying attention, and that what he was doing now would alter things forever.

That merged into a similar scene. He was still on stage, though it felt different. Before, there had been a sensation of hope, of great promise, of reclaiming something long lost. Now the tone was far sharper, angrier, and more bitter. The faces around him were closed and filled with rage, but not aimed at him. No, their fury was directed outward, as was his. And this time his attire, his face paint were not that of a chieftain but of a war chief, one gearing up for combat. This, he knew, was the eve of a great war, and he was about to fire the first shot.

More fighting flickered before his eyes after that. Scene after scene of battle upon battle, himself and many others—all of them Native American, he realized belatedly, as they had been from the start—fighting men and women dressed in the uniforms of the U.S. military branches.

And losing.

They were outnumbered, he knew. Outmanned. Outgunned. And outpositioned. The United States had the forces to simply surround them wherever they appeared and then close in, tightening each deadly circle until nothing within was left alive.

If they were going to survive, much less win, they needed to change the nature of the battle, level the playing field, upend the board.

And Cole evidently had a way to do that.

Now the scenes he saw were familiar ones, the same ones he had been living in his dreams since the heist in Denver: the mountaintop, the wind, the great red eye, the struggle in midair, the pain in his chest, the cave. Only this time he finally saw the end of that titanic clash.

This time he was there as his hands tightened around the creature, even as his mind lashed out and enveloped the eye, binding it in chains of magic and sheer will, trapping it and stripping its defenses away until, finally, there in the dark, it bowed and dwindled and submitted.

He emerged from the cave triumphant, the red eye clenched in one fist and held high over his head, its form now coalesced into a gleaming red crystal shaped like a wedge.

An all-too-familiar wedge.

Cole saw the elders approach, awed by what he had done. The one in the center held forth a golden disc that had been prepared, and Cole accepted it from him. He pressed the red crystal into its center, and the gold melted away and then reformed around it, so it was as if the crystal had always been a part of the amulet. Tiny words glowed around the wedge, further fixing it in place and slaving its powers to the talisman as a whole and to the man who wielded it.

The man who now placed that amulet around his neck and then led the elders and the rest of the shamans on a great circuit, visiting place after place, four corners of a massive square. And at each one he confronted an element and bent it to his will, and at each one he and the shamans prayed and performed an elaborate ritual.

Finally they reached the last corner, the final destination, a great flat mesa overlooking a wide valley. They performed the ritual one final time, and the earth itself answered their plea. It fountained and split and erupted, not here but elsewhere, in many places all at once, hot lava and steam billowing up from below as the earth trumpeted its rage at the way its people had been mistreated.

Now Cole saw himself, at the head of his pack of shamans, meeting with other men. Military men and politicians. They were sitting at a long table, and they were discussing how to put this horrible conflict behind them. A document was drawn up, a treaty, and it was passed around so each man in turn could sign it. Cole signed last, and watched as his hand took the pen and scribed his name onto the bottom of the paper. A name he knew all too well, and now recognized as his own. A name that had haunted this job, this journey, from its very beginning.

The name Daniel Howling Coyote.

He remembered, now.

He remembered it all.

The Ondian reservation where he had been born and raised. The Abilene re-education camp where he had grown to adulthood and come into his power and led his people to break out. The broadcast where he had announced the formation of the Native American Nations, and the later one where he had formally declared war on the United States of America. The battles between the two nations. Realizing that they could not win as they were, and setting out to find an ancient legend, an air spirit of immense power. Battling the creature and finally subduing it, binding it into the amulet so he could control it properly. Using its power to aid him and his shamans as they enacted the Great Ghost Dance, causing the volcanoes to erupt and finally cowing the United States into suing for peace. The Treaty of Denver, which ceded vast tracts of land to the NAN. The time on the NAN's Sovereign Tribal Council after that, and the great sense of betrayal when first Aztlan, and then Tír Tairngire seceded to form their own separate nations. Stepping down himself and disappearing from public life—and hiding the amulet so that no one else could ever make use of its powers to tear the world apart as he had.

He was Daniel Howling Coyote. The amulet was his. It had always been his. And now it was his once more.

Footsteps roused him from his stupor, cutting through the haze of memories that had overwhelmed him. Sharp footsteps, not at all like Doc's clumping or the booted thud of military men. Cole—he still felt a connection to that name, even though he knew it was not his real one—glanced up and found himself staring at a woman with glossy black hair and sharp features.

The NAN woman he'd spoken to on the phone.

The one who had ordered the job to steal the amulet, and then had sicced her sniper and thugs on Cole and his team once they'd had it.

The woman responsible for all this.

He glared at her as best he could, considering he was still half-dazed, and she smiled in response. It was not a pleasant smile, more like the baring of a knife.

"Welcome back," she said, her words just as clipped as they had been on the phone. "We wondered how long it would take you to figure it all out, if you even would." Her smile widened, and her eyes glittered, once again reminding Cole of a great bird about to pounce. "Not that it matters now. We already have everything we need."

# TWENTY-NINE

Cole stared at her. "Who the hell are you?" he demanded. "And what do you want from me?"

Her smile slipped, her lips dipping into a narrow line he suspected was her default expression, much like one of the women who'd taught him English at that re-education camp back in his youth. His youth! His brain still reeled from the sudden unleashing of all those years of memories, all dropping down on him at once like a tidal wave. He forced that back for now, focusing on his present predicament instead.

"I'm sorry," she was saying in that tone that declared she was anything but. "We haven't been formally introduced yet. I'm Nita Ayelen. And you are—"

"Daniel Howling Coyote," he finished for her. "Yes, I know."

To his surprise, she burst out laughing, so hard she nearly doubled over. When she finally straightened, struggling to breathe, there were tears streaming down her face.

"Oh, thank you for that," she managed between choked gasps. "I needed that. Daniel Howling Coyote! Ha! What are you, eighty-one? My, you look good for your age!"

She was right, Cole realized. That didn't make any sense. There was no way he was that old. But he had not just seen the famous man's life, he'd experienced it firsthand. So if he wasn't Daniel Howling Coyote, who was he?

Maybe that didn't matter right now. There were more important questions to be asked at this particular juncture. Like the one he threw at the woman now: "What do you want?"

"Well, for starters," she said, closing some of the gap between them until she was only a few meters away, "I'd like our amulet back, please."

"Yours?" Cole couldn't help it—he laughed at that, at her presumption and her claim, and her apparent calm now that she'd recovered from her laughing fit. "This isn't yours." He held the amulet aloft, dangling it between them on its leather cord. "If anything, it's mine."

"Yours?" She considered that for barely an instant before shaking her head. "No. It was Daniel Howling Coyote's once, but he set it aside, which meant it reverted to the Ute, and thus to the Pueblo Corporate Council. It has never been Cole Danvers's, and never will be. It is ours, and we'd like it back. Now." The last word came out like a spear, so pointed it nearly ran him through, and between that and the narrowing of her already pinched gaze Cole could see that she was rapidly losing what little patience she possessed.

But he wasn't done yet.

"Back off," he warned, pulling the amulet closer to him. "Back off, and tell your men to stand down."

That was when Cole noticed the silence. At first, he'd thought the security teams were all still busy fighting Hazard, or trying to shut down Alaric's digital deviltry, or backing the shamans up against Goyathlay, but it had finally dawned on him that the world around him had gone too quiet, too still for that much chaos to still be occurring.

A quick glance around had confirmed it. The wind-wall appeared to have stabilized again, its surface providing a smooth expanse of rippling, shimmering air that effectively hazed out the world beyond. The klaxons and lights and sirens had all ceased, leaving the camp almost eerily silent and still after all that sensory disruption. Regular voices and footfalls sounding strangely flat and muted by comparison. A small cluster of soldiers stood off to one side around a small, slumped figure, and between their boots Cole could just make out the tufts of hair sticking out beneath the edges of the figure's helmet. Doc. A larger group had gathered near the front of the camp, and Cole could hear groans and growls but no screams—given the men's posture, backs straight, weapons raised and trained on a fixed point, he was guessing they'd managed to subdue Hazard as well, or at least force her to surrender. Even a troll couldn't stand against a dozen high-powered assault rifles, and Hazard was too smart to throw herself against such odds.

So Cole was probably on his own, and surrounded by the enemy. His only way out was to bargain for his freedom—and to do that he had to have some sort of leverage on them. But what? "Back off or else."

"Or else what?" Her voice had gone velvety smooth, which was even more alarming than her usual sharp-edged manner because the edge was still there. It was just coated now, like a blade dipped in poison.

Cole hadn't really thought that threat through, but now it came to him. "Or else I'll break it," he finished, wrapping his other hand around the amulet. "You need it, you came all this way for it, did all this for it—killed my friends for it. Back off or I'll grind it under my boot. Good luck using it then." Because they did mean to use it, he suddenly realized. Not display it or sell it or lock it away or award it as a medal—they'd gone too far, done too much for any of that. He flashed back to what Rodrick had said when he'd looked at the talisman back in that café, about how it had immense power. And his dreams—his memories—had confirmed that, had even shown him the kind of power it possessed, the air spirit bound into the red ruby that had been its eye. That was why they wanted the amulet: to harness that power, to control that spirit.

But in order to do that, they'd need the amulet intact.

Nita Ayelen didn't look terribly concerned, however. "You wouldn't really do that," she said, still in that slippery tone. She edged a few steps closer. "Would you? After all, it's a national treasure. Daniel Howling Coyote created it, wore it, used it. How could you possibly destroy something that valuable, that historically significant?"

"I can and I will," Cole insisted. His fingers tightened around the amulet, its dulled edge biting into his skin. "Try me and see."

She studied him for a second with those dark, glittering eyes before finally nodding. "Yes, I think maybe you would," she admitted softly. Then, surprisingly, she smiled. "Go ahead."

Now it was his turn to stare. "What?"

"Go ahead," she repeated. "Destroy it. Grind it to dust if you like." She laughed, and it was like shattering glass, shrill and taut and jangling. "It isn't real anyway."

He glared at her, trying to figure out what game she was playing. "What're you talking about?" he demanded. "Of course it's real. I know what I stole."

"Do you?" Her smile had morphed into a wide, nasty grin. "Then look at it. Take a good, long look. Make sure you're right and I'm wrong. Go ahead. I won't try anything."

Not trusting her, Cole shifted his hand and his head so he was holding the amulet between the two of them. Then, trying to keep one eye on her past the metal disc, he trained the other on the talisman he clutched so desperately.

It was the same golden disc, the same red ruby wedge, the same leather thong. Everything about it looked right.

Except—

He remembered when he'd held it before, the zing it had sent into his hand, up his arm, straight to his chest. That thrill, that jolt, wasn't there.

And neither was something else, he realized. The real talisman had text etched minutely around the crystal. This one did not.

It was a fake.

But how was that possible? "I know what I stole!" he shouted at Nita Ayelen, lowering the fake amulet so he could glare at her directly. "It was the real deal!"

"Was it?" She widened her eyes in pretend shock. "Oh, no! Whatever could have happened to it? Wherever could it be?"

This time he did hurl the amulet at her, straight at her head. "What kind of sick game are you playing?" he demanded.

She didn't even flinch, didn't look away, but her hand flashed up and snagged the flung fake out of the air, those long, blood-red nails closing around it like a spider enveloping its prey. "This is no game, Mister Danvers," she replied, all levity stricken once again from face and voice. "This is deadly serious. And I'm afraid we still need one more thing from you."

Cole heard something behind him, and twisted to see what it was. But he was too late. A shadow rose behind him, a shadow clutching something in one hand, and then that hand fell with terrifying swiftness. Pain exploded through Cole's head, and he slumped, the soft cottony veil of unconsciousness once again rushing in to surround him. He didn't even feel it when he hit the ground.

# THIRTY

"Uh... What...?"

Cole's first, muddled thought upon waking was *at least I didn't have any of those weird-ass dreams again, the ones about the wind and the eye and me.*

Then he remembered that they hadn't been dreams at all, but memories. And now he had all those memories back, so his brain probably didn't need to keep feeding those images to him masked as dreams. The time for his head to be clever with him was apparently over.

But the time for it to hurt like hell had clearly just started.

"Ah!" A sharp, searing pain lanced down through his forehead, like he'd been stabbed there with a long, sharp blade. His eyes popped open of their own accord, desperately searching for the source of that agony.

Nothing was stabbing him in the head except for a piercingly bright light that made his eyes water even when he glanced to the side. He tried to turn his head, but couldn't. A strap of some sort was cutting into his forehead—maybe that had been the source of the pain?—and another was tight around his chin, holding him firmly in place.

Next he tried to lift a hand to adjust or remove those straps, but found his wrists and upper arms bound as well.

So were his ankles, thighs, shoulders, and waist.

In short, he was trussed up like a Christmas turkey about to be carved. Which wasn't exactly a reassuring comparison.

"Ah, you're awake," a voice noted, and then a face swam into view. It was between him and the light, which at least gave Cole some relief from that blinding illumination. As a result he couldn't see too much of the man clearly, but enough to tell that he was male, Native American, older, clean-shaven—and wearing what looked like a smock of some sort, pale blue and high in the collar, and a matching skullcap that came down over most of his forehead. Something dangled about the man's neck; Cole guessed it was a face mask waiting to be tugged into place and tied securely.

The fact that he was obviously facing some sort of surgeon and was bound to what could easily be an operating table made him even less happy about his current accommodations.

"What the hell's goin' on?" Cole demanded, his words fuzzy as they emerged from lips and mouth and tongue that still weren't entirely functional. "Who're you?" It occurred to him that he was asking those two questions a lot lately, a clear sign that he needed to be better informed before diving into such situations. He'd keep that in mind in future—provided he had a future.

The man smiled. "Marcus Twinfeather, at your service," he answered, sketching a little bow. His tone was far less acidic than Nita Ayelen's had been, though that was certainly a low bar. But he sounded almost friendly, and Cole figured he could work with that.

"You're a doctor?" he asked, forming the words slowly so they'd be clear. His head still rang from where he'd been struck, and jolts of pain lanced through his chest as well. Evidently all the activity had exacerbated the bullet lodged there, and he tried to slow his breathing and calm his pulse in the hope that would help.

"I am," Marcus Twinfeather replied. "A surgeon, to precise. Thoracic."

"Thoracic?" Cole frowned, then winced as the motion caused the straps to pull painfully at his skin. "That's the chest, right? So, what, you're going to take this bullet out?" That didn't make much sense to him, even though his head was finally starting to clear. They'd shot at him before. It was their fault the bullet was even there against his heart, and now they wanted to remove it? The only reason to do that would be to keep him healthy, and Nita had claimed she already had everything she needed.

Unless, he realized with a fresh splash of fear like cold water in the face, kicking his brain into overdrive, part of what she'd needed was *him*. Daniel Howling Coyote, back and aware with all his memories intact—even if she was right and that didn't make any sense, somehow it still seemed to be the case. And now that she had him, she wanted him to survive long enough for her to use him in whatever she had planned.

Marcus was smiling above him. "Yes, something like that," the doctor agreed easily, reaching to his own neck with both hands and raising the face mask. "And I suppose we'd better get started. I'm told time is of the essence here."

"Really? Why?" Cole asked quickly, hoping to stall until he could figure something out. He had just realized that his arms were only secured at the shoulders, biceps, and wrists.

But his arms extended. Apparently they hadn't remembered that. He might be able to push his hands free. If he could, he had enough reach that he could loop his arms around and undo some of these straps. And if he could get free, this would be a whole different situation.

He couldn't do that with Dr. Marcus Twinfeather looming over him, though. And although he couldn't see anyone else, Cole had to assume there was at least one guard standing watch nearby, if not more. Nita had proven that she wasn't about to be that careless.

Although he and his team had still managed to break into this little enclave, Cole realized. That seemed out of character for her. Though perhaps she'd just underestimated them—like she had when she'd sent her sniper to take everyone out before, and he had gotten away.

Or, no, not gotten away, he admitted. Been caught. And about to be killed before he was saved—by a freak thunderstorm.

And lightning that had conveniently taken out the men attacking him.

A new hope leaped into his head. If that had happened once, maybe it could again?

But there hadn't been any lightning when they'd fallen into the pit. Or when the Huns had cornered them. Or during that flash flood. Or earlier tonight—assuming it was still night, though he guessed it was because it didn't feel like he'd been unconscious that long—when he'd faced off against Nita.

So, if the lightning hadn't been a weird coincidence, what was the difference between then and all those other times?

He'd been holding the amulet then, he realized. And not since. Not even earlier, since that had proven to be a fake.

Why even have a fake amulet, though? That didn't make any sense. Even if they'd known Cole was coming to try stealing it back, why not just beef up their security so he couldn't get in? Why lure him in with a fake?

Unless they'd needed him to grab it, thinking it was real, to spark his memories back into place. The words, too—they'd left those there deliberately, hoping he would be stupid enough to recite them again. Which he had. And it had clearly worked—and had left him here, strapped to this table.

"I'm sorry," the doctor was saying, and Cole forced his attention back to the man, who now had on gloves as well. "Normally I'd have knocked you out, of course, but I was told that you couldn't have any sort of anesthetic. Ms. Ayelen worried it might mess up your bloodstream, with . . . unpredictable results." The doctor's hands rose, one holding a wad of cloth, the other what looked like a soft sponge. The sponge descended to Cole's chest, and only now did he realize he'd been stripped to the waist, and the bandages Doc had affixed over his chest wound were gone as well. Even though he still wasn't fully awake, Cole felt the cold dampness of the sponge touching his skin, raising goosebumps as the doctor carefully, even gently washed away the last traces of dried blood around the still-healing wound. Next came the cloth, drying the area with a feather touch.

"You've got a light hand," Cole said, forcing a smile. "Guess I'm lucky to get such a good doctor."

Above him, Marcus Twinfeather chuckled, the sound distorted through his mask. "Thank you. I try." He poked gently at Cole's wound, and his brow furrowed slightly, dragging the skullcap lower over his eyes. "Are these staples? I'd have used thread, though I suppose these can withstand more activity."

"Doc likes staples," Cole agreed, letting his head sag back against the table for a second. That eased the pressure from the forehead strap, which felt like a breath of cool air wafting across his face.

Or, no, that *was* actually a breeze that had snuck in through the tent flaps. Either way, it felt nice, and he tried concentrating on that. He suspected it would be the last pleasant sensation he'd have for a long while.

"I'm going to have to remove these, I'm afraid. It won't feel good, but I'll try to get it over quickly." The doctor did sound genuinely contrite, and Cole felt a little bad that such a kind man should be forced to do such horrible things. Especially to him.

Marcus turned away for a second, allowing more of the breeze to reach Cole and ruffle his hair. Cole closed his eyes, escaping the bright light of the operating lamp, and relaxed as much as he could, enjoying the touch of the breeze on his face and chest. Now that he thought about it, he could actually hear the wind whipping up outside. Too bad he was stuck inside this stuffy tent!

When the doctor returned, he held what looked like a pair of needle-nosed pliers, only with the tips flattened out like thin screwdrivers. "Sorry about this," he muttered as he leaned over Cole again.

Cole grimaced when he felt the cold metal touch his chest, and couldn't hold back a quick yelp of pain as they dug into his skin in order to push under the first staple. Then the doctor squeezed the pliers shut and, with a quick twist and a yank, pulled that staple free. The pain from that was a flash, sharper than before but over quickly, and Cole struggled for breath as Marcus turned to drop the staple into a small metal bowl nearby. "One down, seven to go," Cole heard him mutter as he returned to the task, and steeled himself for the repeated bursts he knew would follow.

In an effort to distract himself from the pain, Cole focused on what he could hear happening outside. There was a howling somewhere beyond the tent, and after a second he recognized it as the cry of a strong gust through narrow valleys and sharp peaks. There was a taste to the air as well, he now noticed—a sharp tang overlaid with a thick moistness like a live wire in the midst of a fog.

A storm was coming.

Marcus pulled the last staple free with a grunt of satisfaction, and set both it and the pliers aside.

"Now comes the worst part, I'm afraid," he warned as he yet again stepped away to gather new equipment. When he slid back into Cole's view, he was holding a scalpel in one hand—and a pair of small metal forceps in the other. Cole had seen forceps before, at Doc's and elsewhere, but these looked particularly wicked, with long gleaming sides that flared out at the hinge before arcing back in to meet in a pair of sharp, saw-toothed, claw-like tines.

"L-Look," Cole stammered, struggling now to pull his wrists free and cursing himself for not trying sooner, doctor and guards be damned. "You don't have to do this!"

That at least made Marcus pull back for a second, eyes widening slightly. "Of course I do," he replied, and although he still sounded apologetic, he also sounded resolved. "It's necessary, I'm afraid. You'll understand later."

And he reached down with the scalpel and quickly, cleanly cut Cole's wound back open, the razor-sharp blade parting the flesh so easily Cole only felt the burn a second after it was done.

Despite the doctor's comment about "later," suggesting that they did indeed want to keep Cole alive, he was not reassured. Instead he resumed his struggles, though his thrashing didn't seem have much effect beyond tiring him out and chafing his skin where the straps rubbed against him. But he wasn't about to give up, especially since Marcus was now approaching him with the forceps.

"I really do need you to stay still for this," the doctor advised. "I'd hate to nick your heart in the process." When Cole didn't stop, Marcus sighed and raised his hand, beckoning to someone just out of view. A second later, a big man in dark clothes stepped up to the other side of the table.

"Hold him down, please," Marcus requested, and with a grunt the soldier slung his rifle back over his shoulder and brought both heavy arms down onto Cole's chest, one above the wound and one below. The added weight, and the guard's strength, were more than enough to lock Cole in place.

"Try not to think about it," the doctor advised as he leaned in, absently adjusting the light so it was pointing straight at Cole's wound. "I'll be as quick as I can."

And then he stabbed the forceps down into Cole's chest.

"*AAAHH!*" Cole couldn't help it—he screamed. It felt like someone had torn his chest apart with their bare hands and then shoved a burning-hot poker into the wound, setting every nerve ending aflame with agony. Tears burst from his eyes and sweat from his forehead as he bucked uncontrollably, his whole body spasming against the pain racing through it, centered in the spike against his heart.

And then the tent blew away.

For a second, amid the screams and shouts of the doctor and the guard and the noise of the wind and the sudden sheet of water pouring down on him, Cole didn't understand what had happened. Then he blinked past Marcus and the guard and the light and saw stars up above, visible even through the heavy gray clouds overhead, and understood.

The storm had struck. And its winds must have increased to hurricane levels, because they had slammed through the enclave despite its protective wall, battering everything in sight—and tearing tents clean off their stakes and moorings, carrying them out into the ravines beyond.

Cole and his operation were now exposed to the elements and visible to anyone nearby.

Not surprisingly, the doctor had been stunned by the sudden change in conditions. But now, blinking away water, he turned back to Cole and the guard.

"We need to finish this!" he shouted, gesturing, and the guard—who had taken a step back out of sheer surprise—returned to his previous position.

As did Marcus. And the forceps he wielded, their tips now red with Cole's blood.

Cole screamed again as the stabbing intrusion resumed—and the heavens answered his cries. The thunderclap that rang out was loud enough to blot out all other sound, temporarily deafening him—and then the lightning followed in its wake, so bright its afterimage seared into Cole's eyes, its intense energy sizzling the air all around them and vaporizing every drop of water in the vicinity.

The lightning struck the guard, spearing him through the top of his head, and Cole winced and tried to look away as the man screamed, his skin instantly crisping, his flesh boiling, his eyes bursting from the heat and the pressure. Then he crumpled to the ground, nothing but a smoking corpse.

Immense winds lashed at them, and even as the guard fell a sudden gust lifted Marcus Twinfeather clear off the ground and tossed him aside like a paper airplane thrown against the breeze. Cole twisted around to see the doctor land some twenty feet away, hitting a van with a thud he could feel but not hear, and a part of him hoped the man was only stunned. Despite the agony he'd been inflicting, Cole couldn't find it in himself to hate the man, or wish him ill.

Then he realized that, in watching the doctor's flight, he'd turned to the side. The straps were no longer holding him down—they had apparently been burned away by the lightning's proximity, and now were nothing more than charred leather bits.

He was free.

Staggering to his feet, Cole grabbed a nearby towel and pressed it to his chest, trying to stanch the blood now flowing from the open wound. Then he looked around, peering through the rain, trying to figure a way out of here.

What he saw, instead, was Nita Ayelen, pushing through the rain like she was fighting her way through heavy curtains. Her hair was slicked to her head and her clothes sodden, but she was still unbowed, her eyes as bright and her smile as sharp as ever. It was the person behind her, however, that made Cole pause, and straighten in shock.

Because directly behind the woman, an aura radiating out from him and blocking the rain from penetrating, was a short, stocky figure Cole knew all too well.

Goyathlay Seevers.

"You!" Cole shouted, lurching forward and closing the distance between them so the shaman would hear him. "You did this!" A flash of memory—recent, for a change, not old—stitched itself back together in his head. There'd been a man earlier, someone who'd clubbed him from behind. He'd only seen the shadow then, but now his mind filled in the form to go with it and Cole's scowl deepened. "You knocked me out!"

If he'd thought to embarrass the shaman or make him feel guilty, he failed—Goyathlay only spread his hands wide and nodded. "I did," he admitted, not smirking but not shamefaced either. "It seemed prudent to end the attempted standoff as quickly as possible."

"You never left the PCC, did you?" Cole accused, raising a hand to jab it in the shaman's face.

They were close enough that he could see pain and anger flash across the man's tattooed flesh. "I did," Goyathlay replied, old hurt visible in his eyes. "What I told you was all true. But Ms. Ayelen approached me shortly after your theft, and made me an offer I couldn't refuse."

Cole sighed, some of his anger burned out of him, and swiped water from his eyes. "You set this up," he said to Nita where she stood to the side, watching the showdown. "You planted Goyathlay in our path because you knew we'd need magic with us, and he'd be the perfect choice."

Her smile widened as she nodded, as sharp a gesture as the rest of her movements. "I did. It seemed prudent," she said, echoing the shaman's earlier statement.

"Why?" Cole shouted at her, and thunder rumbled behind him. "What was the point to all this? You had the amulet already, but you set out a fake for me to steal. You were bringing the real one back to Cheyenne, but first you took a tour of Colorado, hitting each corner in turn. You knew I was after you, but you not only let me live, you planted someone in my team to lead me from place to place. And I'm guessing you engineered it so we could break in here tonight, too?" He could see the confirmation of that in her eyes, and the way she lifted her chin triumphantly. "But *why?* Why go to all this trouble? Just to give me back my—Daniel Howling Coyote's—memories? Then what? What the hell are you up to?"

At first she didn't reply, and Cole saw that, all around them, the guards were starting to close in. Off to one side, Dr. Twinfeather was beginning to stir as well. Soon enough they'd have him surrounded again. Then they'd subdue him, and it would be back under the knife once more.

*Well,* Cole, decided, *I've had about enough of* that.

Thunder sounded again, and lightning lit up the sky. Wind tore at their clothes. Rain lashed at their faces.

And Cole smiled. He knew he must look an absolute fright, standing here in nothing but his pants, blood soaking the towel pressed to his chest, shaking and shivering from stress and pain and cold.

But he was done cowering. He was done running. And he was done begging.

"Tell me what is happening here," he insisted, his voice quiet now, and the wind died down as he spoke so everyone could hear him clearly. "The truth. Now."

A bolt of lightning shattered the stone of the mesa directly in front of him, forcing Nita Ayelen and her traitorous pet shaman to jump back.

Cole didn't budge. He just stared them down.

And, after a second of stubbornly meeting his glare, Nita dropped her gaze.

And nodded.

"What," she asked quietly, her usual venom noticeably absent, "do you want to know?"

# THIRTY-ONE

For a second, Cole wasn't even sure how to respond to that. He just blinked at her. Then again. Then, finally, he laughed, loud and long.

"Everything!" he cried when he was done. "Tell me everything!"

Nita Ayelen frowned. "Can you be more specific?"

"Fine." He sighed. "Start at the beginning. Why did I—why did Daniel Howling Coyote—hide the amulet in the first place?"

A cunning look flitted across her face, gone almost before he could register seeing it at all. "You mean you don't remember?"

Cole ground his teeth together. "No."

"Oh. Well, you see—"

His control was clearly increasing, because this time the lightning actually tapped the front toe of her leading foot. But it was a much smaller bolt than before, barely a flicker, so all it did was make her hop backward, clutching her foot and screeching in pain, her hair standing straight out like the rays of the sun.

"The truth," Cole warned. "I won't remind you again."

"All right, all right!" She blinked away tears and slowly, gingerly, set her foot back on the ground again. "He hid it," she started again. "From us."

"From you?"

"Not me personally!" she snapped. "How old do you think I am?"

That brought Cole back to before, when she'd laughed at him. He studied her for a second, frowning. "You said before I wasn't him," he said slowly, his mind racing to figure out how these new bits of information gelled together. "I...he...was born in 1991. It's 2072. If I am him, you're right, I should be eighty-one years old." He raised his hands in front of his face and stared at them. "There's no way I'm that old. But...I remember everything, his whole life. How does that work?"

A familiar sneer settled onto Nita's face. "Oh, well, as to that—"

"No, never mind!" Cole cut her off. She looked far too pleased with herself for him to be happy about whatever she'd been about to say. "Back on track! We're talking about Daniel Howling Coyote. Why did he hide the amulet from you—from the NAN?"

Her sigh made it clear he'd just deprived her of a great deal of fun, but under his stern gaze she finally continued. "He thought it was too dangerous. He didn't trust anyone else to use it properly." Now she was the one clenching her jaw, anger radiating from her like her hair still did, in almost visible waves. "He performed the Great Ghost Dance, but stopped too soon. 'It was just a demonstration of our power,' he said. 'To remind them what we could do to them if we had to. Now they'll have to listen to us. They'll have to negotiate.' Feh!"

"But—they did negotiate," Cole reminded her, surprised at her vehemence. "I remember. That's why we have a treaty at all, because he—I—scared them so much they were willing to give up land in order to end the war."

"Some land, sure," she retorted, stomping past him to the edge of the mesa. "Look at it! Look at what they gave us!" She waved out at the darkness, at what Cole knew was an open range filled with canyons and valleys and ravines and peaks and plateaus. "It's pretty, right? But so what? We can't grow anything on it! We can't dig anything out of it except more useless rock! We can't even live on it! They tricked us! They stuck us with a whole lot of drek land and a little bit of useful space, and washed their hands of us—again! No wonder Aztlan and Tír Tairngire split away from us! They knew we'd been had, and they refused to stand for it anymore! Lots of people wanted to get back at them for that. But not him! Oh, no!" She marched back over and got right in his face, glaring up at him, her dark eyes wide and a little crazed. "Not the great Daniel Howling Coyote! 'Peace requires sacrifice,' he said. 'We can make do with this, in exchange for being allowed to control our own lives.' Hah!"

Cole stepped back a bit, both so he didn't have to feel her hot breath against his chin and so, if she got too out of control, he could hit her with another lightning bolt without frying himself in the process. "So you want to perform the Great Ghost Dance again," he summarized, "and you need the amulet—the real one—to do it?"

Nita controlled herself with visible effort. "That's right," she said, her voice dropping back down to a more normal level, though still with her usual razor edge. "It's like a magical amplifier. It boosts the power of whoever wears it. But it's more than that. Much more."

Cole remembered the red eye in the sky, the focal point of the creature he'd battled long ago. "It's alive, isn't it?"

"It is." She tried to slick her hair back down, to little effect— even with the rain still pelting them, the charge from the lightning still caused it to stick out in crazed spikes. "It's an air spirit, an incredibly powerful one. He fought it, defeated it, and forced it to submit to him. Then he took its heart, its soul, and bound that into the talisman. Anyone with magic can use the amulet to boost their own power, but you have to know the incantation to even awaken the spirit. And then you've got to bind it to your will all over again."

With a sinking feeling in his gut, Cole thought he knew what she was going to say next. But he had to be sure "How do you do that?"

Her smirk had returned. "You retrace the steps Daniel Howling Coyote took when he first attuned the amulet to himself," she answered slowly, clearly enjoying this part. "You visit each of the four corners of this state, and at each one you battle a different element."

Cole thought about their journey, and about the strange encounters they'd faced along the way. "Fire," he said, recalling the doomed town of Dinosaur. "Water," for the flash flood they'd faced in the canyons near Durango. "Earth" was the pit they'd tumbled into, out by Campo. And now they were here, on a mesa up by Sedgwick. "And air."

"Exactly!" Crazed hairdo and all, Nita still preened like a hunting bird that had just delivered a handsome pheasant or a plump hare to its master. "We led you to each location, and you faced down each element, just like he did before. It was perfect."

"Why me, though?" Cole asked, clenching the fist that wasn't still holding the blood-soaked towel to his chest. "You're telling me I'm not him, so why did you need me for any of this? Why not just attune it yourself?"

"You don't think we would have if we could?" Nita all but snarled at him. "We tried! Over and over again! Shamans, warriors, philosophers—it didn't matter! Nobody could get the damned thing to work! We figured it out, of course. It made sense. Howling Coyote didn't trust anyone else with this kind of power, even then. So he made sure nobody else could use it, ever. Not only did he attune it to himself, but he locked that in so it could only *ever* be attuned to him." She grimaced, hands twitching like she wanted something to rake her claws across. "We thought that was it, that we were stuck, that we'd never be able to use it." Then that smirk returned. "Until we found you."

"Found me? What does that mean?" Cole demanded. "Was I lost?" He had been, though. He knew that. He'd been wandering around Denver, unaware of who he really was. In fact, he'd had no idea whatsoever. Not until all this.

But Nita's grin hadn't faded. If anything, it had gotten even wider. "You were wondering how you could be eighty-one years old, weren't you?" she all but purred. If she'd had a tail, it would have been twitching with glee. "You don't look eighty-one. You don't feel eighty-one. Do you know why that is?"

He shook his head, then tensed as she leaned in close and lowered her voice to a whisper, forcing him to bend down to hear her say, "that's because you aren't eighty-one. And do you want to know something else?"

Again he didn't answer, but she knew he couldn't resist. Nor did he. He stayed right where he was as she crooned in his ear, "you are not Daniel Howling Coyote."

"What?" Now he did straighten, lurching away from her, the wind and rain picking up to match his agitation and his confusion. "That doesn't make any sense! You said the amulet didn't work for anyone else! That's why you needed me!" He raised his fist, and lightning danced across the sky. "Could I do this if I wasn't him? Would I remember everything if I wasn't him? No! So why are you lying to me?"

"I'm not, I swear I'm not," she insisted, her tone turning slightly desperate as her eyes flicked toward the sky, as if she'd suddenly remembered that taunting a man who could strike her with lightning was perhaps not the best idea. "You aren't Daniel Howling Coyote. Not really."

"Explain." Thunder punctuated his command, and she flinched.

"We needed him to control the amulet," Nita said quickly, hands up in front of her as if to claim innocence or at least appear weak and deserving of mercy. "But nobody knew where he was, or if he was even still alive. It'd been over thirty years since he disappeared! But then we found the next best thing." Her head dropped, her last words muttered into her chest.

"What?" Cole stomped toward her and grabbed her chin, forcing it up until she had no choice but to meet his eyes. "What. Did. You. Find?"

"Traces of his DNA," she gasped, the words still almost chased away by the howling of the wind. But Cole heard her this time, each word piercing him to the core. "We used it to fertilize an egg, and that gave us you. His son. Kwinaa Howling Coyote. The nurse named you."

"So...you bred me just for this," Cole stated.

She nodded. "We hoped you'd share enough of his DNA to unlock the amulet. But we weren't sure it would work, that you'd be close enough." A smirk formed on her lips again, as if she couldn't stop herself. "So we decided to hedge our bets."

Somehow, he knew what she meant. "His memories," he growled down at her, his fingers tightening on her jaw and eliciting a mewl of pain from her. "You gave me his memories."

"Yes," she managed, reaching up to grasp his fingers but not trying to pry them loose yet. "We still had some of his things, and there were physical traces of him on them. We had our shamans call forth the memories embedded in those pieces, all of Howling Coyote's past still remembered in each cell that had once belonged to his body, and we transferred those to you."

"What. Happened?" Cole asked. He had to resist the urge to squeeze until her jaw cracked, but he forced himself to tamp down the rage building within him. Killing Nita wouldn't get him answers. And he needed to know. All of it. No matter how bad.

Her flinch this time had nothing to do with his hand on her face. "Something went wrong," she admitted softly, looking away from him as best she could. "The process didn't work.

Trying to cram a second person's thoughts into your head—it overloaded you. Caused a feedback loop, blew the equipment. You were wounded pretty severely. Maimed, even. We tried, but we couldn't save you."

Cole thought back to his earliest memory—not Howling Coyote's but his, Cole Danvers's—which was him collapsing on a street somewhere in Denver, barely alive. "So you tossed me out like so much trash," he said, almost spitting the words in her face.

She didn't deny it. "We thought you were dead," she countered. "You were as good as, anyway. And there were... complications. We were doing this off-grid, in borrowed space to avoid attention, and had to clear out in a hurry. There wasn't any time to do a proper clean-up. So, yes, we canned the project and disposed of the evidence."

Now it was Cole's turn to sneer. " 'Disposed of the evidence,'" he mimicked. "What a nice way to say, 'we dumped the body.'" He leaned in so close their foreheads brushed. "But I survived," he growled at her, the words vibrating through them both. "Doc found me, stitched me up, rebuilt me. I lived."

It explained so much, he realized now. How badly messed up he'd been when Doc had found him. Why he couldn't remember anything that had happened to him before that point. And even little things, recent things, like how he'd been able to feel the amulet too, or how Goyathlay had reacted when they'd first met. His face had been badly damaged, he knew, and Doc had been forced to reconstruct parts of it, like his jaw and his cheeks. That had changed his appearance—it was why he didn't look like kin to the portrait he'd found of Howling Coyote. But the shaman had seen the resemblance anyway. Either he'd been told about Cole's true heritage and was looking for it, or he'd simply recognized in him a mangled, twisted relation to the legendary leader.

Either way, he'd survived. Which wasn't anything the NAN had planned.

Except that Nita looked pleased again as she tilted her head up so she could meet his angry gaze. "Yes, you did," she agreed, her tone brisk and businesslike again. "And once we found that out, once we realized exactly who you were, we knew our old plan was back on the table. We just had to put it into motion."

That was one part that still threw Cole. "How did you find out about me?" he asked, releasing his grip on her and pulling back so he could watch her whole face.

"DNA," she said, rubbing at her jaw with one hand. "On one of your recent jobs, you left traces, saliva or sweat or some such. Sloppy." She actually waggled a taloned finger at him like a stern parent correcting a willful child. "It was a partial match to Howling Coyote's, and we still had a standing search order out for him, so it tripped our program as well." She shrugged. "We erased the record, of course, but now we at least knew you were in Denver. Then it was just a matter of time until we found you and sent you after the amulet." Her smile returned. "You have to admit, it's a nice twist, hiring you to steal the amulet your own father once owned—and then hid away so no one else could find it."

"Yeah, swell," Cole muttered. He was still going back over the job itself, all the little bits and pieces that had seemed strange at the time. "Did you tell Mace who I was?" He answered himself before she could. "No, that would've been stupid. He could've held me and the amulet hostage and demanded a lot more money. But you told him to make sure I held onto the amulet, didn't you?" He saw from her expression that he was right. "And he didn't know about the ambush any more than the rest of us—but you did make sure I was the one who read out those words. They activated it, started the attunement process." Nita nodded. "And then you shot me."

Her face twisted into something he thought might be regret. Or maybe it was just irritation. "Yes, we shot you," she agreed. "But Nathan was under strict orders. And he carried them out brilliantly." She nodded at someone else standing nearby, and Cole glanced over to see a familiar figure with long, silvery hair and steel-blue eyes. The sniper nodded and tipped a finger to his head in recognition. "Everyone else got armor-piercing rounds, to make sure even the ork went down fast. You? You got a soft jacket, with just enough oomph to lock up your spine and put you out of commission. Then we just had to bring you back in and carry you around to each location, attune you, and take you through the Great Ghost Dance."

Cole stared at her. "That was your plan?" he asked. "To paralyze me and carry me around like some kind of throw pillow?"

"Not a throw pillow," she corrected. "A holster. A container. You were the setting for the jewel that was the amulet. We needed you to hold it, to attune it—we just didn't need you to be conscious or mobile yourself."

"But something went wrong." He remembered lying there, staring up at Nathan and his goons. "The lightning."

"The lightning," she agreed. "We didn't think you'd be able to control it yet, and you weren't. But it answered your need anyway. And clearly it was going to keep doing so as long as you were still alive—we weren't sure if turning you into a vegetable would even be enough to stop those strikes. So we had to come up with a Plan B." She smirked again—it was clearly her favorite expression. "And that worked perfectly, if I do say so myself."

Cole tried to make sense of that part. "I woke up," he recounted slowly, remembering, "and your people were gone. I'd been stabbed in the chest. Then I blacked out again."

She said nothing, just waiting, clearly eager to see if he could figure it all out on his own.

"Doc told me whatever stabbed me broke off in there. Right up against my heart. He couldn't remove it." Now a cold chill passed over Cole, making him tremble in a way that the incessant rain never could. He stared at her, this woman who had manipulated his life so completely, as a horrible idea dawned on him.

"You said the amulet was a fake," he said. "But that I had to be attuned to the real one. I had to carry it to those places, had to face the elements with it. But I wasn't wearing it. You took it back, your men did, when they knocked me out. But then—"

He lifted the towel from his chest and stared at it, and then at the hole it had been covering up. He couldn't see through the blood and torn flesh, of course, but it felt like he could at least feel inside, feel a jagged shape that shifted with every heartbeat.

A shape much like a crystalline wedge.

Nita's laughter startled him back to himself. "That's right," she crowed, all but dancing with mirth, her eyes alight. "You got it—literally! Since we couldn't drag you from place to place, we had to get you to go there on your own, with the amulet—but we couldn't risk just handing it to you. You might figure out how to control it on your own, and shut us out. So we hid it." She leaned in toward him again, her face as sharp as ever, her grin as nasty. "Inside. We buried it in your chest, and you followed us right down the path like a good little pack mule. And now—g" she all but hissed the words at him, raising her hands to pinch her nails together in front of his eyes like a hungry bird about to peck them out, "—now we just have to cut you open and take it out. Or maybe we'll leave it there, just chop off your hands and feet and tongue and put out your eyes so you won't be any more trouble." She looked like she was ready to start mutilating him herself, right then and there. "You did exactly what we wanted, and now we have the amulet and we have you, too."

Cole enjoyed the way her eyes widened in shock when he laughed in her face. "No," he corrected when he could speak again, realizing he was pushing the edge of hysteria after all he'd been through but managing to find a calm, cool center in the midst of all the craziness. "You have that wrong."

Her brow furrowed, and he wanted to laugh again but held it back, speaking instead in a loud, clear voice, each word punctuated by thunder overhead and by lightning that split the sky:

"*I* have the amulet," he corrected. "And now it's awake— and *so am I*."

And then the storm fell upon the NAN like the angry hand of an enraged god.

# THIRTY-TWO

Many times, on a job, Cole had experienced what he'd heard referred to as "tunnel vision." Now was no different. The world around him faded into the background, a feat made far easier by both the dark of night and the obfuscation of the storm. He knew, in some part of his mind, that there were other people around, and that most of them were not on his side. He vaguely wondered what had happened to his friends, two of whom he'd last seen being held captive right before he'd been knocked out. But even that was secondary to his current focus, the only thing that stood out sharp and clear—the three people directly in front of him.

Nita Ayelen, the instigator of all this chaos and bloodshed. The reason some of his friends were dead, his other friends dead or captive, and his life a shambles.

Mr. Steely-eyed Sniper, AKA Nathan, the man who had shot and killed Lorelei, Rodrick, Tish, and even Mace, and who had been directly responsible for embedding the amulet in Cole's chest.

Goyathlay Seevers, the so-called renegade, the turncoat who had led them here, lying to them the whole way, and then had betrayed them. Had betrayed *him*.

Cole didn't care about anyone else who might be around. But these three? These three had to die.

Something sizzled in front of him, and Cole glanced down briefly to discover that his hands were glowing, his fingers and palms surrounded by crackling energy. The lightning no longer lived solely in the sky—now it apparently resided in him as well.

And that meant he could wield it directly.

"Die!" he shouted, hurling his hand toward the trio. Lightning shot from his fingers, arrowing straight for Nita and forking to target Goyathlay and Nathan as well. It leaped the gap between them, so bright Cole could barely watch its progress, yet he couldn't turn away. Instead he stared, squinting against the glare, as the lightning reached its victims—

—and rebounded, slicing off to the side like a steam of water striking a window. Sparks showered down on the trio, illuminating them in a series of tiny bursts, but none of them appeared hurt.

Then Cole noticed Goyathlay's eyes were glowing, and his lips were in constant motion, muttering something impossible to hear over the tumult. But Cole knew what that meant.

The shaman had blocked his attack.

"Yeah?" Cole shouted, incensed by the idea that these three might somehow escape justice. "You think you can stop me? Do you? Well, stop *this!*"

Leveling both hands at the tattooed man and his two companions, Cole unleashed all the lightning at his command. Bolts shot from his fingers. More, larger bolts crackled down from the sky. The area around them lit as bright as day, brighter, a growing globe of blue-white light that seemed to burn the very air. Cole blinked, glancing away, unable to continue looking.

When he was able to turn back a second later, the trio was gone.

"What?" He stared, checking the ground where they had been standing. But there weren't any ashes there. He hadn't burned them to a crisp, as he'd hoped. Which meant—

—something shifted in his peripheral vision, something narrow and dark and moving rapidly.

Cole threw himself backward, staggering and barely maintaining his balance as a spear arced by, followed by another, and another, and another. Each one barely missed him, and each one vanished after it had flown past—not just lost from sight, swallowed up by the night and the storm, but actually disappeared.

Like they hadn't existed in the first place.

But they had all come from the same direction, and Cole turned to face that way. There, perhaps three meters away, were the hated trio. Still very much alive.

"You possess power, yes," Goyathlay called, his words carrying over the wind and the rain. "More power than any other shaman since Howling Coyote walked among us, and more than all but a few even before that." He shook his head, and Cole couldn't tell if the gesture was sad or sympathetic or mocking. "But you have no skill, no control," the traitorous shaman continued. "You have might, but you cannot wield it to its full extent. Whereas I—" Goyathlay spread his arms wide, and fire sprang up between them in a soaring, dancing arc, "—have spent decades perfecting my skills. And the talented novice is no match for the experienced master."

Then he hurled the sheet of fire directly at Cole's head.

"Holy hell!" Cole flung himself to the ground, the hair on the back of his head crisping as the flames roared directly over him. He lifted his head after a few seconds, half-expecting to find Goyathlay leaning over him, preparing for the kill.

Instead, he saw Goyathlay and Nita arguing. Over him.

"Let me finish him!" the shaman shouted.

"We still need him alive!" she yelled back.

"Why? The talisman is active," Goyathlay answered. "I can feel it."

"Active, yes," she agreed, "But it still only answers to him. We need him, or else the talisman's useless."

She laid a hand on the shaman's arm, and he shook her off. "He is an abomination," he insisted. "Two souls forced into one body. Nothing good can come of allowing him to exist."

"We need him!" was her only reply.

"Gee, do I get a say in all this?" Cole asked, lurching to his feet and stalking toward them, lightning beginning to play about his hands once more. "'Cause if so, I'm gonna vote for 'I live, *you* die!'"

Before he could throw another bolt their way, however, Goyathlay waved a hand, and the air between them began to spin and swirl. It picked up speed, roaring as it gained more momentum, the rain that struck it or neared it sucked into its hungry maw. It was like a tiny sideways tornado, and the shaman had aimed it straight at Cole.

"No, you have no voice here," the traitor declared, sneering at Cole over the wind spout. "And soon your stain will be removed from the earth." The funnel twisted, its pointed end aimed straight at Cole's chest as it rocketed across the mesa toward him.

Cole knew he should run, or duck, or something. But he didn't. Instead he stood up straighter and held both hands out, arms stretched wide. Then, just as the funnel's tip neared him, he chopped down, bringing the bottom edge of both hands crashing down onto the wind spout—

—and shearing through it like was made of cotton.

As his flesh touched the minuscule whirlwind, it shattered, its threads of wind pulling apart and fraying in an instant. Then it was gone, as if it had never existed.

Cole glanced up, met Goyathlay's wide eyes, and grinned.

"Never mind all that!" Nita Ayelen insisted, stepping between the two of them and shoving Goyathlay back behind her. "Get him!" she shouted, pointing at Cole—

—and a dozen heavily armed men stomped out from behind the various vans and Jeeps and tents, raised their heavy assault rifles, and took aim.

Cole didn't know how the shaman had created his little whirlwind, and he didn't have time to experiment. He wasn't even sure how he was doing any of this—Goyathlay was right about one thing, he was operating on pure instinct, powered by the amulet and the spirit it contained. But this was no time to worry about all that. So instead he used what he already knew best, even better than lightning:

Wind.

The tempest that struck the NAN men had all the force of a full-blown hurricane. It lifted them off their feet and flung them back a dozen meters or more, slamming them against trucks and cliffsides and anything else handy. More men were already stepping forward, though, and Cole discovered he apparently only had a certain amount of power within him or the amulet or both at any given time, and that the sudden pocket hurricane had taken everything he had. He was effectively tapped out, at least for a few seconds, maybe more.

And a few seconds was all the time those men needed to fill him full of holes.

So he turned and ran.

He could hear the heavy report of automatic weapons firing behind him, and dove to the ground, crying out as his wound collided with the hard ground, but rolling to the side and popping back to his feet just in time to dive between two parked Jeeps. A hail of bullets tore up the closer of the two vehicles, shredding its soft top and perforating its sides, and

Cole cowered down, hoping the metal frame would give him some protection. Damn it! What was the point in having all this power if he couldn't even use it to swat some stupid thugs?

Suddenly Cole had an idea. A clever, clever idea. He held his hands up in front of him, and could already see the glimmer of magic returning. Another minute, and he'd be able to act again.

Assuming he could last that long.

More gunfire pounded into the Jeep, and Cole ducked down even further, covering his head with both hands. He waited for the sudden lurch of those same bullets tearing into him next, and when that didn't happen, he dared to glance around.

He was still alive.

And, if that feeling like he'd latched onto a live wire was any indication, sending a spasm threading its way up his arms and into his chest, his magic had returned.

Meaning now was the perfect time to turn the tables on the NAN.

Concentrating on his immediate surroundings, Cole waved his right arm around in a tight circle, like he was winding up to punch the next assailant he saw. As he continued the corkscrew motion, Cole heard a whistling, faint at first but growing louder. It took him another second to realize the sound was coming from him—or more precisely, from the air beside him. The same air that was being wound around his right arm like a bolt of heavy cloth or a length of cord.

The same air that Cole unleashed directly against the shattered Jeep, sending the torn-up vehicle slamming and sliding and skidding and scraping across the mesa—directly toward the same men who'd just cut it to pieces.

It was almost as if the damaged vehicle had come to life and was seeking its revenge.

Men dove out of the way as the Jeep hurtled toward them, but several were unable to dodge in time. Cole could almost hear the *squish* of the heavy vehicle squashing those men as it rolled over them, or the screams as it slammed other men off the mesa before following them into empty air itself. The Jeep seemed to hang there for an instant, almost like it were floating, before it plummeted out of view, falling toward the ground far below. Its path left an empty swath right through the NAN camp, and as Cole rose to his feet again, breathing heavily, he studied that space and the madness still swirling around beyond. It seemed he'd taken out many of the guards, at least temporarily. Though he spotted other men and women here and there, there no longer seemed to be a sizeable force of them on hand to attack him.

The problem was the small group of men and women now marching toward him. They didn't carry guns, nor were they dressed in black combat gear the way the security forces had been. These newcomers were more standard clothing, but each of them carried fetishes and staves and wands. Still, it was the glows emanating from their hands, their mouths, their eyes that really gave Cole pause.

Clearly Goyathlay was not the only shaman the NAN had brought along on this trip.

And now all the rest of them were coming straight for him.

# THIRTY-THREE

"Oh, drek," Cole muttered, raising his fists in front of him like he could punch his way out of this. "Here we go."

The shamans stopped several meters away from him, which was good—at least they weren't rushing him physically. But Cole also knew they were spreading out so that he wouldn't be able to target all of them at once.

For a moment that seemed to stretch on, they all stared at each other, this group of NAN mages on the one side, and Cole all by his lonesome on the other.

Then they attacked.

It was just one of them first, a tall, rangy woman with a flowing silver braid. She raised both glowing hands in the air and energy shot out of them in twin beams, aimed directly at his chest. The energy had no real color to it, but it glittered slightly as it soared toward him, like watery arrows or icy spears, clear but glistening.

Cole knew that he wouldn't be able to call wind or lightning fast enough to stop those bolts. But Goyathlay had blocked his attack earlier. Could he do the same here? Something deep inside him said yes, he could.

These thoughts took less than a second, and even as they flashed through his head Cole was stepping forward, holding his own hands out in front of him, arms extended, fingers together, palms straight out to block the incoming spell. Words appeared in his head, words he didn't remember learning, and rippled out of his mouth. A gleaming barrier formed just beyond his hands, like a sheet of condensation forming on an invisible glass pane. The beams struck his shield and glanced off, bouncing to either side. Cole grinned.

"Is that the best you've got?" he taunted.

The woman didn't answer. She merely stepped back among her peers. No one said a word.

The second attack came suddenly, and in force.

It was more magical bolts, this time emanating from each of the men and women, eight in all. Cole felt like the disco ball in a laser light show, beset by glowing beams on all sides. Somehow he had the presence of mind to repeat the words he'd called out before, and even as the onslaught approached his shield extended, wrapping all the way around him. But would it be enough?

The ricochet of the beams told him it was. And Cole couldn't help but smile as one of those reflected beams struck one of the NAN shamans in the shoulder, knocking the woman backward and almost to her knees.

If they wanted to take themselves out, he was happy to sit back and let them.

Unfortunately, the shamans weren't that stupid. They backed off again after that failed attempt, whispering amongst themselves. Too winded and drained to press the attack himself, Cole instead took advantage of the brief lull to look around.

Most of the NAN soldiers had picked themselves back up by now—those who hadn't been cooked by lightning, anyway. They were gathered in small clusters all around the enclave—including one that seemed to be on guard detail. Cole peered again at that particular group, and was sure he spotted horns rising from someone in their midst. Aha!

He couldn't rush over there, not with these shamans blocking the way. But Cole no longer needed to physically approach something in order to wreak havoc on it.

Casting a quick glance at the shamans to make sure they were still focused on making plans, he turned his attention on that cluster of soldiers and began reaching out with his mind, grabbing and gathering and directing the storm that still hung overhead.

After a long, agonizing moment, the clouds slowly lurched into motion and drifted slowly, ominously, toward that other part of the camp.

When he thought the clouds were directly over the group, Cole spiked the poor weather construct with his mind, jabbing at it until it released its load with a loud groan of pain. Water dumped down upon the guards and their charges, making the soldiers jump from the sudden, stealthy deluge.

That was all the opening Hazard needed.

Cole saw sudden motion from the pile. Then a massive arm reach up, shreds of a belt-thick zip tie still attached, and grab one of the soldiers. After shaking the man violently for several seconds, a second colossal hand removed something from the man's side. Then the hapless officer was tossed aside like a sack of moldy potatoes.

Ten seconds later, Hazard rose from the pack's midst like a tree suddenly shooting up over surrounding bushes.

Then that tree reached out and thumped the nearest guard on the head with a fist as large as the head it just smacked.

Hazard was free.

Cole wanted to look for Doc and Alaric, but just then the shamans launched their latest offensive, and he was forced to respond.

Their first move was to kill the lights. A wave of darkness settled over them all and absorbed every bit of available light. Suddenly it was too dark to even see your own hand right in front of your face.

But Cole didn't need pure sight to see. His enhanced hearing allowed him to navigate blind to some degree, and thanks to the enhancements he never forgot how far they'd gone or where they'd already walked. To some degree he actually enjoyed the dark. It was nice to have to rely upon the other senses for a change, and to slow the pace down a bit. It was also a good way to find objects before you ran into them.

The shamans had been edging forward under cover of darkness. For an instant, Cole considered stepping out of their way and letting them continue, right off the edge of the mesa. But perhaps they could sense their way through the dark as well. Plus, he didn't know if every one of them was here willingly, in which case they might need help in escaping the NAN's clutches. That meant Cole didn't want to kill them if he could help it—not until he'd had time to check on each one personally and figure out if they were willing participants or reluctant slaves.

He did, however, hold out one hand, palm down, and mutter several ancient words.

Just in front of him, a short shriek arose, swiftly followed by a muffled *thud*. Then a series of short, sharp curses.

That happened several more times, as more shamans slipped on the sheet of ice Cole had conjured beneath their feet. Finally the darkness began to fade, turning to merely heavy shadows and then finally absorbing back into the night. By the comparative brightness, Cole could see half the NAN shamans picking themselves up off the mesa floor, nursing bruises and clutching limbs and sides and heads. That seemed to have taken at least some of the wind out of their sails!

A motor suddenly roared to life a handful of meters to Cole's right. Squinting, he could see the dark outline of some sort of vehicle, but he had no other details to work with. Was Nita Ayelen escaping? Was Goyathlay? But he doubted either of them would run as long as the fight was still taking place.

Then a heavy truck came barreling through. It rammed two of the surprised shamans aside, then swerved so it could charge straight at Cole—and all the NAN soldiers gathered between him and the oncoming vehicle. Most of them scattered from its path; a few stood their ground and were immediately run down.

Now Cole could see the truck more clearly. It listed to one side, like it had already taken substantial damage, but still it stayed the course. Then he spotted the driver. So small only the tip of his head was visible behind the steering wheel, and that tip was little more than a collection of stray wisps.

Doc!

Cole wanted to cheer at seeing his old friend out and free and taking the fight to the NAN, but he didn't. Better for Doc if they didn't think about it long enough to remember that he and the others had all snuck in together. Let the NAN deal with him and Doc and Hazard—and Alaric if he was still around— separately, rather than lumping them all in together. It was safer for his friends that way.

Unfortunately, that did still leave him as the focus for most of their ire. The shamans appeared to have regrouped again, but this time they weren't alone. The remaining NAN security forces were now gathering with them, flanking them like shadowy wings on some vicious little flying beastie. Cole felt a shiver of dread at the idea of soldiers and shamans working together against him, but did his best to shake that off. He'd been able to hold each of them off separately, so he didn't see any reason why he couldn't handle them all together.

He thought that right up until another globe of darkness descended upon him—and then the soldiers opened fire into it. *Of course*, he realized as he dove to the ground, desperately weaving a shield above him like a warm blanket to fend off any downward-aimed shots or ricochets. They were all facing him from the same direction now, lined up on the side away from the mesa's outer edge, where they could fire toward the ravines below and at least know they wouldn't take out any of their own people. That was bad, especially when bullets started flying into the shrouded area as well. His shield was deflecting them, but how long could it withstand such punishment?

*I need to give them something else to think about*, Cole told himself grimly. He concentrated, trying to remember what lay behind the shamans and soldiers within the encampment. There were several other trucks and vans, he recalled, all grouped to form the enclave's outer edge. Those would do. Reaching out with his mind, Cole grabbed something large and bulky and metallic that he really hoped was a truck.

And then he pulled.

He heard a faint groan off in the distance, like the sound of metal grinding against itself. Then a screech, but not from any human throat. The object was resisting, not by force of will but simply from weight and inertia, but he continued to haul on it with his mind, and gradually he felt it give. Then the rest of its resistance vanished all of a sudden, and Cole felt a gust of air against his face as the object answered his call.

The darkness vanished all at once, winking out of existence as the truck slammed back into the mesa with a heavy *thud*, a loud *crunch*, and the shriek of collapsing metal. Screams accompanied its impact, and now that he could see again, Cole observed that several shamans and soldiers had fallen to the ground. It looked like one or two also might have been crushed beneath the falling truck, and Cole certainly wasn't going to complain about that. The fewer enemies massed against him, the happier he'd be, and right now he didn't have the luxury of worrying about anyone attacking him. If he survived, he'd feel guilty about hurting unwilling participants later.

The problem was, he wasn't sure how long he could hold out against them. Especially when they were capable of coordinating their efforts like that. All it would take was one lucky shot to knock him out, or worse. And if they could take him without killing him, they'd have the amulet back, and him with it.

Cole knew with deadly clarity that he couldn't let that happen.

For a split second he considered killing himself. But he wasn't sure that would be enough. Would they even need him to be fully active and aware now that he'd accidentally attuned and activated the amulet for them? Could they preserve his heart, keep it beating, press the amulet into it, and fool the air spirit within enough to use it in the Great Ghost Dance? He had no idea. But clearly whether he lived or died wasn't the most important thing.

The amulet was the key. Without that, they had nothing. And there was only one amulet. If he could manage to deactivate it—or better yet, destroy it—they'd never be able to harness that power again.

But of course, the amulet was still embedded in his chest.

Cole suddenly realized what he had to do.

That made him doubly glad when the stomp of heavy feet drew his attention, and he glanced up to see Hazard marching toward him, shredded restraints still clinging to her wrists, a pair of heavy NAN machine guns in her hands. Doc was right beside her, limping a little but carrying what looked like a flamethrower. Alaric was there as well, his deck still slung over his shoulder somehow, a nasty cut dripping blood over one eye, a machine gun in one hand and a big, nasty-looking knife in the other. All of them looked battered and bruised and sported various cuts and scrapes but seemed more or less intact.

"You okay?" Doc asked as the trio reached him. The dwarf glanced around. "Looks like you been holdin' your own." If he was afraid of what Cole had become, of the power he could now wield, neither face nor voice showed it, and for that Cole was immensely grateful.

"I'm okay," he replied, staggering to his feet beside them. The NAN were still shaking off his latest volley, so he took advantage of the momentary quiet to turn to his friends. "Listen, I need you to do something for me."

"Kill 'em all?" Hazard growled, hefting her guns. "'Cause that can be arranged."

Cole shook his head, then nodded. "No. Yes. I don't know. Look, kill them all you want, but I—there's something I have to do. I think it could end all this. But I can't do it if I'm fending them off."

Doc nodded and clapped Cole on the shoulder. "Do what you gotta do," the dwarf inventor told him. "We got you covered."

Alaric and Hazard nodded.

"Thanks." Cole turned away, facing out toward the mesa's edge and the yawning darkness of the ravine, as his three friends stationed themselves between him and the NAN forces. He knew they wouldn't be able to hold off both soldiers and shamans for long, but he only needed a minute. He hoped.

Assuming this would even work.

But he had to try.

Holding out both hands, Cole summoned the lightning again, channeling it into his fists. It came eagerly, like a puppy excited to see its master once more, and Cole thrilled to feel it coursing through his veins, filling him with power. He could get used to this.

But if he let the magic seduce him into trying to keep it, he could wind up dooming them all. So he fought down the temptation as best he could, focusing on the lightning but not the sensation, and then he raised his hands—

—and jammed them both hard against his own chest, right over his wound. Forcing the lightning to spark and leap out, straight into that place where he'd been carved open—and where the amulet was stored.

He spasmed, falling to his knees as sheer agony ripped through him. If Dr. Twinfeather's forays with the forceps had hurt, this was a thousand times worse. It was like someone had just stabbed him in the chest with a live wire—which was basically what he had done. To himself.

But Cole didn't let the pain stop him. He kept going, pouring as much energy as he could muster into the attack.

His whole body was seizing, every joint and muscle locking up from the pain. Spots appeared before his eyes, his vision darkened, and his breath came in short, sharp gasps.

But still he continued.

Then, suddenly, Cole heard a loud *crack*, like the world had just split in two. He felt it as well, vibrating through him like a massive bell had just been struck, with him at its center. He felt like he had been caught in the heart of an enormous thunderclap. A sudden force seemed to rip clear of his chest, the force of its passage throwing him almost flat on his back as it pushed its way free and then disappeared with only the faintest ripple of the night air.

And the lightning vanished from his grasp. Cole reached for it, but it was gone. Nor did the storm overhead respond when he called.

His control of the elements had disappeared. Despite his pain and fatigue, despite being completely wrung out and limp and shaking, Cole dragged himself back up to his knees and smiled.

He'd done it. The air elemental was gone—he was sure of that. Which could only mean one thing.

The amulet had broken. The elemental that had been trapped within it was now free.

Even if they were to capture him now, the NAN couldn't use Cole to perform the Great Ghost Dance. They'd never be able to call upon the amulet's power for that ever again.

He'd just saved the world.

Unfortunately, the sound of many guns being cocked made him turn to peer past his three friends, at the small army assembled there against him.

And now Cole no longer had the amulet's power to wield against them.

*I might have just saved everyone else*, he thought sadly, *and killed myself in the process.*

# THIRTY-FOUR

"Hey, Cole? Cole! You still with us, man?" Alaric called back over his shoulder. The blue-haired decker was so pale and shaky it was amazing he was still standing, much less aiming a machine gun at the NAN forces, but his voice was surprisingly steady as he continued, "'Cause now'd be a great time for more of that lightning, you know?"

"Yeah, don't think that's gonna be happening any time soon," Cole admitted, pushing himself to his feet. "Lightning's all gone now." That strange ache in his chest and his head had also vanished, and for the first time it occurred to him that those had been the effects of the amulet's influence and bond all along.

"So, what, you got nothing?" Hazard asked. "Frag. We're hosed."

Studying the forces arrayed against them, Cole had to agree. There were simply too many of the NAN soldiers still standing for him and his friends to take them all out with their paltry collection of guns. They really needed magic on their side.

Then a thought popped into Cole's head.

*I'm the son of Daniel Howling Coyote*, he admitted to himself, finally owning his heritage, twisted as it was. *The greatest shaman of the modern age. And obviously I've got an affinity for the stuff, just like he did. So I don't have a crazy-ass air elemental at my beck and call anymore. But I felt it—when we first got the amulet. I sensed its presence. And I just let it go. Maybe, just maybe, I can call it back.*

"Okay," he muttered, raising his hands and staring at them as if they were going to reveal some hidden truth. "Time to get serious."

He closed his eyes and reached out with his mind, searching for the elements, magic, spirits, anything. Anything he could use. Anything that would answer his increasingly desperate call for help.

The feeling, when something did answer, was indescribable.

*I hear you, Kwinaa, son of Daniel,* a voice said, the merest whisper in his ear, but reverberating inside his head. *You released me, and I am in your debt. You have asked for my aid, and you shall have it.*

It was a little like sliding into a warm bath, and a little like stepping outdoors in crisp autumn weather and feeling the wind wrap around you, but gently. It was like pulling on a good pair of gloves, or revving your motorcycle's engine and leaning in to feel its power as it carried you forward.

It was like the warmth you felt when you looked at your friends, and knew that they *were* your friends, and that they had your back, no matter what.

It was the sensation of reconnecting with something you'd been missing without even knowing it was gone in the first place.

When he opened his eyes, he was completely unshocked to see that his hands were now glowing, trailing sparkles of light every time they moved.

Cole grinned.

"Come and get it!" he shouted, and pointed at the troops arrayed before them.

And nearly started cheering like a madman when beams of energy shot from his hands and stabbed into the front row, causing the men he struck to convulse and clutch at their chests and drop to the ground, writhing.

"Nice!" Alaric hollered. "That's what I'm talking about! Come get some!" And he opened up on the soldiers with his gun, spraying them with a barrage of bullets. Hazard and Doc joined in, and more NAN forces crumpled.

Of course, the soldiers weren't just standing around being targets. They raised their own guns and returned fire, but Cole was ready for that. He pictured the shield he'd summoned before, only this time it was stretched out in front of him and his friends, and the NAN's attacks were turned away.

It was perfect.

Movement behind the soldiers distracted Cole from congratulating himself, and he focused, trying to see past the men and their weapons. There! He spotted one of the NAN shamans, the woman with the long silver braid, sitting up and shaking her head. It looked like they'd been knocked on their asses by that same backlash he'd felt when he broke the amulet, and they were just starting to recover.

If they regained their feet and their wits and their magic, he probably wouldn't be able to hold them all off again.

He'd have to deal with them now, before they got out of hand.

Cole concentrated. He pictured an enormous, soft blanket, the big fluffy kind it was impossible not to fall asleep clutching every time you were snuggled down into it. Then he summoned the blanket out of the air, or at least the feel and smell and warmth of it, and settled it atop the NAN shamans. The illusory blanket was so warm, so comfortable, so comforting, and after all their exertions already the shamans were certainly all tired, and stressed, and a little panicked. A nice nap would do them all good. Then, when they woke up, they could resume whatever they'd been doing, no interruptions. The NAN would be so pleased.

By the time he got to that last thought, it was all done. All the shamans had lain back down, and appeared to be sound asleep. Even, in a few cases, snoring.

Now he and his friends were free to focus on the ground troops again.

Cole started to say something to the others when something red flashed off to the side. Something like a little red dot, or the start of a long, thin red beam.

"Everybody down!" he shouted. He dove to the ground, as did the other three, and just in time—another loud *crack* resounded across the mesa, and it overwhelmed his senses for a second, just like when a flash went off near you in the dark.

Stone chips and dust rose from the spot where the mesa's very surface had been splintered by a particularly effective bullet.

Fired, Cole was absolutely certain, by the mysterious Nathan. AKA Mr. Steel-eyed Sniper.

Calling up his visual enhancers, Cole quickly swept the entire crowd with his gaze. Then he remembered the last time he'd had to deal with Nathan. He also pictured Nita Ayelen and Goyathlay Seevers, and then set a search program into effect, applying their physical characteristics. This way the computer side of him could run a search of his surroundings while he did other things—necessary things—and if it spotted any of those three, it would immediately alert him.

Which it did, only a few seconds later.

The sniper had climbed atop one of the NAN vans, and was shooting from there, toward the front and its perimeter fence. Cole wasn't sure he had enough magic left to take the man out, especially from here, but when he raised one hand the van's roof buckled and rippled like an angry horse trying to shake the sniper off its back. The man—Nathan—yelped and grabbed the roof's edges with both hands, losing his grip on his rifle. It slid off and hit the ground with a loud clatter. That, hopefully, took care of him. At least for now.

Next Cole scanned again, specifically for Goyathlay. He located the shaman toward the back of the crowd as well, and he appeared to be...

...running away?

Startled, and more than a little bit angry at the thought of the older shaman getting away, Cole shouted, trying to get Goyathlay's attention.

Instead he watched as something that looked like a cross between a large pointed spoon and a small bird of prey appeared in the night sky. It swiveled its long, sharp-edge head from side to side as if tasting the air, and then nodded and twisted midair, redirecting its path before flapping its wings and arrowing across the encampment.

The strange magical construct slammed into Goyathlay's back. The shaman screamed in pain as its sharp beak stabbed into him just below the kidneys, and he swatted at it, trying to drive it away, but this was no ordinary beastie. And it seemed to already have its orders. Cole decided the wise move was to simply let it go for now. As long as it was after his foes, he didn't much care where it had come from or why.

That left the third member of this unholy triumvirate, the woman who had put all of this in motion. Nita Ayelen. Cole wasn't having any luck finding her based on his scan, but he kept looking. All the while he was running through options, places, and even people for anything that might lead to ending this threat, not just for himself but for his friends and others who might one day follow in his footsteps.

It was on his third sweep that Cole noticed something strange. Most of the NAN's tents had been blown down or torn apart by now, leaving great swaths of silk waving in the wind. All except for one of the smaller tents—

—which was currently creeping its way quickly and quietly toward the encampment's far end. Away from the fighting. Away from Cole. And toward the road out of here.

He was as certain Nita was within that tent as he was that that sun rose in the east and set in the west. Some things were simply impossible to refute.

Concentrating, Cole tried to summon a wind to lift the tent out of the way. All he got was a mild breeze. Instead, frowning and bunching his fists at his side, he focused only on the tent itself—

—and laughed perhaps a little too shrilly, when the tent's dark silk suddenly flared upward like a drawing come to life, glowing brighter and brighter as its fabric caught fire. In an instant the entire thing was burning.

He thought he could actually hear Nita's screams as she tried to claw her way out of the refuge-turned-prison-turned-fiery deathtrap. One red-taloned hand emerged, tearing its way out and reaching upward, struggling to pull free before spasming and then splaying wide, frozen in a death rictus. Watching the burning tent collapse in on itself, taking Nita with it, Cole thought of the people of Dinosaur, immolated as a mere backdrop to her plans. He hoped that, somewhere, their spirits could rest a little easier now, knowing the architect of their demise had suffered a similar fate herself.

Motion drew Cole's eye back toward the mesa's far end as a stray NAN man recovered enough to raise his rifle and shoot at Cole and his friends. Cole quickly switched enough of his attention back to the ongoing firefight that he could block the man's shots. Hazard fired back at the man, who collapsed in a heap. One less opponent to worry about.

The combat soon fell into a sort of macabre rhythm, with Cole blocking their foes' shots or disarming them or causing their guns to misfire and Doc, Alaric, and Hazard then shooting the distracted NAN soldiers. More and more of the men and women lined up against them dropped away, and soon it was down to only a handful versus a handful.

One of that handful, however, was Nathan, the steely-eyed sniper.

"Face me like a man!" he shouted, pointing at Cole. "Or are you too scared to do anything but hide behind your friends?"

Cole knew he shouldn't, but he tapped Doc and Alaric on the shoulders and slid between them when they turned. "All right," he called back. "You want me? Here I am."

Nathan stepped forward, waving his remaining men back as he did. He had a rifle in his hand again, but he held it out away from him and let it drop with a clatter to the stone of the mesa, leaving him armed with only a long knife. "Come on," he demanded, holding the blade up so it caught the light from the camp's perimeter. "Just you and me, man to man, blade to blade."

"Don't do it," Hazard warned just loud enough for Cole to hear. "He's good, I can tell by the way he moves. He'll cut you to pieces."

Cole smiled up at her. "Thanks for the concern, but I'll be fine." He was no longer bleeding, for one thing—it seemed the elemental had healed that when he was not looking. And he felt good. Powerful. Like he had lightning in his veins and wind in his blood, giving him the speed and strength he needed.

"Suit yourself." She offered him a knife from her belt, and he accepted it, even though in his hands it was more like a sword. He also recognized the strange red glow around its edge. Hazard caught his eye and grinned. "No sense making it easy for him," she said with a wink.

Feeling slightly better about his chances now, Cole nodded and marched into the space between his friends and the remaining NAN forces. Nathan was waiting for him, his knife held out in front of him, weaving the blade back and forth like a silver snake preparing to strike.

"All right, Mr. High and Mighty Howling Coyote Returned," the sniper taunted as Cole closed the distance between them. "Let's see what you've got." And his blade flickered out like a streak of lightning, ready to bite Cole on the wrist.

Cole tried to block the attack, and succeeded but only barely, even with the elemental's gifts. The faint smile that crossed the other man's lined face said that he knew they weren't evenly matched. He was planning to toy with Cole, that much was clear.

So Cole didn't give him the chance.

Just as Nathan reared back to strike again, Cole lunged forward, his knife held high, blade aimed to plunge down into his opponent's shoulder and neck. It was an easy strike to block, a beginner's mistake, and the sniper grinned more broadly as he raised his own knife—

—and then Cole's other arm lashed out and wrapped all the way around his rival. He yanked hard and pulled the sniper off his feet, dragging the man toward him so quickly Nathan's knife fell from his hand. Nathan struggled but couldn't break free, the steel cable of Cole's arm tight around his chest, and then he was jerked the last few feet forward—

—and right onto the blade of Cole's knife, which he'd brought back down and extended before him.

Eyes wide with surprise and pain, the sniper glanced down at the blade jutting from his chest. His mouth was already going slack, blood trickling from it, as Cole shifted, forcing the knife up into the sniper's heart.

"That was for Lorelei, Rodrick, Tish, and Mace," he said as he retracted his arm and stepped back, letting the dying man fall to a heap at his feet, sliding off the bloody blade as he went.

No one moved as Cole turned and retraced his steps to his friends. He nodded to Alaric, who nodded grimly back, and then reversed the knife and offered it back to Hazard hilt first.

"Okay," he said, turning and facing the last few NAN soldiers once more. "Let's finish this."

# THIRTY-FIVE

The sky was starting to lighten—had they really been battling the NAN the entire night?—and Cole took advantage of the steadily increasing light to study his opponents.

Only a handful of NAN soldiers still faced him. The rest were presumably either dead, unconscious, immobile, or fled. The shamans were just beginning to stir behind them, but none of them had actually awakened yet.

Cole intended to make sure they didn't get the chance.

The first thing he did was concentrate on the enchanted slumber he'd wrapped around those rival shamans. Picturing it again as a great big fuzzy blanket, he could actually see that it was beginning to fray and thin, now more like a light throw than a sturdy quilt.

That wouldn't do.

Pouring energy into the image, Cole thickened the blanket again, and tightened its hold on the NAN shamans, enveloping them firmly once more. Those who had started twitching and muttering quieted and stilled, and soon the shamans were again solidly asleep.

Next he turned to address the NAN soldiers. "Listen," he started. "You've seen what I can do. There's only a few of you left, and you know there's no way you're gonna take me. So just drop the guns and back off and I'll let you walk. Simple as that."

Several of them wavered, their gun barrels dipping toward the ground. *They're going for it*, Cole thought happily. Which was good, since in truth he was wiped. It was a wonder he was still standing, much less speaking coherently and presenting like a badass. He only had to front a little longer, though.

But just as it looked like the soldiers would break, a voice called out from behind them: "Stand fast!"

And then the men and women parted like waves receding from a jutting spike of land, to reveal a short, stout, bald man striding through their ranks.

Goyathlay.

The shaman looked battered and bruised, and blood dripped from a nasty wound in his shoulder and several cuts on his head, face, and arms. But his steps were still strong, his jaw set, and his eyes sharp as he marched toward Cole. "Your time is over, abomination!" he shouted, his eyes beginning to glow again with that familiar white light. "Back to the hells from which you came!" Then the glow brightened and coalesced into a searing beam that lanced straight at Cole.

The energy bolt struck Cole dead center in the chest, right in the heart, and the impact staggered him back a step. He'd barely had time to think about calling up a fresh shield, and no chance to cast it before him.

But it seemed the elemental infusing him with its power had stopped the blow from taking full effect, because though shaken, Cole found the burst of pain was already fading, and he straightened up again, glaring at his tattooed adversary.

For his part, Goyathlay's eyes widened and his jaw dropped. "Impossible!" he breathed. "That spell would kill any man!"

Cole grinned at him, bluffing as hard as he could. "Not so tough now, are you, Goyathlay?" he taunted. "Yeah, you're a big bad shaman, right? But guess what?" He deliberately took a slow, stomping step forward, and laughed as the other man flinched back instinctively. "I'm the son of Daniel. Howling. Coyote. You can't even hope to compete!"

Raising his hand, Cole summoned energy to himself, drawing it from the rocks and the sky and the wind and the trees and even the people and vans and equipment all around him. He pulled that power in until he felt like he was going to explode from the magic swirling inside him, and then he fired it back out at the man who he'd thought was his friend, but who'd betrayed him.

But it didn't blast from his hand. Instead the energy bolt emerged from Cole's chest, straight out of his wound, and it hit Goyathlay Seevers like a freight train. The shaman screamed, his entire body seizing up, every limb locked at full extension as the magic played across every inch of him.

Then, with a blast of noise like a boulder crashing to the ground, the energy burst free, radiating out from the shaman's spasming form like a silent explosion.

*Our debt is paid,* the elemental declared, speaking directly into Cole's head once more even as it fled his body. *Live well, Kwinaa Howling Coyote, and may the wind be ever at your back.* And it was gone.

When the onslaught ceased, the tattooed man slumped to the ground, nothing more than limp, cooling flesh and glazed, staring eyes. The magic had taken his life force with it when it had dispersed.

Everyone there stared at Goyathlay's corpse for a moment. No one spoke. Then, finally, Cole cleared his throat. He could sense that the magic was gone, all but the little bit that was his own birthright, and he felt utterly wrung out, but he did his best to appear still confident and in control.

"So," he started, "about my offer—"

"Here!" One of the NAN soldiers declared. He hurled his rifle away from him, and unhooked his gunbelt for good measure, dropping it to the ground at his feet, pistol and knife both still secured. "Take it!" Then the man turned and ran.

That did the trick. The other remaining soldiers discarded their weapons as well, and backed away. Some did it carefully, cautiously, keeping their cool. Others panicked, ditched, and ran. Cole and his friends let them all go at their own speed. As long as they were willing to go without trying to fight again, he was fine with that. The elemental had healed him, but he was still just one man.

"Looks like you got that sorted," Doc commented. "Nice."

"And you paid him back for turning on us," Hazard added, gesturing toward Goyathlay's remains. "Good."

"We about done here?" Alaric asked. "'Cause there's a thing or two I wanna do before we go, and some of those guys might be calling for reinforcements." He grinned. "Even though you're a big badass stormbringer now, I don't think we really wanna be here when they show up."

Cole nodded. "Let's get out of here," he agreed, and, moving a little gingerly, led the way through the jumble of bodies and tents and vans and other wreckage. Hazard detoured at one tent and re-emerged with a large carry bag slung over her shoulder, and Doc and Alaric both ducked into tents at some point as well—none of them explained why, but

Cole figured they would when they were ready. They paused by the perimeter for Hazard to reclaim her Valkyrie, which was surprisingly still mostly intact after her mad charge the night before, but the other bikes would be waiting for them down at the base of the mesa, where they'd made camp. From here, Cole knew they could pick their way south until they hit Highway 76, which would lead them straight back down to Denver.

It was time to go home.

# THIRTY-SIX

"You always have such drek taste in bars?" Hazard asked as she stomped over to their table. There was no way she'd be able to slide into the booth, so instead she grabbed a chair from another table, spun it around, and planted herself on that. The chair groaned in protest, but it held.

"It's a talent," Cole admitted, leaning back. Amusingly enough, this was the same biker bar where he'd swiped that motorbike on his way from Doc's to Mace's, right after he'd recovered from the ambush in the mountains. It felt like ages ago—practically another lifetime—but it had actually been less than a month.

"They've got decent beer. That's enough for me," Alaric offered, sipping his pint as if to prove the point. Beside him, Doc nodded and took a hefty swig from his own glass. Hazard had carried a drink over with her, and Cole had one of his own, so for a second they all contented themselves with enjoying the fact that they were back, they were clean and rested, they were sitting somewhere comfortable, and they had cold beers in their hands.

"You said you wanted to meet," Cole reminded the big troll eventually. "Is it about the debt I owe? Because if so—"

"Debt's paid," Hazard rumbled, wiping her mouth with the back of one hand. "You're good."

"What?" That was from Doc, scowling over at her around Alaric. "How? We didn't bring back—"

But Cole had already figured it out. "That bag," he cut in, watching the big enforcer carefully. "The one you found on the mesa."

She grinned at him, her tusks winking in the bar's dim light. "Yep. Lots of folks, they take a long trek like that, they bring along some cash for spending money, roadside expenses, and so on. Figured they'd have a bundle." She shrugged. "More than enough to cover your debt. What I wanted to tell you."

Cole studied her. "Thanks," he said slowly. "And thanks for all your help. We wouldn't have survived without you."

Surprisingly, Doc nodded. "You're a good one to have around in a fight," the dwarf agreed, not scowling for once. He raised his glass in Hazard's direction.

"Definitely," Alaric chimed in, adding his glass to Doc's. Cole raised his as well, and the three of them all stared at Hazard, who glowered back at them. But maybe with less ire than she used to.

"Oh, fine," she said finally, sighing as she lifted her own glass to clink against theirs. "You all aren't totally useless either, I guess." She downed the rest of her beer, then rose to her feet, the chair sighing in relief as her weight left it. "You get in another scrape like that, give me a holler. Might be good for a laugh." Then, with a quick wink, she turned and tromped away, the bar's other denizens melting from her path.

"Gee, I think she likes us," Doc muttered after she'd gone and the door had swung shut behind her, and Cole laughed.

"Yeah, I think you may be right," he agreed.

Now Alaric cleared his throat. "So, that night on the mesa?" he started, suddenly fascinated by the way his long fingers pushed his glass across the scarred, stained tabletop. "When I said I had something I needed to do?"

Cole nodded but didn't say anything, just waited for the decker to get to the point.

"Well, yeah. Here it is." And he offered Cole a data stick.

"What's this?" Cole asked, warily accepting the tiny plastic storage device.

"Money," Alaric burst out, a slow, sly grin creasing his face. "I found their secure datalink, used it to access the PCC's main servers. First thing I did was wipe all the footage from that night. Then I rooted through their system and erased everything they had on Project: Shadow Dance—that's what they were calling it. Sent a virus through that into the rest of the NAN, too, tracking and wiping any mention of it in any of the other nations' systems." He tapped a finger against his glass, producing a clear, ringing tone. "Could be somebody else knew, of course, or that there's printouts somewhere, but any official records about you and the amulet and all that? All gone."

Cole considered that. With Nita Ayelen dead, and Nathan as well, there couldn't be very many left who even knew he existed, or about his heritage. Possibly no one at all. He'd been keeping his head down since they'd gotten back a few days ago, expecting more NAN agents to show up and try taking him back, but thanks to Alaric that might actually not happen. "Thanks," he replied. Then he reprocessed the first thing the decker had said, and the data stick he held. "Wait, you said this was money?"

If possible, the blue-haired elf's smile grew even wider. "Yeah, so while I was in their systems I had access to their financials. And, well, maybe I figured they'd put us through the wringer, really mucked with us, killed my brother, the whole bit. So they owed us."

Cole stared at him. "What, you stole money from them? From the PCC?" He had the sudden urge to drop the data stick in his drink and run screaming the other way.

But Alaric didn't look too concerned—and, for a change, neither did Doc. "Yeah," the decker admitted. "A little. Don't worry, I was smart about it—I shifted some stuff around, drew off from an expense account or two, funneled it into an offshore I had tucked away for a rainy day." He shrugged. "That's why I'm only giving you this now—it took a few days once we were back for me to bounce the money around enough times, but there's no way anybody's gonna be able to trace it now. And hey, we earned it."

Cole couldn't argue that one. Instead he asked, "how much?"

"Well—" the grin was back, "—Rodrick had told me what you guys were supposed to pull down for that job in the first place. So I went for that—the full amount, not just what would've been your cut." He laughed. "With maybe a little more tacked on for, you know, hardship pay."

"The full amount plus some? Holy hell..." Now Cole felt like he was gripping the data stick too tightly, as if it were some precious artwork or rare flower or something. The pay for the job had been high—too high, honestly, suspiciously high, the kind of paycheck you're wary of because it's just too good to be true—and this was that plus more? Damn. "And you two got the same?" Doc and Alaric both nodded.

"I had one for Hazard, too," Alaric admitted, holding up a second stick. He shrugged and tucked it away again. "If we do see her again, maybe I'll give it to her." Then he grinned. "Maybe."

"Ha, fair enough," Cole agreed. He pocketed the data stick. "Thanks."

Doc cleared his throat. "I got you something too," he declared, and pulled out another data stick, which he slid across the table to Cole. "I found what was left of their med tent, did some poking around. They had a terminal set up there, and it'd had all your medical files downloaded to it. Both yours and everything they had on your...sire."

Cole tapped the data stick with a fingernail. "Daniel Howling Coyote's records are on here? And mine?"

"Yeah, well, they didn't have a lot," Doc warned gruffly. "A lot of his got lost or destroyed during the war, I'm guessing. But what they did have, and everything from after, it's on there. And what little they had about you." He frowned, stole a quick glance at Cole, then looked away again. "I figured you might like to see where you came from. Who you came from."

*Who you were before they destroyed your mind*, Cole thought, frowning down at the little storage device before him. That's what Doc meant. And it was awfully tempting to learn something about Kwinaa Howling Coyote, who had apparently grown to adulthood before the NAN had found him and experimented on him, but who he didn't remember at all. Conversely, he had a lot of Howling Coyote's memories in his head, but he'd realized that they felt distant somehow, like he was watching someone else's life rather than reliving his own.

Which was exactly the case.

Finally he pushed the data stick back across the table. "I appreciate it, I really do," he told his old friend. "But you know what? I think I'm good."

And now that he'd said it, Cole realized it was true. He was good. He didn't need to know more about who Daniel Howling Coyote had been, or even about who he'd been before. He knew who he was now. That was enough.

"So, what're you gonna do now?" Alaric asked as Doc shrugged and reclaimed the data stick, tucking it back into a pocket. "Pull more jobs?"

Cole laughed. "Maybe. Why, you want to work together again?" It had actually wound up being a pretty tight team, now that he looked back on the whole trip. They could pull off all kinds of work if they wanted to get back together again. And once he had some proper training, he might not need to hire a shaman, either.

But Doc was already shaking his shaggy head. "Not me," he avowed. "I'm done with all that nonsense. I'm gonna go back to my lab and get back to work—only now I can afford whatever parts and supplies I need." He rubbed his stubby hands together, eyes bright, and Cole made a mental note to stop by regularly to drag Doc out to lunch or dinner or something. That way he'd at least know the old dwarf was eating *sometimes*.

But he still hadn't really answered Alaric's question. "I don't know," he finally said, going for full disclosure. These were his friends, after all. "I don't think I've figured that out yet." He leaned back against the booth's wall, feeling the smooth wood against his back. "I do know one thing, though."

He raised his glass in a toast, and outside thunder suddenly boomed, making most of the other bar patrons—including Doc and Alaric—jump. Cole didn't budge or flinch, but he did smile.

"I'm done dancing to anyone else's tune," he told his friends. "From now on, the only dance I do is the one I can call my own."

"Hear, hear," Doc crowed, and raised his glass to meet Cole's. Alaric did the same, and the three friends sat there, toasting and drinking and enjoying each other's company while a sudden thunderstorm raged outside.

Some nights I sleep. Some nights I drink until my body's fooled. Some nights I can't quite manage either one, and I sit in my office, half-awake, a Target's sweet tobacco stink burning away until the cherry reaches my knuckles and I realize I've been fretting.

*Fretting*, I tell ya.

Brooding, sulking, worrying at old cases like a dog chewing a bone or a devil rat chewing a dog. I'm not in the world's cleanest business, and I'm sure as hell not in the world's cleanest city. What's more, I've got a Transys Avalon supercomputer replacing a good chunk of my grey matter and storing an awful lot of data, a bog-standard addiction to White Brite betel gum to sharpen my senses, and a top-of-the-line Lone Star detective headware suite—enhanced and auto-recording vision, hearing, the works—to make sure I always pick up all of life's little details. When I get to being all Byronic and dwelling on old jobs and everything comes up in crisp ultra-high definition and crystal clarity, it ain't never an easy night, I'll tell you that for free.

And some nights, when the beer doesn't cut it and the harder stuff's too expensive to keep handy, when the darkness crawls in, and even Ariana's perpetual sunshine dims a little too much, I do what any sensible sumbitch does; I call a friend.

Sometimes it helps. Sometimes it just gets us *both* into a mood. Sometimes it's a little bit of both.

Me an' Pink, we spent three, four hours on the line. He'd started the call wrapping up a stakeout before calling it a night and leaving a few drones behind. The boredom had worn at his nerves, and our talk had turned maudlin. Sour. Complaint piled atop complaint, the entire process lubricated by alcohol. That's how friends work, ain't it? Something was bothering him, some topic wanted out, and it was my job as a friend to let him say what he had to.

"You remember that kook with the chainsaw? What's-his-name, what'd he call himself?" I glanced away and made a face as I tried to remember. "Growler or something, wasn't it?"

"Gary Growls," Pink shook his head, making a face of his own. "Yeah. He left a damned mess, brother, I tell you that much. What was it, seven, eight bodies before he got pinched?"

"Hell, forensics worked it out to like ten, last I heard. All mix-and-match pieces, hacked to bits, took the poor bastards forever to sort it all out. What kinda asshole installs a chainsaw in a cyberarm, anyways? Nastiest damned thing...worst damn case..." I trailed off, my empty glass clinking against the desktop as I let out a sigh.

"Naw. Burns," Pink scowled into his commlink, expression as dark as his African-UCASian skin, "Burns are the worst, brother. Fire's great for steak, but bad as hell for people. And the smell!"

"You ain't lyin'." I—unironically, I was just smoking at the time—blew out a light blue stream, a fresh Target in my hand. "You remember Devil's Night, what was it, three years back? When the 'Weeners had that stash of Kamikaze to go balls-out with?"

He shuddered. I didn't blame him. The Halloweeners were, at best, politely described as a band of hardy urban survivors with an uncanny knack for maximizing the combat and psychological effects of fire. At worst, and perhaps just as accurately, they're a bunch of fuckin' pyro psychos. Mixing their natural tendencies with the street's hardest combat drug hadn't done Seattle any favors. Especially not with emergency services already stretched thin, Devil's Night being Devil's Night, and a great many devils living in Seattle.

I swirled a few pieces of ice around that all-too-empty old-fashioned glass, then set it down on my cracked smartdesk. I could call Pinkerton—I could call just about anyone—with just my headware, but sometimes I liked the point of view of having a camera. It made it feel like more of a conversation, and less like talking to myself. He cleared his throat, drawing my attention away from my long lost drink.

"Hey, speakin' of burns..." Now he trailed off. I arched a brow. His dwarvish hands worked nimbly just barely at the edges of my field-of-view, and I knew he was tickety-tacking something into his commlink. "I got a case might be up your alley."

He meant, politely, he was offering me a job. A hand-out. A second-rate gig Pink didn't need himself. I got a chirp from my Transys headware, just as politely informing me of an inbound file.

"Yeah?" I'd open it later.

"You remember Polo?"

"I didn't figure you for the high society, horseback type of guy, Pink," I gave him a grin. Truth was, I didn't know much about Pinkerton's life before Lone Star. "But I guess it makes sense, you and all the fancy Downtown cops up on those little horsies, wearing those little hats, swinging those, what do you call 'em, those mallet-things around? I bet you're a real dapper figure up there, buddy."

"Not the sport, di—"

"Yeah, yeah." There went that joke. "Polo. The goat kid?"

"Yeah. Changeling kid, with the horns and all that."

"Runs with the ACE, don't he?"

The Alley Cat Express were a bunch of free-running fanatics, walking a tightrope halfway between being a legit business and a street gang. They got legal, bonded, courier gigs from time to time, but mostly worked the grey and black markets, making deliveries, running messages, handling messenger and delivery work for folks too Matrix-insecure (or just paranoid) to trust more conventional means. I knew a few of 'em. The Cats weren't too bad, as a rule. They didn't like drawin' inside the lines, and I respected that.

"He'll run with 'em again, once he decides what kind of legs he wants."

"Hmm?" I arched my other brow at that. I'd only seen Polo work once or twice, but everything I knew about the kid said he was fast, smart, and tough as nails. His quirky genes'd seen to that. "He lost a leg? Or he just goin' in for some chromed-up goat-leg upgrade?"

"Hell, Jimmy, he lost 'em *both*. He and a couple other kids got burned, literally, earlier tonight. Changelings, or whatever SURGE-kids are calling themselves these days? This whole little group, all Changelings. 'The Woof Pack,' they called themselves. What happened to 'em, it's bad stuff." Pinkerton's attention slid off-screen, eyes a little out of focus, and I realized he was skimming over some notes. "Polo, Polly, and Pantherine. All three vics were SURGE-positive, so I'm thinking hate crime. Burned bad. Molotovs or some sort of incendiary grenades probably wouldn't do this, so it may be something else."

'Something else' was Pinkerton-ese for 'magic.' He and mojo didn't get along. It made him squirm.

"Burned bad enough to lose his legs, but not dead?"

"Yeah. Torched to nothing, above the knee. Even with that ACE DocWagon contract and help coming in fast, they were in real trouble. It was nasty. Polo's on the meat market for both legs, another kid died, the third one, she's still laid up. Burns on more of her body, but not as nasty. She wants a little get-back, she's got some nuyen saved up, she called me as soon as she woke up. Five large, plus expenses."

"Uh-huh." I wasn't sure if he was kicking the case my way because it was tied to my neighborhood, because he knew I could use five grand more than he could, or because he thought it was magic; I wasn't overflowing with power, but Pink was downright mundane. Only way to find out was to ask.

I cleared my throat, figured I'd cut right to it. "Where'd it happen?"

He looked away from the camera, like he couldn't quite meet my eyes. Like he knew I'd hate what came next.

"Out back of Our Lady of Ash."

"They were doin' a run on a church?" Pink knew how I'd feel about that, especially *that* church.

"No. They sideline as shadowrunners, I hear, sure—" He was right, half of the ACE kids do, "—but they swear up and down they weren't on a job. They were stopping by to drop off some stuff, ACE surplus, you know how the Cats are. Some charity pieces for the parishioners, they say. On the up and up."

"Then they got jumped?"

"Firebombed or whatever, yeah."

My headware alert kept blinking at the edges of my field of vision, letting me know the file was waiting for me to open it.

"And you're sure you don't need it?"

That was my polite way of saying, "Brother, I need a case."

"You take it. Your neighborhood, more your style."

That was his polite way of saying, "I get paid by Downtown-desperate folks, you get paid by Puyallup-desperate. Those're two different tax brackets."

I pretended to think it over, like I had such a busy schedule I could afford to let a case pass me by. Like I could make rent without a new caper and a quick resolution. Like I was doing him a favor, not the other way around.

I tried not to think about the church itself.

"All right," I shrugged down at my smartdesk display, rather jauntily if I do say so myself. I toasted him with my woefully empty glass. "I'll take it off your hands."

Then I said the dumbest piece of shit words anybody's ever let slip past their idiot lips.

"How bad can it be?"

# TWO

"Bo-osssssss! Are you reaaaaa-dyyyyy?"

As I finished getting dressed, a glowing girl ghosted her way through my bedroom wall, voice high-pitched, teasing, innocent.

Ariana? She never sleeps. It's just not in an ally spirit to do something so wasteful. When she's around, she's around. When she's not, she's not (and normally I can call her). Sometimes she flits over to Skip and Trace's place, sometimes she's off on another plane, sometimes she's just in the next room, thinking really hard about whatever it is ally spirits think about.

So, the morning after my late-night call to Pink, while I was bleary-eyed, in need of a shave, and of an entirely sour disposition—my usual charming combination—she was raring to go, as bright-eyed and cheerful as ever. She loved a new case to solve, new people to help, new places to go. She loved everything.

Ariana's my opposite that way. She's my opposite in basically *every* way that counts. Ironic, given she's a sliver of my soul.

I made her. Named her. Whipped her up from astral energy and elemental magic, carved out a place for her in reality, willed her into being by reshaping natural laws thanks to complex formulas and hard-bitten stubbornness. Back in those days, I'd been one of Lone Star's up-and-comers, a golden boy, a proud graduate of U-Dub's magical studies program, and a tactical-trained Department of Paranormal Investigation shooting star, all full of piss, vinegar, and an Initiate's expert magical ability.

Then had come the vampire, and great big chunks of my power and potential falling into darkness amid bloodstained fangs. Then had come getting fired. Then had come the drinking, the better-than-life chips, the drugs. Then reality'd slapped me in the face real good, spit at me a little, too, shoved me down and dared me to get back up.

Ariana? She'd been there for all of it. Right by my side, the best friend and partner a soul could want. But none of it had touched her.

She was left flawless by it all, all shining and pure. A testament to my former ability, a dream put together by my fancy magical know-how and raw elemental power; she smiled like platinum, winked at children with emerald eyes, had hair like silver, skin like gold. All my old power, all my sorcerous strength, all my overt elvenness—she had too-high cheekbones and too-sharp ears, not like my scruffy-ass self, who'd never even bothered to learn Sperethiel, the elfy-elf language most of "my" folks loved so much—and she was all of my stupid, worthless, old hope and brightness and optimism, too.

She was so eager to tackle the world and solve all the city's problems.

Me? I needed a paying gig, and had nothing better to do.

Plus I knew what I was heading into, or so I thought. A DocWagon clinic, to talk to an injured gal. Burns. Burns are never good.

But I still went. I still half-assed my tie, tucked in my shirt—more or less—and shrugged on my longcoat. I still holstered my Colt, checked my wand in its nylon sheath, plopped my worn old fedora on my head.

Like an idiot.

My Ford got us across town to Puyallup's northernmost—and as such, most respectable—DocWagon clinic in almost record time. The car had the body of an Americar, but the growling engine of a bulky limo about twice the size. An old friend and I had done a number on it, when we weren't busy doing numbers on each other, and it was a real Frankenstein's monster. Turbo Bunny hadn't yet been a legend in the Seattle shadows, but she'd had her greasy thumb even back then, her knack for getting the most out of a junkyard, the most out of a car, the most out of anything but the people around her. The car was an ungodly brute that probably got the worst miles-per-gallon of any of Seattle's growling electric-hybrids, but it could haul ass on Puyallup's ash straightaways like nobody's business. I wanted to hit the hospital first thing, as early as they'd allow visitors. The clinic wasn't far, so the drive wasn't long at all.

The contrast, stepping over that mantle, was as stark as ever. Outside was drifting ash and dirty streets, every fourth or fifth car a rusted hulk even this far north in the district, every meter of wall tagged and re-tagged, marked by gangers as surely as dogs lifting their legs. Kids working the corners all day to peddle chips, men and women working the corners all night renting something more fleshy but less personal, everybody using everybody.

Inside? Inside was cleaner and sharper, but no more human. Hospitals gimme the willies, they have since I was a kid; too clean, too white, too antiseptic. Life's dirty and rough-edged.

I'll take the streets of the Barrens over the hallways of a hospital any day.

It was too early for me to feel like talking to the corp-perfect receptionist, so I strode right past him and his little corp-perfect kiosk. I spun up my Transys headware and let the augmented reality overlay guide my path, sending thought-queries to the helpful dog-brained nodes of the building itself, inputting patient information—Pink'd shared the DocWagon ID numbers of the kids I was after—and asking for room numbers in exchange. Easy-peasy.

My longcoat flapped as I stalked the hallways like I'd been here a hundred times before, and Ariana glowed and hovered in my wake. Her features, always mercurial, were shifting between a scrunched-nose "eww" face at the too-clean, too-sterile, too-harshly perfect nature of the place, and a wide-eyed "aww" face as she picked up the pain and fear of every patient to ever lie in a bed in this place; and the final terrors of those who didn't recover, the guilt and frustration of doctors and response teams who'd lost patients, and on and on and on.

She's a good kid, Ari. Got a bright soul. I drag her to some ugly places, sometimes. I hate myself a little bit for it, sometimes. I remember to give her an out, sometimes.

"Hey, kiddo, you remember what I told you about detective-client privacy?" I said over my shoulder as I took a left, then a right, following the imaginary footsteps the AR-overlay put down for me. She bobbed her head. Good kid. "I need you to make sure we stay private in here, yeah? You've got to be my eyes outside the building. Go play watcher spirit and do laps for a bit, lemme know if any shady characters try to sneak into the joint, okay?"

"On it!" she snapped off a sharp salute, shot me a sunny smile, and swooped away. She was eager to please, but also eager to be elsewhere. Ariana's not stupid—hell, she's smarter'n me. Smarter'n any human, in her way. She's a special flavor of innocent, and maybe even a bit naïve, but she's not dumb. I think she knows when I give her an "out" like this. I think she feels it. I hope so.

I took off my hat as I turned into the room I was after, finally. *DOE, J* was on the AR door placard; just like a great many DocWagon contractors; the emergency response company cared about the nuyen, not the name.

"Polo?"

I knew the answer before I asked. My top-notch eyeware suite saw to that, even though I kept the black-and-white filters on more often than not, they didn't miss much; I knew the kid on sight, even had helpful facial recognition protocols reminding me of it. He was a Seattle mutt, but with more Pac-Islander than some; sun-bronzed skin from a lifetime of running around outside, jet black hair save a few blue-dyed highlights, angular brown eyes. He was a Changeling, too, though, and there he took a jaunty sidestep away from standard human descriptors, even more than my elven-ass self. His widow's peak was flanked on either side by high-set horns, curling up and back as big as a troll's or a billy-goat-gruff's. He wasn't technically a satyr—a Mediterranean-centric brand of the Orkish metatype—but there was no denying the horns marked him as an "other."

And normally, mind you, he also had what he called The Legs.

Even among the free-running cult of the Alley Cat Express kids, he was a runner and a jumper. Someone'd bet he was an Adept once, but I'd eyeballed him on the Astral and collected; he was mundane except for his SURGE-mutation, he even had some muscleware instead of magic, but those legs were all the edge he'd needed. He had an exaggerated hindcannon and hoofs in lieu of feet, those backwards-slanted legs we thought of as horse's or goat's or—fancifully, when cybered—raptor's. They were something else. They were something special. They were something magical.

Or...they *had* been.

"Oh, shit, kid."

There was no missing how the starched white sheets were laid across him, how they dropped off not fair from his waistline. Stumps.

They were gone. Burned off, no mistaking it. No denying it.

Polo didn't answer. He was out cold. Instead of any sort of greeting, I got a rhythmic *beep-beep-beep*, and a long pause punctuated by a ventilator's hiss. Three more *beeps*, another pause-hiss. I knew the model number I'd see before I looked up. I'd memorized every detail of that ventilator long before I'd gotten my headware installed, long before I'd dosed up on Sideways and gotten my gene-crafted attention to detail.

*Beep-beep-beep-hiss*, that had been the sound of the machines my mom was hooked up to in a hospital not far from here, but a couple decades removed from this one. A Puyallup clinic had to make do with the old stuff, I guess, because damned if it wasn't the same model, the same rhythm, the same pace, the same maddening not-quite-to-the-beat as I'd heard all those years ago. *Beep-beep-beep-hiss*, that'd been the sound of my mother's artificial breathing, the fake lungs fooling her body into not giving up, the sound of her dying slowly right before her young son's eyes.

I let out a long, low sigh, sagging against the doorframe and picturing someone besides Polo lying on a cold hospital bed.

Dad hadn't been there at the end. He'd been busy working a 24 up at McMillin, busy being warden, busy with corrections, busy with prisoners and putting a roof over my head and food on my table. Dad was out of paid time off, so he had to put in hour after hour at the prison, paying for the treatments that kept his wife half-alive while he didn't have time to see her. Dad had just dropped little Jimmy Kincaid off and left him to do his homework, left him to talk to a mostly-corpse, and left him to listen to that *beep-beep-beep-hiss* until it finally, mercifully, stopped.

My jaw clenched, back in the here and now. I dragged my cybereyes away from where I'd started to busily memorize the ventilator's serial number for no good God-damned reason.

I spun from the room, slumped my back against the wall, and sucked in a long breath. I wanted a smoke. I wanted my mom back. I didn't get either.

"New patient," I said aloud, even though the clinic's onboard AR system could respond to mental cues. I rattled off the *other* patient number I had; hell if I was hanging around that ventilator, waking Polo up. Lord knew the kid needed his sleep. I didn't know if he knew about his legs yet, and I wasn't gonna be the one to tell him. So Polo was out cold, Polly was dead. That left Pantherine.

My long elven legs ate the distance—if I'd been in an uncomfortable hurry before, *now* I was fighting the urge to break into a full-on sprint and get out *out* out of this fucking place—and I barged into the next *DOE, J*'s room without knocking.

An honest-to-Buddha *catgirl* blinked up at me, halfway through slurping down a Yum-E-Freeze treat. She had ears sticking out of her hair, cat-slit eyes, little whiskers, and a tail swished under her blanket. Her ears lifted in curiosity, then laid back in annoyance. Those big yellow eyes blinked at me after taking in my working clothes.

"Uhh, *rude*!" Pantherine's tongue was bright blue as she stuck it out at me. "Don't they have knocking in, like, A Hundred-Fifty-Years-Ago Land?"

This fuckin' job.

# THREE

"Yeah." I nodded, sighed. "Yeah, they've got knocking in, uh, what you said."

"So?"

I pointedly lifted a hand and knock-knocked on the doorframe. "Can I come in?"

She tilted her Yum-E-Freeze like a queen toasting with a goblet. Her ears flicked again.

"Listen, ah..." I remembered the likeliest fake name after another glance at the *J DOE* nameplate. "Pantherine sounds silly in a hospital. You want I should call you Ms. Jane Doe, I gu—"

"Jhes," she interrupted, "With an h."

"What?" Where the fuck do you cram an 'h' into Jess?

"J-H-E-S." Cat-slit eyes bored into me with infinite patience.

"Not Jane?"

"Not Jane. I look like this—" she giggled, half-drunk on either painkillers or blueberry Yum-E-Freeze, "—why bother worrying about the first name, as long as I still give 'em a fake-ass SIN?"

Fair enough.

"Jhes it is, then. May I?" I hung my hat on the foot of her bed and sank into a chair after another queenly nod. "My name's Jimmy Kincaid. I think I saw you and the other ACE kids a few times."

"Mm-hmm. I know you, Jimmy Kay. Everyone does," she waved her blue concoction grandiosely, taking in half the world.

"I'm sure you're aware of Knight Errant's ah, lack of interest." That was my polite way of saying, "The cops don't care when Changelings get lit up."

Her ears laid back. She was aware.

"You and your friends—" Shit. One was dead. "—er, *friend*, Polo, hired an associate of mine, Mr. Pinkerton, to help with your investigation. He's asked me to take it over for him. I was hoping to ask you a few que—"

"Why?"

"So I can get a better picture of what happened."

"Not that," that blue tongue flashed in childlike annoyance again. I was reminded of Ari, almost. "I know why you'd ask someone questions, duh, to get answers. I mean why did Pinkerton hand us off to you?"

No humble way to say it, and hell if I'd ever gone outta my way to try for humility, anyhow.

"Puyallup's my beat, not his," I shrugged a little, leaned forward to put my elbows on my knees. "Pink's a Downtown guy, I walk closer to the Barrens. I know the neighborhood, the people in it. I know you guys, at least a little bit. I'm a better fit."

"So you'll find whoever did this to us?"

"I'm gonna try."

"And then what?"

"Hmm?" I tried to play innocent. I wasn't any better at that than I was at humble.

"After you find him. Then what? What will you do?"

"I'm a private eye, Jhes. Licensed and everything. I'm not a shadowrunner. Not a hitman. I figure things out. Once I do that, I let you know."

"Fine," she rolled those cat-eyes, ears flopped in faux-relaxation, then carelessly tossed her empty cup away. "So what do you need to know?"

"Let's start at the beginning. Pink said you three dropped some goodies off, yeah?"

"'Firmative, cap'n," she slurred a bit, tried to mark off a sharp salute despite all sorts of stuff hanging from her arm. "Right on schedule, Alley-Cat-O-'Clock, like we always do. After hours stuff, we just drop it off and scoot, like a ding-dong-ditch when you're a kid, right?"

I hadn't played that particular game. I grew up in Puyallup, ringing doorbells got you shot and running marked you as prey. Jhes must've been a Downtowner, slumming it by playing 'runner.

"Right." I didn't belabor the point.

"So we leave behind a couple strays packs, is all. Nothing major, jus' some candy bars, powdered soy-dairy mix, bunch'a socks. Figure he can use it to—"

"He? He who?"

"Father Esposito, down at the church."

"So this is a regular thing?"

She shrugged, tail lashing idly. "If we've got excess goods..."

Which meant stuff they'd bartered for or stolen.

"...and we're in the neighborhood..."

Which meant anywhere halfway nearby—to the Alley Cat Express free-runner weirdos, "in the neighborhood" was pretty flexible.

"...then we drop some stuff off, yeah. Esposito gives it out to poor kids or homeless folks or whatever. Good karma, you know?"

No, I sure as hell didn't. Me an' good karma, we don't go way back.

"Sure." I didn't belabor *that* point, either. "So you drop off a couple backpacks of charity treats for good karma, you leave, and then what? Walk me through it."

"Not much to walk through. That's about it, really. We drop off the stuff, we start to leave, and boom." Her ears flattened against her skull. Fear. Pain. "The street's on fraggin' fire."

A monitor started to beep. Her tail lashed. Her ears flicked back and forth, through a half-dozen emotions. All of 'em ugly.

"It was like a dragon or a jet engine, this roar. This whoosh. It just filled the whole world, the light and the sound of it. Shouting about freaks and mutants, almost as loud as the fire. And then over it, mixed with it, I heard Polo screaming. And then someone else. And then I realized the someone else was me, and I couldn't get the sound to stop, and it all jus'...jus' *hurt* so bad, and I looked around and didn't see Polly no more. Not at all."

A window-in-view blinked up and I reviewed Pink's notes while she talked. Yeah. There hadn't been much of Polly *left* to see. She must've been ground zero for the explosion.

"No...shots fired? No launched grenade, no sound before the fire?"

She shuddered, and turned it into a shake of her head.

"Just the burning," she said, and something near her beeped again, more insistently. "The burning and the screaming."

A nurse strode in, giving me that universal nursely scowl. *It's-my-job-to-heal-this-person-and-you're-upsetting-them-and-in-my-way,* it said. I got that scowl almost every time work brought me to a hospital. I ran from it every time. Never cross nurses. I took my cue.

I snatched up my hat. "I'll be in touch, Ms. Doe," I said, hurrying out.

As I passed Polo's room, my damned cyberaudio suite saw to it the beeping and hissing chased me clean out of the clinic.

*All* those fucking machines sounded like my mom dying and the silence of my father being somewhere else.

# LOOKING FOR MORE SHADOWRUN FICTION, CHUMMER?

## WE'LL HOOK YOU UP!

Catalyst Game Labs brings you the very best in *Shadowrun* fiction, available at most ebook retailers, including Amazon, Apple Books, Kobo, Barnes & Noble, and more!

## NOVELS

1. *Never Deal with a Dragon* (Secrets of Power #1) by Robert N. Charrette
2. *Choose Your Enemies Carefully* (Secrets of Power #2) by Robert N. Charrette
3. *Find Your Own Truth* (Secrets of Power #3) by Robert N. Charrette
4. *2XS* by Nigel Findley
5. *Changeling* by Chris Kubasik
6. *Never Trust an Elf* by Robert N. Charrette
7. *Shadowplay* by Nigel Findley
8. *Night's Pawn* by Tom Dowd
9. *Striper Assassin* by Nyx Smith
10. *Lone Wolf* by Nigel Findley
11. *Fade to Black* by Nyx Smith
12. *Burning Bright* by Tom Dowd
13. *Who Hunts the Hunter* by Nyx Smith
14. *House of the Sun* by Nigel Findley
15. *Worlds Without End* by Caroline Spector
16. *Just Compensation* by Robert N. Charrette
17. *Preying for Keeps* by Mel Odom
18. *Dead Air* by Jak Koke
19. *The Lucifer Deck* by Lisa Smedman
20. *Steel Rain* by Nyx Smith
21. *Shadowboxer* by Nicholas Pollotta
22. *Stranger Souls* (Dragon Heart Saga #1) by Jak Koke
23. *Headhunters* by Mel Odom
24. *Clockwork Asylum* (Dragon Heart Saga #2) by Jak Koke
25. *Blood Sport* by Lisa Smedman
26. *Beyond the Pale* (Dragon Heart Saga #3) by Jak Koke
27. *Technobabel* by Stephen Kenson

## ANTHOLOGIES

## NOVELLAS

## NOVELLAS (Continued)

In the year 2079, shadowrunners do the jobs no one else wants. There's plenty of work to do, and plenty of obstacles to overcome. Backstabbing corporate pawns, aggressive law enforcement, and other shadowrunners angling for your payday can get in your way. Your job is to beat them to the punch and make the big score before they can stop you.

Shadowrun: Sprawl Ops puts players in control of their own team of shadowrunners, selecting who they'll hire and then building up the cash, gear, and abilities the runners need to survive the streets. Only one team will complete the final mission that scores a huge payday and wins the game. Do you have the guts, wiles, and treachery it will take to make it to the top? Time to find out.

**WWW.CATALYSTGAMELABS.COM/SHADOWRUN**

Made in the USA
San Bernardino, CA
11 February 2020